"That's no prowler, miss. That's Mr. Kendall."

Fancy blinked and slowly shifted her gaze to the hulk lying next to her on the floor. "*Lucien* Kendall?" she asked, praying it wasn't so. Not her guardian. Not here. Not now. Not like this!

"In the flesh," her victim answered. "Or what remains of it, at least."

Fancy closed her eyes, wishing she could disappear. Of all the men in all the world, why did it have to be *this* man her brother had appointed as her guardian? She had kissed *this* man—and enjoyed it.

He moaned then, and she started. Concerned, she leaned over him. "What's the matter?"

He cracked open one eye. "Other than the fact that I've been shot, you mean?" He looped a long strand of her hair around his fingers and tugged her head down until he could whisper in her ear, "Another kiss would greatly ease the pain."

5

Naughty or Nice

Also by Melanie George

The Pleasure Seekers
The Art of Seduction
A Very Gothic Christmas
by Christine Feehan and Melanie George

Naughty or Nice

MELANIE GEORGE

POCKET BOOKS

New York   London   Toronto   Sydney

An *Original* Publication of POCKET BOOKS

 POCKET BOOKS, a division of Simon & Schuster, Inc.
1230 Avenue of the Americas, New York, NY 10020

ISBN: 0-7394-4747-5

Back cover illustration by Gregg Gulbronson
Original lettering by Iskra Design

Manufactured in the United States of America

To my mom, Barbara . . . Thanks for always
being there to listen.

I want to thank David—my biggest supporter, my pep club president, my cheerleader, my fan, and my friend—for lending me his ears, common sense, and regular humor in the face of my wavering faith. Keep the matzoh ball soup coming, petunia!

Naughty
or Nice

One

From a connoisseur's standpoint, the backside so sweetly hoisted heavenward twenty feet in front of Lucien was the most provocative one he'd ever had the good fortune to admire: lushly rounded, firm, high, and leading to well-shaped legs and dainty feet. The entire effect was so enticing that even the god-awful breeches of indeterminate gray did little damage to the overall presentation.

The sight made up for all the misery he had suffered thus far, including the everlasting drizzling that had not let up for the three days since his coach had rumbled into the rutted, gorse-infested purgatory of the Cornish wilderness.

Now, if only he could see the rest of the package that went along with that sweet bottom, Lucien thought, leaning against the stable door.

But the little thief continued to rifle through the drunk's pockets. He was out cold, his snores resonating louder than a logging mill, which might account for why the girl had not heard Lucien arrive, horse in tow. His coach had struck one of those deuced gouges so prevalent in this wretched nexus of the universe, leaving it and Tahj, his Buddhist shadow and conscience, stranded until Lucien could send assistance.

Content to watch, he adjusted his position to a more comfortable one, too much the cad to alert the girl of his presence. Might as well enjoy himself now that an opportunity had arisen—and it had most definitely arisen.

A delirious haze descended as he stood there wondering if one could be smitten with a backside, and idly curious as to what the lass was intent on stealing, as she didn't seem to be taking anything.

The thought was relegated to obscurity as the girl's floppy hat tumbled from her head, unraveling a silky banner of blue-black hair that puddled on the floor in a glossy pool beside the drunk's head.

Lucien's hands fisted at his sides as his arousal swelled to a nearly unbearable throb, reminding him quite forcefully of how long it had been since he'd had carnal knowledge of a woman.

Five months, six days, and twelve hours, give or take a few minutes.

He had begun keeping track, wondering when this anomaly would pass. He should be glad business had called him away from London; otherwise his reputation as a first-rate libertine would be completely shot to hell. His oath as a Pleasure Seeker was at stake, and it seemed he had finally found a cure in the form of a lush pickpocket.

Divested of her uninspired disguise, the girl muttered a rather amusing curse, quickly rolled her silky mass of hair on top of her head with slim fingers, and jammed the hat back into place. Straightening, she stared down at the unconscious man, the slump of her shoulders conveying she had not found what she was looking for.

The least Lucien could do was lend some assistance—preferably of a more compelling variety.

"Need any help, sweetheart?" he inquired.

The little robber whirled around so fast she very nearly dislodged her hat again. She had no such luck with the grimy scarf meant to obscure her face. It slid down to her throat, leaving Lucien dumbstruck.

He had long ago reconciled himself to the fact that the Lord generally didn't align all a female's features equally, that the Almighty enjoyed the jest of giving a woman a lush body but a sparrow's face, or the face of a goddess but a body like a Buddha.

But this . . . Good sweet Christ, the little larcenist was a fetching piece, from her dark winged eyebrows to her wide-set, exotically tipped eyes, a piercing shade of green, her pert nose, high cheekbones, and a mouth so damn full and wide he was already contemplating its possibilities.

She treated him to the same perusal he gave her,

starting at the tips of his mud-splattered boots, over his less than pristine clothing, his shirt bearing a stain from a futile attempt at repairing the damage to his coach, his hair and greatcoat both damp. Overall, not his best appearance.

Rallying herself, she took a step back and said, "Don't come any closer." She made the wasted effort of covering her face again, a vision he would not forget for the remainder of his days. Eventually his luck would run out and someone would succeed in putting a bullet through his heart—but hopefully not before he'd had a taste of the lush fruit in front of him.

"And what might happen if I dared come closer?" He took a step forward, amused at having this slip of a girl toss out warnings to him. He could tuck her under his arm with little effort—restrain her with one hand. Span her waist with those same hands and settle her on top of him, poised like a goddess on his erection, impaled fully, fragile and delicate, nipples taut, skin flushed with pleasure.

She dispelled the image, saying in a surprisingly calm voice, "Then I guess I'd have to shoot you." A gun appeared from behind her back.

His delicate wildflower had turned out to be a determined wildcat. "That is dire, isn't it?" His gaze flicked to the hand holding the gun; it trembled like a leaf. Clearly she was not cut out for a life of crime.

"I mean it."

"I'm sure you do. But might I suggest that in the future you pick a less frequented spot to rob your victims?"

"I wasn't robbing him. I was—" She stopped and frowned at Lucien.

"Was?" he prompted.

She lifted her chin. "That's none of your concern."

"But you've made it my concern, now that you're holding me at gunpoint. What do you plan to do with me, by the by? I don't intend on putting up even a modicum of resistance. Indeed, I promise to be the most willing of captives." Provocative new images replaced the old: his hands tied to a bedpost while she did her worst to him. Maybe this godforsaken wasteland wasn't hell, after all.

She leveled the pistol at his heart. "You'll move out of the way, please."

Lucien had looked down the barrel of a gun too many times to think death might decide to take him in a dimly lit stable, by the hand of a beautiful, dirt-smudged pickpocket.

"As you wish," he said, lowering his arm from the jamb and waving her by. He had to rein in his amusement as she hesitated, wariness in her eyes. Smart girl, not to trust him.

She edged along the perimeter of the stalls until she reached the doorway, barely five feet separating them. In one lunge, he could pin her to the wall, an idea that held great temptation as she stepped into a wash of moonlight that haloed her slim figure in its pearlescent beam.

Had it not been for the womanly beauty of the green eyes focused so intently on him and that impressive backside of hers, he might have thought her a child, she was so petite. Though, as his gaze skimmed over her, the front side was equally impressive. The baggy linen shirt did little to camouflage her curves.

Uncomfortably aroused, Lucien leaned back against the doorframe. She waved the gun at him. "Stay where you are."

He extracted a cheroot from his pocket. "I'd much rather stay where you are."

She scowled at him. "Turn around and count to one hundred."

Lucien decided not to remind her that he had already seen her face, so if she intended any sort of escape, she should put a bullet in him, or at the very least check him for weapons—a prospect he would no doubt enjoy. But all that seemed counterproductive.

He turned to face the inside of the barn and lit his cheroot, blowing out a stream of smoke before saying, "Next time you might want to cock the hammer. Your threat would have been much more impressive."

"Start counting," she snapped.

"One . . . two . . . three . . ." She had until five, then the chase was on.

On the count of four, something bashed him in the back of the head. As black spots wavered before his eyes and his knees buckled beneath him, Lucien's last coherent thought was that Tahj was going to have himself a bloody good laugh if he ever found out his best pupil had been felled by a girl.

Then he hit the dirt.

• • •

What rotten luck, Fancy thought as she stared down at the prone form of quite the most handsome man she had ever seen. Black hair, thick and straight, hung well below the collar of his greatcoat. His chiseled profile was limned by shadows and moonlight, the leaves overhead casting patterns on the ground beside him, framing the glorious Goliath.

She winced when she saw the blood on the back of his head. She hadn't planned on hitting him with the rock. Frankly, she hadn't thought she had enough strength to incapacitate him, just daze him a bit so she could make her escape. The wicked glint in his eyes had been the deciding factor. He hadn't looked the least concerned about her shooting him, as though he had known the gun wasn't loaded. But she couldn't take the chance that he would follow her, or report her to the authorities too soon. She only hoped he hadn't gotten a good enough look at her face to give an accurate description.

Kneeling beside him, Fancy pressed two fingers to his neck. Relief coursed through her as she felt his strong, steady heartbeat, his skin taut and warm. His jaw was roughened with whiskers.

He had the most sinfully long lashes, she noted, and they had framed the most memorable eyes, a pale aquamarine that was startling against his swarthy skin. It had taken her a good minute to catch her breath when she'd spotted him leaning in the doorway.

Where had he come from? And was he staying at the inn? She should hope the answer was no, but the thought was oddly depressing. So few exciting things happened in her part of the world.

Itching to touch him, knowing she'd never get another chance, she lightly feathered his hair through her fingers, smoothing the soft strands back as she whispered in his ear, "I'm sorry."

Reluctantly, she pushed to her feet and stared down at him, shamelessly admiring the way his trousers molded his backside. He was so well built, so broad and tall. Not even Heath, her neighbor and long-time friend, whose stature and breadth was impressive, could match this stranger.

But this was no time to be acting bird-witted. She had to find the drunk's cohort and pray he would give her as little trouble as his friend, who had conveniently passed out in the stables. She needed to obtain proof that Rosalyn's stepbrother, Calder, was behind Rosalyn's attempted kidnapping that morning.

Without proof, it would be Rosalyn's word against Calder's. And now that his father was dead and he had appointed himself the district's magistrate—ousting the fair and honorable man who had held the post for nearly twenty years—finding allies who would bear witness that Calder was low enough to force his stepsister into marriage would be next to impossible.

Just the thought of what could have happened to her best friend made Fancy shiver. Calder had been furious when he learned that his father had left a considerable fortune to Rosalyn—a good portion rightfully due her from her deceased father's trust—enough so that Rosalyn would be independent of Calder or any man, should she so choose.

Everyone knew that Calder's uncontrollable gambling and expensive tastes would lead him to bankruptcy within a few years, even though he had inherited several profitable estates, including Westcott Manor, where Rosalyn had lived until she had fled two days ago.

At present she was at Fancy's house, Moor's End, protected only by Jaines, her grandmother's beloved but ancient butler, and his wife, Olinda, the housekeeper. Both of them had worked at Moor's End since their youth, and though Fancy could barely pay them, they stayed on.

Had it not been for her grandmother, she and her brother, George, would have found themselves in an orphanage when their parents died. Her father's family would never have lifted a finger to help them. When Colonel Samuel Fitz Hugh, Earl of Porthaven, had met and married a common Cornish woman, his family had dissolved any relationship with him.

Fancy was all alone now. Her grandmother had died a year earlier; George, two months later. She had been devastated when she received the news of his death. Only a few weeks before, he had written to say he was coming home.

While she had desperately wanted him home, she knew he was returning because he still thought of her as the fourteen-year-old sister he'd had to leave behind while he fulfilled his duties to God and country, rather than the mature twenty-year-old woman she had become. But she would welcome his overprotecting ways if it would bring him back.

And with her best friend in danger, they sorely needed a man's help. She had underestimated Calder's determination, but she would not be so naive again.

The thought stirred Fancy to action. She took a final look at the stranger, a pang of regret stirring inside her at the thought of never seeing him again. With a heart-felt sigh, she blended into the night to seek out her quarry.

Lucien awoke with a dull pounding at the back of his skull. Memory returned quickly of a pistol-wielding spitfire whose intent he had obviously misjudged. He never would have believed she had it in her to harm a fly, let alone brain a man who outweighed her by at least five stone.

Wincing, Lucien rose from the ground. He figured he'd been unconscious for a few minutes, long enough for the thief to escape. Damn, he'd been outfoxed, and he didn't like the feeling one bit.

His horse had ambled into the stable and was munching on hay. Lucien listened, hearing nothing but the wind through the trees and the drunken revelry coming from the tavern a short distance away, where he intended to enjoy one more night of freedom before reluctantly taking charge of his ward, Lady Francine Fitz Hugh. George's sister.

Lucien dragged a hand through his hair, coming

away with blood on his fingertips. That was his reward for his honorable behavior and foolhardy agreement to come to this benighted place. George would be here, if he'd protected the boy better. He had been the lad's commanding officer, after all. From the first day, George had been overzealous, eager for action, eager to please—and he should have stayed the hell back in Cornwall, with his family.

Instead he had landed in Lucien's regiment, all battle-hardened soldiers who understood that their leader was fallible and who weren't foolish enough to worship him. Most knew how he had earned the nickname Renegade.

Christ, he should have gotten out sooner. Before his demons had taken control of him. Before he had caused the death of a twenty-four-year-old boy.

Familiar anguish twisted in his gut as he grabbed the bay's reins and led him into a stall, removed his bridle and saddle and brushed him down, before stocking his hay and water.

As Lucien was leaving, the stable boy ambled in, a disheveled ragamuffin with sandy brown hair and a pale, freckled face, rubbing the sleep from his eyes, which widened upon spotting Lucien.

"Cor, mister . . . y' scared me." He blinked as his gaze traveled up Lucien's tall form. "Y' is a big 'un, ain't ye?"

The boy's reaction was not uncommon. At six-four, Lucien generally received a second look. He had to duck to enter most taverns, a damnable nuisance when one was inebriated.

"Where've you been, boy?"

A flush spotted the lad's apple cheeks. "I fell asleep in the back loft, sir. It be the only dry spot on a night such as this."

"Do you have a name?"

"Aye, sir. Jimmy."

"How old are you, Jimmy?"

"Ten, sir."

Bloody hell. The boy should be at home in bed at this hour, asleep under the watchful eyes of his parents, not catering to a bunch of drunken swines on a damp night.

Lucien eyed the lad's bare feet and shabby clothing. They were glaring reminders of how miserable being poor could be, when children had to work to feed themselves and their families, and common necessities were luxuries. Lucien knew that life too well, seeing the youth he had once been in the boy staring at him. He didn't like the feeling.

"Please don't tell nobody," Jimmy beseeched. "I promise it won't ne'er 'appen again."

Lucien knew the boy would be out of a job if his employer got wind of his falling asleep. And the loss of even those meager wages could be devastating to his family.

Lucien had grown up in London's rookery amid filth and squalid misery, was taught about survival by beggars, prostitutes, scavengers, and swindlers. That life stayed in a man's blood and forever tainted him.

"I've got a job for you," Lucien said.

The boy eyed him warily and took a hesitant step back. "Wot kind o' job?"

A bitter taste rose in Lucien's throat as he realized what Jimmy thought he was proposing: some men found young boys to their liking.

He pointed to Sire's stall. "Give my horse some extra oats tonight. He's had a long day." Lucien pulled out a pound note and handed it to the boy, who gaped at it bug-eyed.

"Thank 'ee, sir! I'll take care of 'im right an' proper, I will."

Lucien took a step and then stopped, a pair of green eyes flashing in his mind. "Have you seen anyone strange around here this evening?" he asked.

Jimmy canted his head. "Strange, sir?"

Lucien didn't know why he was reluctant to ask the real question, which was if the lad had seen a woman masquerading in men's clothing.

"Never mind." She was best forgotten, anyway.

He headed toward the tavern, where the feeble glow of lamplight shone through the grimy windowpanes, the dregs of humanity within drowning themselves in ale and gin, their gaiety having nothing to do with the coming holiday. Lucien knew their type well; it was the life he was accustomed to. The life he had never managed to escape.

He stepped through the door. A cloud of smoke hovered against the rafters; the beams were darkened with age, the smell of cheap liquor familiar. He needed a drink. He needed a woman. And he prayed to God that tonight he wouldn't need anything more.

He sat down at a table in the far corner, his back to

the wall as his gaze scanned the motley crowd. A plump barmaid sauntered toward him, ample breasts, ample hips, and lust in her eyes.

"Wot can I get 'ee, luv?"

"Bottle of whiskey."

"Plan on 'avin' y'rself a good time, do y'?"

"As good as possible."

"Alone?" Her query was as subtle as the rock the impertinent little thief had hit him with.

"Hopefully not." He couldn't bear another night of solitude.

She smiled seductively. "I get off at two."

Hopefully he'd get off soon thereafter. "Two it is."

Giving him a promising look over her shoulder, she walked away to get his order.

Lucien leaned his head back against the wall and closed his eyes. He was weary. A common malady these days. Why hadn't he just hired another governess for his ward instead of coming here himself? Probably, he thought wryly, because the last two women had swiftly quit, referring to Lady Francine Fitz Hugh as an incorrigible chit who would never aspire to being a true lady. Hopeless, in other words.

Just what he needed: some willful brat who would give him more headaches than he already had. How the hell old was she anyway? He couldn't remember if Fitz had told him. George had always called her his little Fancy—an angel, he claimed. Clearly the man had been too blind to see his sister for the pain in the rump she was. Lucien could only pray the girl hadn't driven off—or killed off—the two old retainers that yet remained at Moor's End.

The barmaid returned with his bottle and a passably clean glass. She leaned over to pour his drink, her mountainous breasts pressing suggestively against him, beginning the foreplay. Normally that would have been enough to stir him, and yet it didn't. He couldn't stop thinking about the lass from the stables. Clearly he had contracted a brain fever.

"Y' are a big hunk o' man. Probably built like a stallion." She shot a glance at his groin. "Ten minutes, and Sugar'll give y' the ride of y'r life." With that promise, she sashayed to the next table.

The first shot of rotgut hit Lucien like a rock rolling down his throat. But it would soon do the trick, benumbing his brain, and that was all that mattered.

He stared into his glass, his mind drifting back a few days to when he had stopped by Northcote, the estate that had once belonged to his friend Caine Ballinger, intending to offer the brooding old boy a bit of season's cheer with a finely aged bottle of brandy.

Caine was one of the first friends Lucien had made upon his return to England. They had been pitted against one another in a round of hazard at Dante's, a crude gaming hell in the bowels of Clerkenwell, the last place Lucien expected to find an earl's son.

Lucien had taken Caine for a considerable sum, but Caine had accepted his defeat with good humor, and they'd both gotten soused thereafter, two drunken fools singing in revelry as they unsteadily wove their way down darkened streets toward Madame Fourche's brothel, as though begging a footpad to relieve them of their money.

They made it unscathed and had one hell of a time that night. The next day Caine had invited Lucien to join a secret society, a group of men that made up a bachelors' club known as the Pleasure Seekers.

Lucien didn't know what would have become of his life had fate not thrown Caine in his path. He had formed the only real friendships he had ever known in those years after he had discovered his family was lost to him. They'd disappeared as though they had never existed, a fact Lucien owed to a dead man, who he hoped rotted in hell.

Caine was the only one who knew the whole story, and it had been damn hard for Lucien to accept the fact that his friend had shut him out. He had only seen Caine sporadically in the two years since Caine's father had died, and those occasions had been tense. The last time, Caine had refused to even see him.

Damn the man for being such a pigheaded ass. Lucien knew his friend was hurting from his father's suicide and from the circumstances he found himself in, an unhealthy relationship with the Marquis of Buxton's widow, Olivia Hamilton—as well as his obsession over the home he had lost, and the rage he concentrated on the Duke of Exmoor, whom he blamed for his father's death. Lucien wished he could get through to his friend, but the blighter had always been stubborn as a bloody mule.

He took another belt of his drink and caught the barmaid's summons, a promise of promiscuous sex in her eyes as she waved to him from the stairs leading to the chambers above.

Lucien contemplated making an excuse—peculiar for a man who had always thoroughly enjoyed women. Perhaps that was why he couldn't banish the image of the fiery little head-basher. She had stirred him, and he had needed to know if the feelings she aroused would carry him through, or if that veil of numbness would descend once again.

Yet the thought of being alone, knowing what awaited him in the hours after midnight when his soul was restless, propelled him to his feet and across the pockmarked floorboards. Grabbing the barmaid by the hand, he pulled her up the stairs.

"Y' like it rough, do y'?" She scraped her nails across his back and purred in her coarse voice, "Good. So do I."

Lucien blanked his mind. This was the best he could ever hope to get; he was destined to confine himself to serving girls and whores. The poor boy from the cesspits of Shadwell, on the East London riverside, could never break free.

He had fought it. God how he fought it. But the savage in him yet remained.

At the top of the stairs, the barmaid shoved him up against the wall, her hand cupping his groin as her mouth found his, her eyes nearly feral with lust.

Lucien took hold of her wrists and backed her up a step. "Patience, dear girl. My room is right down there."

He guided her toward the last door on the left, wondering if he could summon a properly enthusiastic response, since his body balked.

He was contemplating his options when a flash of movement caught the corner of his eye, drawing his gaze to a partially opened door. He spotted a familiar breeches-clad leg, heard a familiar warning, then a familiar thud. A grim smile curved his lips.

"Stay here," he ordered the barmaid as he moved to investigate, his restlessness forgotten as he imagined the reckoning one little thief was soon to have.

Two

$\mathcal{A}$ lack of planning had always been her downfall, Fancy thought as she backed away from the naked man stalking her, his eyes aflame with equal parts fury and desire. The latter concerned her far more than the former.

She could be rash, hotheaded, and—as she had heard far too many times from the governesses her odious guardian continued to foist on her—willful, insubordinate, and completely unsuited for any lifestyle that required associating with the world.

She might be inclined to agree with the part about her being rash. Creeping into a strange man's bedroom while he was engaged in a bath, with only a silk screen between her and discovery, certainly didn't fall under the category of careful planning. But it had seemed her best option, since his clothing was strewn about the floor, just begging to be rifled through. A better opportunity she would not get.

"Comin' in 'ere to rob me blind, were y'? Well, y'll get much more than the beatin' y' deserve." The gleam in his eyes promised he would enjoy both the beating and his lascivious plans.

While he recognized her as female, he didn't recognize who she was. But none of that mattered as he continued toward her until her back was pressed up against the fireplace, where a small blaze endeavored to keep out the chill.

Fancy raised her gun for the second time that night, knowing she wouldn't stand a chance if he called her bluff.

He smirked at her. "Y' ain't gonna shoot an unarmed man, are y'?"

"I will if you come any closer."

"Look at me, lass. I'm naked." His hand moved to his privates with a disgusting flourish, momentarily distracting Fancy, which gave him the opening he needed.

He dove at her, knocking the wind from her lungs as he thrust her hard against the mantel, the gun flying from her hand and landing halfway across the room.

She struggled against him, but he was too strong. A stinging blow to her cheek knocked her to the ground. He loomed over her, an unholy light in his eyes as he reached for her.

Her panicked gaze lit on the fire poker, and without a

moment's thought, she grabbed it and brought it down with a sharp crack against the side of his head. He blinked once and then collapsed in a heap beside her, his left arm dropping across her chest like a wooden plank.

With a muted shriek, Fancy shoved his beefy arm aside and scrambled away, her entire body trembling, her grip on the poker so fierce her knuckles were blanched white.

Before today, she hadn't even been able to lay a trap for the mouse that had moved into her bedroom. Now she was dashing about the countryside clubbing men over the head!

"I'm glad to see it's not just me you feel inclined to injure," a voice drawled from the doorway, bringing Fancy's gaze swinging up to find a booted foot pushing the portal open. The great, muscled hulk with the piercing blue eyes stepped into the room, smiling as he closed the door behind him.

Heavens, in the light he was even more attractive. His presence filled the room, his shoulders nearly as wide as the door. As he surveyed her, his eyes seemed to burn as intensely as the wall sconce beside him.

"I must say that my pounding skull does not sway me toward benevolence at this moment."

Fancy lifted her chin, even as remorse surfaced for hitting him so hard. "You survived, didn't you? Clearly, your skull is too thick to break."

"Count yourself lucky, dear girl. Murder is a hanging offense. And it would be a terrible shame to stretch that pretty neck of yours."

Fancy lifted a hand to her throat. Dear Lord, what would happen to Jaines and Olinda and Rosalyn and Moor's End if she found herself swinging from the end of a noose? Her gaze raced to the thug on the floor.

"He's alive," the man said, uncannily reading her thoughts. "But he'll have a prodigious headache when he awakens. I know from experience." He rubbed the back of his head. "So tell me, sweetheart, how long have you hated men?"

Fancy was too frazzled to heed the danger he presented. "I don't hate men."

"So you like men?"

"Yes . . . I mean, no . . ." She shook her head, flustered by his persistence. "What is it that you want?"

"An apology might be a good place to start. Then we can move on from there."

"I'm sorry. Now go away."

He smiled at her as though she were a toy that amused him. "You really should pick your customers with more care. Perhaps you wouldn't find yourself in such precarious situations."

It took a moment for his meaning to sink in. "You don't actually think—"

His smile broadened. "I can only hope to be so lucky." He folded his arms across his chest and leaned back against the door. "So do you contain your criminal activities to thievery only?"

"I told you, I'm not a thief!"

"Not a very good one, at least."

"I'm not— Oh, why do I bother talking to you?"

"Perhaps because I exude an abundance of charm, and you find yourself oddly drawn to me."

"I'd find the progression of a snail on a slippery rock more engaging."

His bark of laughter was interrupted by a pounding rattle on the door, followed by the gruff voice of the proprietor. "Wot's goin' on in there?"

"Seems we're about to have an audience," the rogue said, amusement in his eyes. "My companion for the evening must have thought crimes of passion were transpiring in here."

Fancy narrowed her gaze at him. "You mean your doxy is waiting out there?" When he smiled, she said, "You're despicable."

"Despicable I may be, but right now I'm your savior."

The wooden door shook. "Open up, or I'm comin' in!"

"Make up your mind, love. A kiss will buy my chivalry."

"That's blackmail!"

His grin grew wicked. "I know."

Keys jangled just outside the door. At any moment, the proprietor—a large brute with beady eyes—would be inside the room and see her standing over a man with a fire poker. Good Lord, she was still holding the thing! She thrust it behind her back and heard her "savior" chuckle.

"Perhaps I should let him in," he said, turning toward the door.

"Fine. You win. I'll kiss you. But only once!" she hastened to add.

"Deal." He winked, and then leaned his shoulder against the door as the owner began to push it open, saying in a perfect Cockney accent, "Sod off, damn y'. I'm busy in 'ere."

The rattling stopped. "Naught's amiss?" the innkeeper queried.

The wicked man had the nerve to look back at her, his single raised eyebrow positively lecherous. Oh, what had she gotten herself into now?

He said to the proprietor, "Y' interrupted me, y' fat lout. Back away from this door, or I vow I'll kick y' until y'r dead."

An indignant snort sounded from the other side, followed by the heavy thud of footsteps moving away.

Her self-proclaimed savior then turned and said in a voice full of sinful intent, "Now, about that kiss . . ."

Fancy took a step back and found a solid wall thwarting her retreat, and the solid man in front of her intent on preventing her escape. The dancing flames in the grate gave his face a saturnine cast and outlined the determination in his eyes. She was well and truly caught.

She flattened her palms against the wall as he leisurely advanced, as though they had all the time in the world. "One kiss," she reminded him, her mouth drying with each step he took.

"One kiss," Lucien repeated calmly, not wanting to frighten her into bolting. He fought his own need, a rising heat infusing his blood, both comforting in its old familiarity and dreaded in its intensity, colored as it was by memories of the past.

He pushed it down and concentrated solely on those sweet eyes regarding him with a mixture of alarm and excitement, widening with each step that brought him closer to her, until she was staring up at him, chin high, a defiant sprite in a floppy hat. He took the ridiculous thing off and tossed it to the floor.

"What are you—"

He pressed a finger to her lips to silence her, then held her gaze as he traced the soft contours of her mouth. Such a mouth, plump and lush and pink as a rosebud. She was made to be kissed. Often and thoroughly.

He shifted forward until he could feel the tips of her breasts against his chest, his body attuned to each subtle inflection, each soft breath. God, she made him feel like a giant, she was so tiny. He would crush her if he were ever on top when they made love—and he hoped to be given that honor, even if it meant saving her from every scrape she found herself embroiled in from now until doomsday, extracting rewards for each act of gallantry.

Then a thought occurred to him, something that had never troubled him before. "Are you married?" He'd had his share of that particular breed, which only cemented his determination to remain a bachelor.

"No," she replied, and then frowned, as though recognizing too late that he had given her a perfect out.

Lucien felt oddly relieved by her answer. "Do you live around here?" It would make his stay much more fulfilling; he suspected she would be as much a hellion in bed as out.

She lifted her chin. "No."

He could tell she was lying, and by God, he wanted her even more. What was the world coming to when a man found a liar and a thief so damned intriguing? Perhaps he would find the answer in her kiss.

"Please," she said in a breathless voice. "Just get it over with."

Was she dreading his touch, or aching for it as much as he was? "Anticipation, my dove." He lightly pressed his thumb against the seam of her lips until she opened for him, the satiny surface glistening like a ripe berry.

He could feel her trembling and wondered if she was truly as innocent as she looked. A girl who frequented such establishments must have some experience. No one this bold and beautiful could be chaste. He would enjoy erasing the memory of whoever had come before him.

Leaning down, Lucien captured her breathy gasp with his mouth, a fist of desire hitting him square in the chest. He cupped her face in his hands and made love to her with his mouth, gently coaxing her to accept his tongue, sliding inside, tasting her sweetness, heat rifling through his blood as he felt her respond.

He slid his fingers into her hair, releasing the heavy topknot and letting the silk cascade into his hands. He twined a fistful of it around his hand and tugged, tipping her head farther back so he could explore the hot, moist depths of her mouth more deeply.

He shifted so that his shirt scraped the hard points of her nipples, the erect little buds telling him that he was affecting her, her soft whimpers driving him nearly beyond control.

His hands skimmed down her side to the soft flare of her hips, and then around to cup her bottom, fulfilling the fantasy that had begun in the stables. The firm globes fit perfectly in his palms, and he lifted her up against his erection, forgetting himself as he rocked gently against her.

She moved in concert at first, but then tore her mouth from his, the small hands that had settled at his shoulders pushing at him. "Stop this! Let me down."

Lucien's body balked, but his mind took over after a momentary lapse. Reluctantly, he gave in, but tortured himself by slowly lowering her feet to the floor, letting her slide along his body, the friction working on them both.

Despite the anger now glittering in her eyes, desire lingered, and she wasn't quite steady as she braced her palms against the wall. "I said one kiss, you black-hearted swine!"

Lucien couldn't trust himself to be that close to her and not touch her, so he backed away and dropped down into the room's one chair, feeling on the verge of a heart attack, he was so primed. God, he needed another drink.

"That was one kiss, dear girl."

"That was nothing of the sort!"

"If my lips didn't leave yours, then it was one kiss."

She looked like she wanted to bash him over the head again. "You got what you wanted; now I'll be leaving."

"If you feel you must. But tell me where you live, and I'll come to you. Or you can come to me. Whichever you prefer."

"I won't be coming anywhere near you," she said angrily, and he was almost convinced she meant it.

The man on the floor began to stir. Lucien glimpsed the concern in the girl's eyes as she glanced down at her second, correction, *third* victim of the night. She was a puzzle. First she brains the poor bastard, and then she feels remorse. He wondered if she had shown *him* any pity. If so, he was sorry he'd missed it.

He rose from the chair, intent on escorting her from the premises and finding out where she lived in the process, but she whipped around to face him, the fire poker thrust unerringly at his manhood. One-eyed Jack and the boys instantly recoiled.

"You do know how to bring a man to a grinding halt, sweetheart."

"I want you to stay back."

"Since you've targeted my most prized possessions, I have no choice but to comply. I might someday wish to procreate."

She snorted. "As if you haven't left your progeny all over the globe."

He could barely restrain his smile. "Such a slur on my character. I'll have you know that I don't have a single bastard. Children tend to hamper a man's free spirit—as do their mothers. But if you're worried about pregnancy—"

"Practice your skills on the tart you left behind," she said frostily. "Now I'll bid you good night."

The thought of losing her again did not sit well with Lucien. He moved toward her, but she brought the poker up between his thighs, the curled spike pressed squarely between his balls.

He raised his hands in surrender. "You win."

She backed toward the door, keeping her gaze focused on him as she bent to retrieve her gun. She made quite a sight standing there with a weapon in each hand.

"Do you always defend your virtue so vigorously?" he asked. She would certainly be a challenge, if so. But he was a man who enjoyed a challenge.

Instead of answering, she peeked out the door and scanned the corridor. Unfortunately for him, the hall was deserted. With a less-than-hospitable glance in his direction, she slipped out.

Lucien started after her, but something gripped his ankle. He looked down to see a beefy hand wrapped around his boot and two bloodshot eyes staring up at him.

"Wot 'appened?" the slimy woman-beater asked in a slurred tone.

"This happened." Lucien's right fist connected with

the swine's jaw, knocking him out again. "Perhaps next time you'll think twice about manhandling my future mistress." Then he headed out the door and barreled down the stairs, a faint aroma of her vanilla scent wafting in the air as he burst into the tavern's courtyard.

He swore fiercely. She had eluded him. Again. If that bloody bastard hadn't held him up, he wouldn't have lost her. Lucien felt just volatile enough to go back up and punch him again for the hell of it.

Hearing the crunch of feet coming up behind him, Lucien jerked around, making the stable boy jump back a good foot, his face paling beneath his curly mop of hair.

"Sorry, mister."

"What is it?" Lucien snapped, then regretted his harsh tone. The boy had done nothing wrong. He sighed and raked a hand through his hair. "Is something the matter?"

He hesitated. "Well, when I saw y' run out, I thought maybe y' might be chasin' after that boy what dashed out here a minute ago."

"You saw him?" Lucien asked eagerly.

He nodded. "I remembered wot y' said earlier. Y' know, about seein' anything strange."

"Do you know who he is?"

"Couldn't see 'is face 'cause of the hat 'e was wearin', but I saw which way 'e went." He pointed toward the east. "He 'ad an old hack tied to a tree."

Lucien glanced off into the darkness, thinking the girl could be anywhere by now. But there was a good chance she lived in the area. That was something, at least.

He dug a hand into his pocket and offered the boy another pound note, recognizing the telltale shaking of his hand as he gave the money to the lad. The ache was beginning to boil up inside his gut; the demon would have him in his grip any time now.

"If you should spot him again, come get me." Lucien headed back toward the tavern, needing to get behind the closed doors of his room.

"I . . . I know where he went."

Lucien pivoted around to face the boy. "Where?"

"Moor's End."

Lucien frowned. That was the home of his ward. Could the girl be one of the Fitz Hugh servants? Could it be that easy?

If he found her, maybe he would also find peace for a few hours and stave off the hunger that rose inside of him in the darkest part of the night. Perhaps tonight he could outdistance the craving.

"Saddle my horse," he said, and stalked toward the stables.

Three

Fancy reined Clover to a walk once she was far enough away from the tavern to feel safe, though it was not Calder's thugs who concerned her, but the stranger whose kiss had nearly melted her.

The things he had done with his tongue, how soft yet demanding his mouth had been against hers, how hard and hot his body . . . She had never thought it could be like that, drugging, mind-consuming, making one forget rational thought. If she had, she would not have agreed to kiss him.

But it had gone much further than a kiss. He had pressed intimately against her, and the feelings he had stirred had sent her senses whirling until fear of her own wanton response made her fight against him.

Her thoughts calmed as the old mare came to a stop

at the end of the long dirt drive that led up to Moor's End. The crumbling gray mansion with its symmetrical gables and steeply pitched roof was the only place she had ever truly called home. It stood like a proud Gothic monument, backdropped against cliff and sky, a profusion of rhododendrons growing wild around the perimeter, the familiar smell of tidal water scenting the air.

Memories crowded in of days spent bathing naked in deserted coves, treading across moorland bogs, of learning how to gut a fish, to scull, to row a boat. Climbing on the rotting hulls of shipwrecked vessels, trespassing upon abandoned estates, and slipping in through shuttered windows to inspect the ghostly interiors.

As a young child, before her parents had died while traveling to China on one of her father's military expeditions, Fancy and her brother had spent months with her grandmother and had grown to love this place.

Many days she and George had crouched among the sand dunes and tufted grass, looking seaward, picturing great lines of high-prowed vessels, their sails aloft as they entered the shallows on the flood tide. Captains who were unable to properly navigate their boats would crash helplessly upon the rocky shoals, bringing out smugglers to feast upon the booty that washed ashore.

But approaching by sea had always been the best way, sailing from southern Ireland to the Hayle estuary, as the first traders did, to get a glimpse of the

Cornish claw thrusting defiantly into the ocean, the forbidding grandeur of Land's End awing even the most jaded sailor, with its hinterland of granite tors and the emergence of St. Ives Bay, its protective arms shaped like a horseshoe.

Fancy breathed deeply. Home. This place was in her blood, and she would do anything to keep it safe.

Giving Clover a gentle nudge, she headed toward the stables. One of the doors hung askew, its loose hinges sunk deep into the rotting wood. Tomorrow she would have to fix it; money was too tight to hire anyone to do the task.

Once she had Clover brushed down and fed, Fancy put a blanket over the mare's back and kissed her nose. "You did well tonight, girl," she murmured, then headed out into the chilly darkness.

Glancing up, she spotted the light flickering through the windowpanes of her bedroom. Rosalyn was waiting for her, anxiously, Fancy suspected. Her friend hadn't wanted her to go after the men, but considering what had happened that morning, Fancy knew Calder would not cease in his attempts to get his hands on Rosalyn unless they found something they could use against him.

She had barely walked through the front door before Jaines appeared out of the gloom of the long corridor, a single lick of white hair sticking up at the back of his head while strands as thin as cobwebs threaded the rest of his balding pate.

His concerned brown eyes peered at her through thick spectacles. "Thank goodness you're back."

"Has all been quiet tonight, Jaines?"

"Yes, miss. But we were worried about you."

"As you can see, I'm fine."

Olinda appeared next, a spry woman whose silvery hair framed a perfectly oval face and brought out the beauty of her dove gray eyes. She looked much younger than her husband, though barely five years separated them. She claimed it was the result of her strong Scottish stock.

"Praise Saint Ninian, there ye are! I was just aboot tae call out the cavalry. Where've ye been, hinny? Ye had us all worried."

"So I've heard."

Olinda *tsk*ed. "Ye always were a vexing child."

Fancy hugged Olinda's thin shoulders. "But you love me, don't you?"

Olinda's voice was gruff, but the pat on Fancy's arm was gentle. "Aye, lass. I love ye. Ye are like one of me own."

Fancy didn't know what she would have done without Olinda and Jaines this past year. There were days after her grandmother and brother died that she didn't think she would make it, but they had pulled her through. Now it was her turn to bear the responsibility that others had spared her from all these years.

Woof! The distinctive bark echoed in the domed foyer and shook the rafters.

Fancy looked up to the top of the steps, where a shaggy head of mottled brown and white came into view before Sadie barreled down the stairs, her massive paws skittering across the recently waxed floor, sending her careening into poor Jaines, who toppled to the ground, Sadie's prodigious weight pinning him there while she treated him to a slavering lick that knocked his spectacles askew.

"Off, you blasted beast!" he demanded in regal tones.

For all Sadie's enormous size—she was a good part wolfhound blended with some other equally massive breed—she was as sweet as a lamb. The poor thing just didn't realize how big she was. Thunder brought her quivering behind Fancy's legs. And she was utterly terrified of the cat, Sassy, a mischievous tabby who loved to creep up on people and pounce, taking special delight in stalking Sadie's tail. It never failed to send the poor hound scurrying into Fancy's lap, one-hundred-dred-fifty pounds of cowering deadweight.

"Come, Sadie," Fancy coaxed. "Leave poor Jaines alone. You're smothering him."

Adoring brown eyes swung to Fancy, bringing Sadie to her feet, her big head nudging Fancy's hand, wanting a scratch behind the ears.

Fancy knelt down and stroked the dog's thick fur. "Did you keep our guest company tonight?" she asked, to which a female voice replied, "She was a delight."

An ethereal vision in a *peau de soie* dress of dark blue stood looking down at them, from the top of the stairs.

No matter how many times a person saw Lady Rosalyn Carmichael, they could not help but be moved by her beauty. She was a stunning, lithe creature, possessed of angelic features and pale blond hair that hung to her waist, the thick mass now a long, braided rope down her back, tendrils escaping to frame her oval face and cerulean blue eyes.

Where Fancy was dark, Rosalyn was light. Where Fancy was short, Rosalyn was tall, with the longest legs Fancy had ever seen. If ever there was an image of feminine loveliness, Rosalyn epitomized it.

"Thank goodness you're back," she said as she glided down the stairs, coming to a stop in front of Fancy and taking hold of her hands. "I was so worried."

Fancy smiled reassuringly at her friend. "No mere man is going to stop a Fitz Hugh." Even as she made her claim, an image of dark hair and jewel-toned eyes rose in front of her. *He* had not been a mere man. Fancy wasn't quite sure what he was.

"I didn't doubt it for a minute." Rosalyn's smile transformed her from angelic to breathtaking, with a hint of sin in that heavenly expression that brought men, young and old, to their knees.

All the girls had instantly hated Rosalyn when she had first arrived in town with her mother. But Fancy had felt an immediate kinship, knowing what it was like to be the new person in a place where generations of families had lived and died, their roots mired deep in the sandy loam.

When she had first spotted Rosalyn sitting by herself at Meadow's Cove, the young girl had looked so sad and lost. Fancy's heart had gone out to her, and she had vowed then and there that they would become the best of friends. And they had.

"What happened to your cheek?" Rosalyn asked, her gaze narrowing suspiciously on Fancy's face.

Fancy turned her head away, having forgotten the blow the horrid thug had managed to get in. "It's nothing; I hit a low branch on the ride home. I wasn't watching where I was going."

Her friend raised a brow, clearly not believing that story. But Fancy knew she would say no more. She wouldn't want to upset Jaines and Olinda.

"Let's get you out of those damp clothes and into a nice warm bath." Rosalyn tugged her along.

Fancy went willingly up the stairs, Sadie at her heels. With a vow that she was all right, she sent a reluctant Jaines and Olinda off to bed.

As soon as they were gone, Rosalyn laced into her. "Who hit you?" Before Fancy could reply, she added, "Oh, why did I let you go alone? I could never live with myself if anything had happened to you." As she spoke, she yanked Fancy's shirt over her head, as though she had suddenly become incapable of undressing herself. "I just knew those despicable men would hurt you. It was pure foolishness for you to track them down. Calder won't give up, you know. No matter what we do." She pushed Fancy back on the bed and wrenched off her scuffed boots. "I'll just have to go to America or some other equally heathenish place and hide out."

"You won't have to—"

"I don't know how I let you talk me into these things. This is my problem, not yours."

"It's our—"

"I'll just have to cut off my hair and wear a wig. Disguise myself as a governess or a charwoman."

"That's going a bit—"

"But we won't do this again." She shoved Fancy down into the copper tub that she had thoughtfully filled and kept warm for her. "If anything had happened to you . . ." Rosalyn's eyes were glossy with unshed tears.

Fancy took hold of her hands. "I'm tougher than I look."

"But your face . . ."

"It's already forgotten." But it would probably show a bruise by morning, which would undoubtedly make Rosalyn feel even worse.

Truth be told, the kiss that had come after the slap had affected her far more. Was the handsome blackmailer still at the tavern? Had he looked for her, even though she had told him not to? Oh, why did it matter?

"If it makes you feel better," Fancy said, "both of Calder's thugs will have splitting headaches in the morning."

Laughter lit her friend's eyes. "You really are the most remarkable woman. Men would love you—if only they could find you out here."

"The same for you. You should be married by now and raising a house full of children."

Rosalyn scrubbed at Fancy's gnarled locks. "We are a pair, aren't we?"

"A force to reckon with." With a wink, Fancy ducked

her head beneath the water and rinsed the soap from her hair.

Rising from the tub, she wrapped a thick towel around her, smelling like a spring garden from Rosalyn's favorite soap.

Using another towel, Rosalyn dried her hair. "So were you able to find anything?"

"No," Fancy replied with a sigh, grabbing her old terry wrapper from her bed. "But I'll come up with something."

"You shouldn't be doing this. You already have enough to concern yourself with. Aren't the taxes coming due on the property soon?"

The reminder lay like a heavy sorrow on Fancy's heart as she moved to the window and looked out, staring off into the distance where weather-pitted granite tombs of ancient earth goddesses and priests jutted from the ground. The stones were tilted to form a roof, set high on the hills amid gorse and scrub, the treasures they once contained long gone, leaving only the aging memorials of a forgotten way of life—as her own life would soon be, if she couldn't turn things around.

The more she wanted things to stay the same, the more the sands of fate shifted beneath her. The weight of responsibility pressed on her shoulders. Unless circumstances changed, and soon, she would lose Moor's End.

She hadn't realized how far behind her grandmother had fallen in her taxes until the tax collector had shown up at her door shortly after her grandmother's death to relay the bad news. Fancy had been given three months to come up with what was owed, or the house would be taken from them and sold.

Moor's End had belonged to her grandmother's family for generations. Every decaying stone and creaking hinge had been special to her, as they were to Fancy. Moor's End had sheltered her through all her troubled years; nothing existed for her outside these walls. After all her grandmother had done for her, Fancy owed it to her to try and save the home she loved. She had only two months left to do so.

Pinning a smile on her face, she turned to Rosalyn. "You worry too much. I already have half the money." She barely had a third. The regulation men had been out in force the past few months, which made runs out of the cove nearly impossible.

"Smuggling is too dangerous. If you get caught—"

"I won't."

"The rocks are treacherous, especially at night."

"I know every crevice."

Rosalyn frowned. "Still . . ."

Fancy padded across the room to stand before her friend. "I promise I'll be careful. Now, we'd better get some sleep. Who knows what antics Calder will be up to tomorrow?" They would have to be even more vigilant from this point on. "Do you want Sadie to sleep with you?"

"No, I'll be fine." Rosalyn paused at the door. "Have I told you lately what a wonderful friend you are?"

"You've told me a thousand times. Don't worry, we'll beat Calder at his own game." Hoping she looked as confident as she sounded, Fancy picked up a small oil lamp. "I'll walk you to your room."

As they stepped into the darkened hallway, Fancy found herself thinking about her guardian. She could only be thankful that he had not deigned to show his face in Cornwall. The last thing she needed was some ex-military man monitoring every move she made.

She wondered what her brother had been thinking to saddle her with a keeper, as though she were incapable of taking care of herself. And worse, a keeper whose antics often appeared in the scandal sheets. George must have been delirious. But as long as her mysterious warden stayed away, all would be well. Or so she hoped.

"What was that?" Rosalyn suddenly whispered.

"What?"

"I heard something downstairs."

Fancy turned her head toward the landing and listened. Nothing but Sadie's panting and the whisper of the wind through cracks in the stones reached her.

Then she heard it. The faint sounds of someone moving around in her grandfather's old smoking room. A chill raced up her arms and raised the hairs on the back of her neck.

"Perhaps it's Jaines," she replied in hushed tones, as she and Rosalyn padded toward the stairs. But Jaines had no reason to be in the smoking room. Her grandfather had been its last steady occupant. Old bottles of liquor still lined the cupboard, well aged and highly potent by now, she suspected. But nobody in the house drank.

Fancy gripped the banister, spying the light shining from beneath the door at the bottom of the steps. "Stay here," she told Rosalyn, who was pressed against her back.

"I'm not letting you go down there alone. It could be Calder."

Fancy didn't want to think that she could have underestimated Calder's determination again. "It's probably just an animal who got in through the chimney." Which didn't explain the light, but she kept that to herself. "I'll be back in a minute."

Rosalyn grabbed her arm. "Let's get Jaines."

Fancy didn't want to alarm her friend, but Rosalyn seemed to think that because Jaines was a man, he could handle any situation. What she failed to recall was that Jaines was seventy, if he was a day, and he suffered from rheumatism.

"Even if I wanted to rouse the poor man, you know that Jaines sleeps like the dead."

Rosalyn anxiously gnawed her lower lip. Then her eyes lit up. "Wait here." Less than a minute later, she was back, pressing something cold into Fancy's hand. She looked down to see it was her grandfather's old gun, which, prior to this evening, she had never even held. "Let's go," Rosalyn then urged, her expression determined as she clutched a heavy brass candlestick in her hand.

Fancy knew when she was beaten. Taking a deep breath, she exhaled slowly. Then she and Rosalyn crept down the stairs, so close together they were almost one. Even Sadie was jammed quiveringly against her thigh.

As they reached the second-to-last step, the door to the smoking room suddenly swung open, casting a large shadow on the floor before an equally large figure emerged into the entrance hall. Their collective gasp brought his head jerking in their direction.

In the next moment, Sadie woofed, and in an unprecedented bout of bravery, she lunged at the intruder. The man went down in a heap of dog fur . . . and the gun suddenly exploded in Fancy's hand.

Four

Sadie barked madly, while Rosalyn's voice curdled into an alarmed shriek. Even Sassy, who had squeezed out of a dark cubbyhole, hissed, her mottled orange-brown fur sticking up in spikes.

Good Lord, Fancy thought, she had shot the intruder! At least she thought so. She couldn't see anything through the dense gray smoke obscuring her vision. The firearm was at least twenty years old, and she had thought it wasn't loaded!

Waving the smoke away from her face, Fancy gasped when she saw the prone figure on the floor. She dashed down the stairs, her hair a wet banner clinging to her wrapper and streaming in black rivulets over her shoulders. She dropped down beside the man and got her first good look at him. Her mouth dropped open in shock as pale aquamarine eyes settled on her.

"Not dead yet," he said with a groan, "but I suspect you'll succeed at doing me in . . . before the night is through." He closed his eyes and grimaced in pain, snapping Fancy out of her daze.

Her gaze lit on his ankle, and she saw the nasty gash where the bullet had deeply grazed him. "You'll need some stitches."

Rosalyn knelt on the other side of him, thinking more clearly than Fancy was at that moment as she tore off a strip of her shift and tied it around his ankle with the proficiency of a trained nurse.

"I'll send Jaines for the doctor," Rosalyn said, starting to rise, but the man's hand whipped out and wrapped around her wrist.

"No doctor. Just . . . sew me up." He turned to Fancy. "You." The word was an order.

Before Fancy could protest, Jaines and Olinda appeared. "Oh, Lord, what's happened?" Jaines moaned.

"We caught a prowler skulking about the house," Rosalyn answered.

"That's no prowler, miss. That's Mr. Kendall."

Fancy blinked and slowly shifted her gaze to the hulk lying next to her on the floor. "*Lucien* Kendall?" she asked, praying it wasn't so. Not her guardian. Not here. Not now. Not like this!

"In the flesh," her victim answered. "Or what remains of it, at least."

Fancy closed her eyes, wishing she could disappear. Of all the men in all the world, why did it have to be *this* man her brother had appointed as her guardian? She had kissed *this* man—and enjoyed it.

He moaned then, and she started. Concerned, she leaned over him. "What's the matter?"

He cracked open one eye. "Other than the fact that I've been shot, you mean?" He looped a long strand of her hair around his fingers and tugged her head down until he could whisper in her ear, "Another kiss would greatly ease the pain."

Fancy nearly lost a hank of her hair, she sat up so abruptly, unsettled by the tingling inside her at feeling his warm breath on her cheek. She scowled at him, and he smiled. Then his smile faded, and he began to shake.

Lord, what was the matter with her? He was hurt. She turned to Jaines. "Do we still have the laudanum we used when Bevil broke his arm?"

"I believe so," he said, and hustled off to find the medicine.

"We should get him upstairs to one of the beds," Olinda suggested.

Fancy nodded, looking at his big, muscular frame. "You take his right arm," she said to Rosalyn. "I'll get his left."

They struggled to lift him to his feet. Fancy had a sneaking suspicion that he was purposely making it difficult, and that he was taking a great deal of delight in leaning most of his weight on her.

A large, dark hand draped over her shoulder and brushed across her breast. To her mortification, her nipple peaked. Her gaze snapped to his, ready to blister his ears, but his eyes were jammed shut, and his jaw was gritted.

The first bedroom they came to was hers. Fancy hesitated, feeling oddly unnerved at the thought of him lying in her bed. But the three guest rooms all were blanketed in a thick layer of dust, and none had sheets on the bed. She would just have to sleep in the study. In the morning, she'd have him transferred elsewhere.

They managed to get him to the bed. As soon as Rosalyn eased away, he fell back heavily against the pillows, dragging Fancy down with him—and over the top of his body, leaving nothing but solid, hard man beneath her.

"That's better." Though he looked ill, he smiled wickedly at her, and this time she knew his intention had been purposeful.

"You'll release me," she hissed only loud enough for him to hear, "or you'll find your trousers sewn to your wound." He chuckled softly at her threat, held on for another moment, and then opened his arms. She moved away quickly, her body warmed where they had been pressed together.

Jaines shuffled in then, a glass in one hand and the bottle of laudanum in the other. He went to pour the potent medicine into the glass, but her patient swiped the bottle from him and took a substantial swig.

Fancy grabbed hold of his wrist. "Don't take too much."

"Worried?" He cocked a mocking brow and then

downed another dose, surely too much, even for a man his size.

She dropped his hand. "If you die, they'll blame me."

"And murder is a hanging offense," he said, taking delight in repeating the words he'd taunted her with earlier.

Fancy kept her tongue behind her teeth with effort and looked over her shoulder. "I'll need the medical supplies."

"I have them," Olinda said, holding up the faded black satchel that contained a needle, thread, salve, bandages, and an assortment of the healing herbs her grandmother had taught her to use.

Fancy noticed her patient unbuttoning his trousers. "What are you doing?" she said in an outraged voice, the voice of a woman who had never seen an unclothed man.

Deviltry danced in his eyes as he looked up at her, though she could see the drug beginning to fade them. "It would appear I'm undressing. You need to get at my wound, don't you?"

"I can cut off the bottom half of your trousers," she told him sternly, praying he didn't go for the next button.

"Are you sure?" he said in that provoking tone.

"Positive."

Olinda stepped up beside her. "I should be doing this, lass. Ye're unmarried." To which she added pointedly to their patient, "Never even touched a mon before, nor let them touch her—she's a good girl, our lass is."

Utter mortification flooded Fancy, made all the worse

when the scoundrel quirked a dark brow at her, blatantly reminding her that she had not only touched a man, but that she had moaned while he kissed her. Cad!

She scowled at him, but the cur simply chuckled. Then his eyelids began to droop as the drug took effect, which suited her perfectly. The last thing she needed was him making this any more difficult than it was going to be.

"Don't take advantage of me while I'm unable to defend my honor, ladies." Then his head fell to the side.

Rosalyn came to stand at her shoulder. "He'll be asleep for quite a while, considering the amount of the laudanum he took."

Fancy stared down at the big body sprawled across her bed and got an image of him wrapped in only a Christmas bow—a well-placed Christmas bow, of course. Any other man would look ridiculous lying on a white ruffled coverlet, but he just appeared larger and more impressive.

She sighed and glanced briefly at Rosalyn, noting the questioning look directed at her. Avoiding it, she turned to Jaines and Olinda, who stood at the end of the bed, fingers lightly entwined, still in love after nearly fifty years of marriage.

"Why don't you both go to bed? Rosalyn and I can handle things from here."

Jaines could barely meet her gaze. "I'm sorry, miss. This is all my fault. I thought you and Lady Rosalyn had gone to bed. I heard a horse thundering up the drive and worried that it was Lord Westcott, come to take Lady Rosalyn away. I'm afraid I met Mr. Kendall at the front door with the old blunderbuss that has been hanging in your grandfather's office. Of course I felt horrible when I found out who he was. I didn't realize he was coming, you see."

"None of us did, Jaines." And Fancy suspected that had been the man's intention; to catch them off guard. He was just that devious.

"I told him everyone was abed and that we had no room prepared for him, but he said he'd bunk down in the study for the evening. He seemed pleased enough to find the liquor cabinet well stocked, and eager to be alone. He told me to go to bed. He didn't look very well, now that I think on it."

Probably due to the clobbering she had given him. Once more, niggling remorse rose in her.

"I don't hold you at fault for any of this, Jaines. Mr. Kendall should have known better than to appear in the middle of the night. Now, why don't you both get some sleep? It's been a long evening." And it appeared it wouldn't end any time soon.

"Are ye sure, hinny?" Olinda asked, then added, "He's a big mon," as if Fancy had possibly missed that fact. "Quite dangerous lookin'—and handsome, as well. The lassies will have a fine time with this one."

The lassies most definitely would. In such a remote outpost as Cornwall, he would be like an angel sent from heaven. And he clearly had no compunction about who he bestowed his favors upon, or under what circumstances.

"We'll be fine," Fancy assured her, trying to assure herself of the same thing.

Olinda finally shrugged. "Come, husband. We have unfinished business. If I recall, ye were in the middle of makin' me swoon with your sweet declarations of love."

"Olinda!" Jaines scolded in a mortified tone as they headed out the door, their soft old voices fading away.

"They really are adorable together," Rosalyn remarked.

"Yes," Fancy said. If only everyone could find the kind of love Jaines and Olinda shared.

Sighing, she looked down at her guardian. Lucien Kendall. Lucifer would be a far more apt name, as he was surely the devil in a stunningly packaged disguise.

Opening her satchel, she dug out a pair of pinking shears and proceeded to cut his trousers away below the knee. A fine dusting of dark hair sprinkled a muscular calf. Her fingers lightly traced his skin before she caught herself.

Carefully, she removed the linen binding Rosalyn had wrapped around the wound. The injury was not as bad as she feared, but it was mean looking, a long gash that left a crescent shape above his ankle. Another few inches, and she might have blown his foot off.

"Would you like to tell me the whole story now?" Rosalyn said as she handed Fancy a clean piece of cotton and a bottle of antiseptic to bathe the wound.

Not looking up, Fancy replied, "I ran across him at the tavern. He took me by surprise when I was searching through one of the men's pockets."

"Dear Lord, what did he do?"

"Nothing." She only wished he had; maybe then she would have had a better excuse for her actions. "It was more what I did."

"Oh, no. What did you do?" *This time,* were the unspoken words.

Fancy faced her friend. "How could I know he was my guardian? All of a sudden he was standing there, smiling at me. I didn't know what to do. I thought that if he sent for the authorities, you'd be returned to Calder and I'd . . . well, I don't know what would have happened. But I doubt it would be inspiring."

"What did you do?" Rosalyn persisted.

"I didn't mean to 'do' anything. Honestly. I just thought if he saw the gun . . ."

Rosalyn groaned. "You didn't."

"I was just trying to make him move out of the way! It wasn't loaded—or at least I didn't think it was."

"You didn't shoot him then, too, did you?"

Fancy's exasperation rose. "I didn't mean to shoot him this time! It was an accident."

"So he just allowed you to leave?"

"Well, yes . . ."

"Something tells me there's a 'but.'"

Fancy glanced away, rooting through the satchel for a needle and thread. "I was afraid he was going to follow me. So, I . . . I hit him over the head with a rock."

Rosalyn sank down onto the bed. "Oh, goodness," she said, sounding calamitous.

"Oh goodness, indeed." Fancy threaded the needle

and began to stitch his wound, his skin resilient beneath her fingertips. "What am I going to do?"

"Perhaps he'll awake in a more forgiving frame of mind." But as they looked at each other, Fancy knew that was highly unlikely to happen. There was also the little fact that she had threatened his manhood with a fire poker.

And kissed him.

"Why couldn't he have simply sent another governess?" she bemoaned. "In the year since George died, he has not deigned to visit here, which suited me just fine. Blast him for choosing the absolute worst time to appear."

"Well, I cannot entirely blame him."

Fancy's hand paused mid-stitch. "And why not?"

"You chased off every governess he sent."

"They all treated me as though I were a child. 'Hold your pinkie up whilst sipping your tea, Lady Francine,'" she mimicked perfectly. "'Back straight, Lady Francine.' 'Pick up your feet when you walk, Lady Francine.'" She huffed. "It was ridiculous. Who is going to care if I drink my tea with my pinkie up or down?"

"You might care, should you someday wish to be introduced into polite society."

"All I wish is to be left in peace."

"That is something I can well understand." A moment of thoughtful silence passed before Rosalyn said, "What shall we do now?"

Fancy sighed. "I don't know."

While she wanted to dislike the man for throwing her life into turmoil, deep down she felt an odd excitement at having him there.

When she had left him at the tavern, a strange sadness had settled over her at the prospect of never seeing him again. Perhaps she had even harbored the ridiculous hope that he would follow her. When she had gotten her first glimpse of him lying in her foyer, she had been secretly thrilled.

Her emotions were in a jumble as she tied off the final stitch, and she knew a sudden urge to run far and fast. Something told her that her life would not be the same from this moment forward.

"Do you think he'll cause trouble?" Rosalyn asked.

Fancy looked down at her sleeping guardian and sighed. "I think he'll cause nothing but trouble."

After Rosalyn had retired to bed, Fancy sat in a chair in the corner, Sadie plunked at her feet, watching the rise and fall of her guardian's chest. In sleep, his face had been washed of its wickedness, and he looked like a fallen angel.

She had been too unnerved to undress him, other than removing his jacket. Dirt and small specks of blood stained what had once been a pristine white shirt with crisply starched points. His pants were ruined. He had not worn a cravat, which in most places would have been unseemly.

But he didn't seem the type of man who'd care about what was unseemly or not. He was most unusual in many ways. He had been in the military. A decorated colonel, George had often boasted in his letters. Her brother seemed to think the sun rose and set at this man's feet.

"He's the bravest person I've ever met," George had said frequently in his correspondence to her, clearly idolizing his commanding officer. "I think you'd like him."

Fancy doubted her brother had meant his words to be so prophetic. She did like his colonel, in the worst sort of way. But her impulsive behavior had set her on a course from which there was no return. She had kissed him, a man who, for all intents and purposes, was to be in charge of her life. Only catastrophe could come from that. But just looking at Lucien tied her stomach into knots and made her fingers itch to touch him.

Abruptly, Fancy pushed to her feet, not liking where her thoughts were going. If she looked at him any longer, she might very well give in to the urge to lay her hands on him, to make sure his heart still beat steady and strong beneath her fingertips.

She padded to the window, staring out into the endless night. The moon glimmered over the sleek edges of the ocean, glittering like diamond points, reflecting prisms off the dirt-streaked windows of the conservatory.

Moor's End had once been a magnificent manor home, giving employment to half the town's villagers. Now the large stable stood mostly empty; the gardens were overgrown, the plum trees unpruned and wild.

In three days, she was to meet Bodie at Mariner's Nook to bundle up the shipment that she hoped would bring her closer to paying off her grandmother's debt. Her guardian's unexpected scrutiny would make everything much more difficult.

A low moan brought Fancy back to the moment. She turned, expecting to see blue-green eyes leveled on her in accusation, but Lucien was still asleep, though stirring restlessly. As she drew nearer to him, he began to thrash in the throes of a nightmare, induced from too much laudanum, she suspected.

She sank down next to him on the bed as he rambled words in a language she didn't recognize, only a few understandable phrases in between.

"No," he muttered, his head rolling back and forth on the pillow. "Don't do it. Don't!" Suddenly, his hands wrapped fiercely around her arms.

Fancy jerked back, startled. But he didn't hurt her, just held on, and she knew that he didn't realize what he was doing. "Ssh," she murmured, seeking to soothe him. "It's all right. Everything is all right."

"Sanji," he said in a guttural voice, his face contorted in pain. "I'm sorry. I'm sorry."

Fancy could hear the fierce regret in his voice and wondered who Sanji was. One of his soldiers, who he had not been able to save, like her brother?

"You're forgiven. Now rest." When he eased his grip, she pulled her arms free, but she did not move away. Instead she cupped his cheek, the muscle beneath resonating with tension. He seemed to calm as she stroked him, her fingers fanning through his silky hair as she whispered softly to him. Then she bathed his brow with a cold cloth; his skin was so hot, she feared an infection had set in.

When she was rinsing out the cloth she turned to find his gaze fixed on her, his eyes foggy with the drug.

"Sleep now," she told him in a quiet voice. "You'll feel better in the morning."

His hand curled around her upper arms, tugging her forward until they were face-to-face, her breasts flush against his chest. Then he cupped the back of her head, bringing her mouth down to his. She didn't resist; she couldn't. She wanted to know if what she had felt the first time had been real, even if he didn't realize what he was doing.

She closed her eyes and let go. His mouth molded hers, strong yet gentle, his tongue sliding inside to taste her, coax her.

The kiss was everything she had expected, and more. But it was over too soon, as his fingers slipped from her hair and his eyes drifted shut. In the next moment, he was asleep again.

Fancy doubted he would remember any of what had taken place come the morning. But she would not soon forget.

Five

Lucien awoke feeling as though an awl had been driven through his skull. Little hammers beat against his temples, and his mouth tasted as if a rat had crawled into it and died. Laudanum, his beleaguered brain tapped out. The poor man's drug of choice.

It took a moment for the fog to begin to clear. Why was there a translucent white canopy above his head and a frilly coverlet pulled up to his chin? If this was hell, it wasn't at all as he had imagined it.

He rubbed his eyes and opened them again. The canopy was still there. The coverlet, too. What the blazes was going on? He vaguely recalled a doxy named Sugar and a searing pain in his ankle.

Then a memory of fern green eyes penetrated his hazy brain, a wavering image of an incredibly foolhardy slip of a girl. He had left the tavern to find her. And he had—much to his detriment.

A strange sound rumbled in Lucien's ear then, and a moist heat fanned the side of his face. Cautiously, he turned his head and found two piercing brown eyes the size of tea saucers staring into his, set in the face of a mammoth dog. Its teeth were massive, its jaw big enough to tear out his windpipe.

The dog cocked its head and stared at him unblinkingly. Then it unfurled its long pink tongue and gave him a slobbering lick.

"Have a care, you accursed hound." Lucien wiped his hand across his cheek. "Dogs are considered a delicacy in some countries."

The threat was lost on the buffleheaded animal, and Lucien practically rolled off the bed when it put its front paws on the mattress to sniff at his crotch.

"Unless you're a female in disguise," he said, pushing the dog's snout away, "that area is strictly off limits." He tried to remove the animal from the bed. "Good Lord, you weigh as much as a Clydesdale. What do you eat? Clipper ships? Down, you—"

The remainder of his demand was cut off as the dog let out a howl that sounded as if it had boiled up from the very bowels of Hades. In the next moment, the beast was sprawled on top of Lucien, trying to get beneath the covers and shaking so hard the entire bed rattled.

A second later, the ugliest cat Lucien had ever seen sprang up onto the bedside table, flexing its claws and testing the sharp tips out on the counterpane, sending the dog into yowls of anguish.

"Oh, goodness!" a new voice added to the melee. "Sadie, down! Sassy, stop that!"

That voice. Lucien peered over the top of the canine's big head and found the skull-basher from the tavern running to his aid. She shooed away the cat, who pranced off, tail waving like the flag of a conquering warship.

The dog glanced over the edge of the bed to make sure its nemesis was not waiting to pounce before removing its lumbering body, which left no barriers between Lucien and the woman warily staring down at him.

If he had thought her beautiful before, she was even more stunning in the light of day. Her black hair swirled in a soft cloud around her face. Her eyes were luminescent, settling into a darker green as he watched. She had been dressed in nightclothes when she shot him. Now she wore a simple cotton morning dress of pale rose that highlighted each curve and hollow.

"We meet again," he said.

"So we do."

"It's fortuitous, wouldn't you say, that one of us is in bed?" He rolled up on an elbow and patted the spot beside him. "Care to join me?"

She ignored him. "How is your ankle this morning?"

Lucien glanced down at the linen bandage wrapped neatly around his wound and then back up at his nurse. "Still attached, I see."

"Do you feel any pain?"

Blessedly, he didn't. Nevertheless, he couldn't make

this easy on her. She *had* shot him, after all. "It hurts quite a bit," he lied.

A slight frown pleated her brows. "Would you like more laudanum?"

"No." He hadn't really needed the potent medicine the night before. At least, not for his wound. "Maybe you could rub my leg?" he suggested.

She glanced at him suspiciously, and then looked at his leg. Lucien could tell she didn't cherish the idea of touching him. Most men wouldn't consider that a good sign. He did.

He planned to play the invalid for however long and to whatever degree he could get away with it. It was the perfect punishment for her, and suitable retribution to appease him. He sensed she had an untapped wealth of passion, and he intended to unearth it.

Hesitantly, she sat down on the bed, so close to the edge he was surprised she didn't fall off. She wet her lips, which drew his attention to them and started a slow-building heat in his groin. He vividly remembered how sweet she had tasted, how good she had felt in his arms.

He closed his eyes as she laid her hands on him and began to gently massage his lower leg. Her fingers were warm and surprisingly expert.

Opening his eyes, he watched her, noting how she wouldn't meet his gaze. "So what's your name, love?"

She stopped her ministration and glanced at him. "Don't you know?"

"How would I know? It's not as if we've been formally introduced."

She stared at his leg and nibbled her lower lip. "Who do you think I am?"

Bloody hell. She was going to torture him. "While this game was amusing last night, I'm not quite up to it today." He groaned to bring his point home and shifted his leg, pleased when she hastily resumed kneading his muscles. "The lad at the stables said you worked here."

Her head jerked up. "He did?"

Lucien shrugged noncommittally. "He might not have said those words exactly, but that was the general impression. So I imagine you were at the tavern last night to make some extra blunt? Are your wages not sufficient enough here?"

Fancy was at a loss for words. Was it possible he didn't realize that she was his ward? Had her brother never described her to him?

It seemed too unbelievable to be true, but it did appear that he thought her a household servant—and worse, apparently. While she should be offended, she couldn't blame him. She certainly didn't act like the mistress of the manor, or dress the part. She couldn't fix a broken stable door or a rotten stair in a frilly gown. Had it not been for the unnerving way he had looked at her the night before, she would be wearing her breeches that very moment.

She started when he suddenly took a lock of her hair between her fingers. "Is money a problem, love? There are men who would pay quite handsomely to have you grace their bed. Myself included."

As he had last night, he used her hair to pull her forward until they were face to face. She wondered if he would kiss her again. And if she wanted him to.

"Perhaps if you locked the door," he murmured, "we could discuss arrangements. I vow to make it worth your while."

Fancy could only stare, mesmerized by the look in his eyes, and the way the color seemed to shift from green to blue. "Are you propositioning me, Mr. Kendall?"

His smile radiated sin. "It seems I am. I won't deny that I'm attracted to you."

Fancy could scarcely breathe. He was attracted to her. She had presumed he had simply been toying with her the night before.

She had never been the kind of female who inspired passion in men, but rather friendship, like the sort she shared with Heath, even though he had started speaking of marriage in the past year. But she knew he felt a misplaced responsibility to take care of her now that George was gone.

Heath and her brother had been close friends as children, inseparable at times. It seemed odd, now that she thought about it, that George had appointed a stranger as her guardian rather than his closest friend, who would have been the logical choice—and one Fancy could have accepted much more easily.

Though Heath enjoyed his lectures, as most men did, he would never have interfered with her plans. In fact, he had assisted her the last two times Bodie had ridden in on the midnight tide to collect the smuggled

French brandy and silks, though the venture was foiled when the gaugers had suddenly appeared. If not for the dense fog that often rolled over the beach in the wee hours of the morning, they might not have escaped.

"What do you say, love?" her patient prompted. "I won't tell your mistress. We could both have a very good time. It would certainly make my stay here much more enjoyable."

Undoubtedly. "You didn't want to come?"

"No," he replied without hesitation. "The last thing I need is the responsibility for some high-strung brat who's terrorized every governess I have sent to see to her welfare."

His comment stung. "Maybe she didn't appreciate your interference. Or maybe she thought you should come yourself, instead of sending hirelings to do your dirty work."

"She told you this, did she?" He canted a brow, and Fancy realized she was giving too much away. But he went on as though her answer was of no import. "I went to a damn lot of trouble to find those governesses. It wasn't easy to convince someone to come out to this desolate rock."

Why, the condescending peacock!

"I was having myself a fine time in London until her ladyship's tantrums interfered," he added.

"Gambling, drinking, and whoring, I presume." She had read about his wild antics in the scandal sheets. He had recently won a large estate from some earl's son.

"More gambling and drinking than whoring," he

said, caressing her cheek with his thumb, sending a shiver chasing over her skin. "Few have truly interested me. But you . . . you have fire. We would be suitably matched. You have a need, and I have the ability to fulfill it."

Fancy couldn't think with him touching her that way. He lured her far too easily.

She stood abruptly and moved to the end of the bed to unwrap his bandage. "So what do you plan to do with your ward now that you've arrived?"

"I intend to take her in hand and let her know precisely how things will be from this point on. Her days of running roughshod over everyone have come to an end. I won't tolerate disobedience."

His words confirmed what Fancy had dreaded. "And what if she doesn't care for your brand of discipline?"

"She'll learn to like it," he replied with grim determination.

"Perhaps she feels competent to take care of herself."

"If she had been capable of that feat, I wouldn't be here. She has succeeded in chasing off two able-bodied caretakers."

Fancy had to bite her tongue. Attila the Hun would have made a better governess than the women he had sent.

"I'd say she's in need of a hand to her backside," he said, as though seriously contemplating carrying through on the punishment.

Fancy's ire rose at that ridiculous statement. "And you think to administer it, I suppose?"

"If necessary."

"I hate to disappoint you, but she's far too old for such treatment." And she would claw his eyes out before he got within striking distance.

His gaze narrowed on her face. "What do you mean, 'too old'? Just how old is she?"

Fancy barely contained a smirk as she replied, "Twenty."

"Twenty!" She jumped back as he flung the coverlet to the floor and swung his legs over the bed, swearing as his wounded foot connected with solid ground. "Good God. This is bloody priceless." He rifled a hand through his hair. "Why didn't anyone tell me?"

Fancy hadn't expected her remark to elicit such a response. "Perhaps they would have, had you asked."

He scowled at her, and he was quite formidable when he looked like that. And now that he was sitting upright, quite large and dangerous, too. "What am I going to do with some twenty-year-old chit?"

"You act as if she's an evil hag."

"She could be, for all the luck I'll have marrying her off."

That statement constricted Fancy's chest. "Marry?"

"What else am I to do with her?" He rubbed the back of his neck, then stopped abruptly and frowned. "There was a blond girl last night. Tall and extraordinarily pretty. Is that her?"

"Her?"

He glared impatiently at her. "Your mistress. Lady Francine."

The moment of truth had arrived. "And if it is?" Fancy evaded. *Tall and extraordinarily pretty.* Fancy had never begrudged her friend's beauty, but at that moment she felt conspicuously plain in comparison.

"Then I'd have to wonder why no man has laid claim to her. She looks like an angel."

"An angel you wanted to throttle not five minutes ago," Fancy reminded him.

He shrugged. "I was angry."

Had Rosalyn been a hideous troll, she doubted his anger would have abated so readily.

"Help me up," he said then, holding out his arm. "I want to see what this hellhole looks like in the light of day."

Ire carried Fancy across the distance she had put between them, her mind conjuring images of using him as a voodoo doll and sticking large pins in his behind.

"Easy, love," he murmured, chuckling as she slapped her arm around his waist and helped him up, no small feat, as she nearly toppled beneath his weight. "Take me to the window." He hobbled along next to her, his arm slung across her shoulders. His nearness was unnerving, and he didn't allow her even an inch of breathing room.

He drew the sheer curtain back to look out. The morning sun had coated the sea in golden streaks, the waves whipped into frothy peaks from the gale that had sprung up the night before, sending little whirling clouds of sand into the air and back to the ground to choke the reedy grass and willows.

Fancy glanced at the man beside her. "How long do you intend to stay?"

He looked down at her, his gaze warm and faintly ironic. "My answer would have been vastly different had you asked me that question yesterday."

"Why?"

"Because yesterday I had no reason to linger."

Fancy trembled inside at his meaning; her thoughts conflicted. One part of her wanted to tell him that the woman he desired was the very same woman he couldn't wait to be rid of. She shouldn't want him to linger. Nothing good could come of it. She had things to do, and he would only be in the way. But, to her dismay, he had already become a fascination for her—the way he moved, with a subtle, predatory grace, how he smelled, like whiskey and smoke and leather, how he was built, as though specifically designed to accommodate a woman's form, hard to soft, dark to light.

She should tell him the truth and send him on his way as soon as possible. But confessing who she was would be more hindrance than help. In two days, she would be meeting Bodie again, and this shipment would bring her much closer to fulfilling the debt she owed on her home. She needed that shipment desperately. Having the last two rendezvous foiled, she could not have him get in the way of this one.

"Lingering will get you nowhere." If she could not

come to a conclusion on anything else, she had to at least set him straight on whatever he thought might happen between them. "It's best that you do what you came to do and be on your way."

His half-grin told her he was undeterred. "So that's the way it's going to be, is it?"

"That's the way it's going to be," she replied unequivocally, meeting his gaze.

"I could change your mind," he challenged in a seductive voice, turning her to face him. His shirt had lost several buttons, and she found herself staring directly at his chest. He put a finger beneath her chin and tipped her head up. "In fact, I feel obliged to try."

The thought of what he might do was too unsettling to contemplate. "You would be wasting your time," she said coolly.

"Perhaps. But time is something I have in abundance at the moment. You *are* going to nurse me back to health, aren't you?"

"You look perfectly healthy to me."

"Hardly. I suspect my recovery will take quite a while. I hope you're up to the task."

Fancy diverted the topic before he completely unraveled her. "Who is Sanji?" she asked.

He went utterly still, the expression on his face tense and shuttered. "You slept in here with me last night?" His words were more accusation than question.

"I needed to make sure you didn't succumb to a fever or infection."

"What did I say?" he demanded.

Fancy shook her head. "Nothing, you just mumbled the name. But you were *hilla*-ridden at the time."

He stared at a point over her shoulder for a few moments, seeming far away. Then, slowly, his gaze drifted down to hers. "*Hilla*-ridden?"

"Ghosts," she explained. "They tormented your dreams."

"I don't believe in ghosts."

Fancy felt silly to have brought it up. He would certainly not understand. "People around here hold a lot of faith in their superstitions. They believe there is a way to rid yourself of almost anything that ails you."

"Even *hillas*?" he asked, treating her to a slow grin; whatever had disturbed him was now gone.

She nodded. "All you need to do is crawl on your hands and knees through the ringed stones at the Men-an-Tol, or bathe in the waters of Madron Wells."

"Interesting. What other odd customs should I be aware of?"

Fancy couldn't tell if he truly wanted to know, or if he was mocking her. Her grandmother had taught her these traditions and legends, and while some she silently rejected as ridiculous, most she took to heart because her grandmother believed them.

"If you are afflicted with madness," she said pointedly, "then you would be bowssened in a pool of water by the burliest men in the county until the insanity had left you."

Amusement lit his eyes. "Insanity, is it? Well, perhaps you're right. I'd have to be crazy to want to stay here. Will I be pushed off the cliff next?" He lightly caressed her arm and Fancy pulled away.

"Let's get you back to bed."

His ready compliance should have been warning enough. Not surprisingly, she found herself far too close to him when he settled back against the pillows.

"I think I'm going to like being laid up. Are you sure you don't want to join me?"

"There would not be enough room for me and your bloated head."

"Well," he said with a martyred sigh, "it seems you've put me in my place. It also seems I've put off the inevitable as long as I can. Bring your mistress to me, if you would."

A moment of panic flooded Fancy's senses. "My mistress?" She swallowed a dry knot in her throat. "I . . . believe she's taking the waters."

"The waters?"

"Yes, there's a hot spring on the west side of the property. She could be there for hours."

"Send someone to fetch her, then."

Persistent ox, Fancy thought, praying he didn't get restless and decide to leave the room. She had to rally the troops and get everyone's agreement to, well, lie, basically. Knowing her guardian's plans for her, she had no choice but to deceive him, at least until she could secure the money she needed to pay off her grandmother's debt.

She turned to go, but he took hold of her arm. "You haven't told me your name. I recall asking, but receiving no answer."

Fancy cast about for a suitable name. "Mary," she said. "Mary . . . Purdy."

He shook his head. "No."

Her heart missed a beat. Did he know she was lying? "What do you mean, no?"

"Mary doesn't suit you."

"Well, that's my name."

"Then I guess I'll have to find you a better one." He thought for a second and then smiled. "I have it. I'll call you Angel. My angel of mercy, come to soothe me with one hand, and slap me with the other."

Oh, she would definitely like to slap him.

"Now that we have that settled, be a good girl and go find your mistress. But, Angel"—he said the name with goading relish, as she yanked her arm from his grasp—"don't go far. I'm an invalid, remember?"

Fancy wished she had something to hurl at his arrogant head, but that would only ruin a cherished knick-knack. She had already clouted him with a rock, threatened him with a fire poker, shot him in the leg, and where had that gotten her? In her current untenable position, that's where!

The best she could do was leave with her head high and her dignity intact—while shutting the door with a resounding slam as masculine laughter followed her down the hallway.

"What madness could have been in ye, hinny, tae be telling the mon such a fabrication?"

Fancy faced the three people who meant the most in

the world to her and felt her resolve waver. What she was proposing seemed much more far-fetched now than when the idea had first occurred.

"I don't see that we have a choice," she replied. "I can't allow his sudden appearance to change all my plans. How will I get out to meet Bodie, if Mr. Kendall is watching me all the time? Besides, he's not feeling very charitable toward me at present." She wouldn't put it past the wretch to lock her in her room, just to spite her.

"He'll feel a great deal more uncharitable should he find out what you're doing," Rosalyn said, ever the voice of reason.

Fancy sighed and glanced at her friend, who was dressed in a lovely sprigged muslin gown that matched her eyes, the high waist accentuating her slender torso and ample bosom. Without even trying, she epitomized the qualities of a gently bred female, even though Rosalyn had been every bit the hoyden Fancy had been growing up. The difference lay in the fact that Fancy had never quite shed her impulsive ways.

"He already thinks you're me," Fancy reminded her. "So this seems the perfect solution to all our problems. I can continue to meet Bodie, and you can charm and distract our guest." She pushed down the image her words conjured. "You know everything there is to know about me. Jaines and Olinda can help keep up appearances. And truthfully, it would make me feel better knowing there was someone else besides the three of us keeping an eye on you."

"I don't know." Rosalyn looked pensive. "It seems too risky, and Mr. Kendall doesn't strike me as the sort of man who takes well to being deceived."

Fancy didn't doubt that. Her guardian was a formidable man. If he wasn't such a nuisance, she might admit that her brother had chosen an unmatched protector. He was ex-military, the elite light cavalry. And he hadn't gotten all those muscles from lifting books.

She remembered the letter he had sent her informing her of her brother's death, the remorse that had come through in every word. How eloquently he had spoken of George's bravery in the line of duty. They had been under heavy attack during the weeks after George's final letter to Fancy. George had saved another man's life; he was a hero, they said. But she would have preferred George back, whole and safe, rather than a hero. He had always been a hero to her.

"How many more excursions to the cove do you expect to have to take, miss?" Jaines asked.

"Three, four at the most. I haven't wanted to risk discovery by having Bodie come too frequently, but I guess we'll have to chance it." Fancy took a steadying breath and met Rosalyn's concerned gaze. "Your lord and master awaits, Lady Francine."

Six

Fancy paced back and forth in the corridor outside her bedroom, which was currently occupied by her best friend and her guardian. What were they doing in there? And why was it taking so long?

She gnawed on her nail, her gaze continually moving to the closed door. Would Lucien believe Rosalyn was his ward? What if he posed a question she could not answer?

Fancy nearly leapt out of her skin when the door suddenly opened and Rosalyn emerged, the smile she had pasted on her face upon entering the lion's den fading as soon as the door was closed behind her.

"What happened?" Fancy asked in a hasty whisper. "What did he say?"

Rosalyn took her by the arm and led her away.

When they were out of earshot, she said, "I think everything went well. I'm fairly certain he believes I'm you. Since he doesn't know much about you, he couldn't probe. He did remark how dissimilar in looks George and I are, though."

"Well, George and I didn't look too similar, either. George's hair was dark red, and his eyes more hazel than green. He took after Mother's side of the family." Fancy stopped. Rosalyn's attention seemed to have drifted. "Has something happened?" she asked, suddenly worried.

"Hmm?" Rosalyn blinked and then stared at her, appearing puzzled. "Has what happened?"

"You looked deep in thought."

"I was just thinking how incredibly handsome Mr. Kendall is, though his hair is far too long and wild for convention. And I believe he once sported an earring. Quite a shock to a girl's senses, I daresay."

"Yes," Fancy mumbled. Rosalyn and Lucien would make a wonderful-looking couple. His height and swarthy features would compliment her sylphlike figure and blond goddess softness.

"He seems to have acquired a fascination for you," Rosalyn said, looking at Fancy closely.

Fancy hated that her heart did a little jig. "Oh?" she replied, managing to sound only mildly curious.

"He asked where you were, and how long you've been in my employ, and he deftly slipped in a question about whether you were involved with anyone. That sounds distinctly like interest to me. Are you sure nothing more happened between you two than an unfortunate confrontation at the tavern?"

It was not like Fancy to keep anything from her best friend, but she just wasn't ready to confess the kiss—two kisses, actually—that she had shared with her guardian.

"Nothing," she answered, expecting a clap of thunder to herald her fib.

Rosalyn looked as though she didn't quite believe her, but all she said was, "He's waiting for you." A bellow vibrated the walls then, and she added with a chuckle, "Impatiently, it seems. Should I chaperone?"

Fancy almost said yes. Her guardian had a thoroughly wicked streak, and she doubted he would behave, but going to his room with reinforcements would only amuse the wretch. Besides, she was supposed to be a servant, which made the rules vastly different. Now that she had made her proverbial bed, she would have to lie in it.

And as she marched toward her bedroom door, back rigidly erect and head high, she thought her guardian would find her comparison vastly amusing.

"Good Lord, woman, where've you been?" Lucien demanded as the defiant chit entered his room, her stern schoolmarm expression conveying she was ready to chastise him. Good. He looked forward to seeing what torture she intended to inflict next. He was agonizingly restless, and had barely made it back to the bed before the door opened. If she knew he could walk, let alone practice his morning drills, life would not be nearly as enjoyable as he intended it to become.

"Still grumpy, I see."

"I'm bored. And my leg hurts," he added as an afterthought. In London, he would be seated in front of a whist table at one of his favorite gaming hells by now. Instead, he was doomed to spend the morning staring up at a spider building a cobweb in the corner.

He watched his nurse move toward him in that surprisingly graceful way of hers, stopping a foot from the bed, where she looked dispassionately at him. Cruel woman.

"If you would refrain from your tantrums," she said, "perhaps you wouldn't feel so badly."

Normally he would have given up trying to seduce her by now. But there was something intriguing about this fiery bit of female that no man could overlook. She gave as good as she got, and he found himself inexplicably drawn to her. She had the beauty and manner of a born lady, but with the sin of the streets in her blood.

"I have an itch," he said. One that had started the night before and that he doubted she would scratch.

"Are your arms suddenly unable to move?"

"I can't reach it."

She narrowed her gaze at him and cautiously edged closer, as if expecting him to make a move. Lucien smiled to himself as he rolled to his side and offered her his back.

Those slim fingers with their short nails gently

rasped across his flesh, touching him as though she enjoyed it. But if he glanced over his shoulder to look at her at that moment, he suspected her demeanor would be less than friendly.

"Lower," he murmured, sensing her hesitation as her hand moved down his spine, her fingers pressing into the arch, making him wish he'd had the forethought not to wear a shirt. He wanted nothing between her hands and his skin. It had been a long time since a woman had touched him so simply. "Lower." He heard the groan in his voice, and her fingers stilled. He cursed himself for ruining the moment.

Rolling over to face her, he saw the conflict in her eyes and felt not a damn bit of satisfaction. A knock sounded at the door, and she whirled around like a guilty party.

His ward popped her head in, still wearing the same charming smile she had bestowed upon him earlier. It was hard to imagine such an ethereal creature being the hoyden he had read about in the governesses' stinging reports.

"I don't mean to intrude, but there's someone here to see Mr. Kendall."

"Lucien," he reminded her.

She blushed prettily and nodded. She really was quite lovely, and he couldn't fathom why no man had made an offer for her hand. Perhaps it was simply that her choices were too few out here in sheep country. He would have to take her to London and employ the help of the only "lady" he had ever associated with, Clarisse Templeton, widow of the late Marquis of Dane.

Clarisse was a social butterfly; she could introduce his ward to polite society. Since Lady Francine was the daughter of an earl, she deserved to find a man who was her equal.

"Who is it?" he asked.

"He says his name is Tahj."

Lucien dropped his head back on his pillow. "Bloody hell," he muttered. He'd forgotten all about the man and his broken coach.

"Who's Tahj?" his reluctant nurse asked.

"I suspect you'll find out in a moment."

His prediction proved correct as a man suddenly appeared on the threshold, with a round face, slanted eyes, olive complexion, and every hair shaved from his head. He was garbed in a loose, flowing orange tunic with a black sash around his waist, orange trousers gathered at the bottom, and black slippers sporting a dragon's image embroidered in red silk thread.

Hands on hips, the man focused his gaze on Lucien, a sharp intelligence in those piercing, dark eyes. He was small, but something about him radiated power.

"One night from my side," the man said in a uniquely punctuated voice, "and already you are in trouble."

Lucien sighed. "Ladies, may I introduce you to my traveling companion, Rahmatahj Vajrayana, or Tahj, as I call him."

Tahj pressed his hands together and offered them

both a bow. "May Buddha bless such heavenly flowers," he intoned, his English nearly perfect but for an accent that Fancy didn't recognize. "You shall both be fruitfully rewarded in the afterlife for putting up with the antics of the *namak haraam*."

"*Namak haraam?*" Fancy queried, puzzled.

"'Unworthy one' is one of its many connotations," Lucien answered. "Lower than the slime scraped off one's shoe after walking through a dung field."

"This is true," Tahj asserted, nodding his head. "That one"—he pointed to Lucien—"is undisciplined, stubborn-minded, and walks in the path of the misguided. Alas, he is my burden."

"I didn't beg you to follow me around for the last ten years, you blistering pain in the rump. You could have stayed in India."

"Buddha has willed that you are to be my tribulation. I cannot ascend to the Final Nirvana until the day you have found the path of enlightenment." Tahj sighed wearily. "I fear I shall wither and die, unholied in my quest."

Fancy bit her lip to keep from laughing. Though she had only known her guardian a day, she completely understood the older man's frustration.

"Why do you lay in bed? What game do you play now?"

"I was shot."

Tahj snorted. "You are perfectly well. You only seek to fool these young women."

"I really did shoot him," Fancy piped in. "I thought he was a robber."

Smugly, Lucien quirked his brow at the odd little fellow and folded his arms over his chest. "See?"

What happened next transpired so quickly, Fancy barely had a moment to blink, as Tahj lunged toward Lucien's bed, leg outstretched, his heel thwapping down where Lucien had been only a moment before. He had rolled off the bed with lightning speed, raising his right arm to block the chopping blow that curved down toward his head, the palm of his other hand thrusting up into the old man's midsection, knocking him back.

"Ha!" Lucien crowed. "You're getting slow in your dotage, old man."

"Never too old to teach a whelp such as yourself a lesson." Tahj gripped the bedpost and swung his legs in an arch, catching his opponent square in the chest, expelling a whoosh of air from Lucien as he hurtled back toward the bureau.

The movements that followed were a blur as arms, hands, and legs blocked one blow after the next in a flurry of feints and parries that were incredible to watch. One moment Lucien was driving Tahj back; the next moment Tahj was cornering Lucien. It was hard to believe such a slight man could hold his own against a brute Lucien's size.

The fight was over a moment later as Tahj swept out his leg, catching Lucien's injured ankle and sending him hard to the floor, Tahj's knee pressed into his chest.

"You have weakened, *vajra*. Your practice has suffered to let an old man beat you."

"You got a lucky break."

"There are no such things as lucky breaks. One makes one's own destiny." He clasped his hand in Lucien's and helped him up. "Now get dressed. There is much left to pummel into that hard head of yours."

Lucien sat down on the bed. "My nurse told me I need to rest." He glanced over at Fancy as though expecting her to save him. "Didn't you, Angel?"

Heat flushed Fancy's cheeks. "I told you not to call me that," she hissed furiously, which only garnered a chuckle from him as she swung on her heel and headed toward the door. "I hope he beats the blazes out of you."

Lucien was still laughing as the door slammed behind her. She was a damn temptation when she was angry; the way her eyes sparked fire and her creamy skin flamed with color. A definite danger to his peace of mind.

He dropped back against the pillows, his aching muscles protesting. Tahj's beating had been another one of the monk's lessons. He believed strength of body brought strength of mind, which he had tried to reinforce through meditation. But Lucien didn't want to delve too deeply into his own mind. He only found himself reliving his past, remembering the two lives he had lived. One of them forever lost. The other, too ingrained to forget.

"I do not like the look in your eyes," Tahj said, standing over Lucien, disapproval showing in full measure on his round face.

"As usual, you're seeing things that aren't there."

"I see very clearly. You have designs on the dark-haired girl."

"And if I do? What business is it of yours?"

"She is an innocent."

"Innocent!" he hooted. "She damn well shot me. And that was *after* she had knocked me unconscious and very nearly unmanned me when I tried to rescue her from some thug." And he still didn't know what she had been searching for.

"She is an innocent," Tahj repeated firmly, either not hearing Lucien or not caring. The latter, undoubtedly. "You have not been practicing your Shaolin. You are slow. Unprepared."

"Unprepared for what? The days of battle are behind me." But never forgotten. He could still see the faces of all the men who had fallen, all the senseless loss of life. For what? To bend a people to British rule? To force them to accept Christianity over their own religion?

But he had done his duty because there had been a killing need in him, a desire for retribution against the people who had imprisoned and beaten him and drugged him so that he could not escape, leaving him a slave to his own weakness even now, all these years later.

"The battles are not yet over for you, *preta*. You still harbor bitterness in your heart."

"You never give up, do you?"

"That I have been with you all these many years should answer your question. You must exorcise the *ashura* to find peace."

A familiar rage built inside Lucien. "Peace? Is that

what's missing? I've lost fifteen years of my life. How do you propose I overcome that? My entire family is gone. Dorian, Jillian, Hugh, Gavin, Jensyn. My parents."

He stalked to the window, watching a raven buffeted by the wind. His family was long lost to him; only rubble marked what remained of the small, run-down cottage where he had spent most of his youth, crowded into one room with his siblings. He had been the oldest, the protector. But he hadn't realized how unprepared he was to protect them when the time came, and his foolish bravado had been the beginning of the end.

But he was no longer that foolish youth. He'd had many years to harden into an embittered man. He couldn't go back and undo what he had done, but he could dole out retribution now that he had the means.

"The hatred will overcome you if you let it," Tahj said as he came to stand beside Lucien, who had been subjected to this same speech since the day he had woken up on a pallet inside the temple walls, the place that would be his sanctuary for the next two years.

"Then I'll let it," Lucien returned.

"You have already sought your revenge against the son of the man you call Redding."

Lucien turned. "Revenge? I won a house, Tahj. Only one of many that Christian Slade owns. Will it bring the bastard's father back from the dead so I can finish what he began? Or bring my family back? Change all the years of hell I lived through?" He clenched his fists at his side. "Will it bring Sanji back?"

"Sanji's death was not your fault."

Lucien fought the urge to close his eyes against the memory. "Yes, it was. Just as the death of my ward's brother was my fault."

Lucien massaged his brow and faced the window again, glimpsing the slim form of his nurse, clad once more in breeches and moving fleet-footed along the top of a crumbling stone wall, hastening toward a clump of trees. The wind clawed at her hair, stealing it from its pins and sending it tumbling down her back.

What was it about her that drew him so strongly? He had encountered women far more beautiful. Some men might even think his ward the lovelier of the two.

Lucien wondered if his lack of attraction toward Lady Francine was due to the fact that she *was* a lady, since he stayed far away from them, Clarisse—Lady Dane—being the only exception.

But there was more to Miss Mary Purdy than her singular upbringing. An exuberance clung to her, a love of life, and he had wanted to get closer, to warm himself in her glow.

His sister Jillian would have been about Mary's age. He suspected the two girls would have been friends, as Jillian had a similar wild streak in her. Where was Jillian now? And the rest of his siblings? Alive or dead? Did they think he was dead? He had left one night to confront the Earl of Redding and never returned. Instead, he had been bound hand and foot and shipped off to a life of slavery in India.

Lucien sighed and shook his head. What had possessed

him to come to Cornwall? He couldn't stay; the restlessness would eat at him soon enough. He had to keep moving, keep ahead of the memories that plagued him.

Since he left India, his days had become a blur of endless places and forgotten nights, women who touched him, but never touched a part of him. He carried an innate coldness in him, an inability to feel. At times it scared the hell out of him, the way it seemed as if someone else looked out through his eyes, that somewhere he had lost an essential piece of himself. His soul, perhaps. It had been left back in India, hanging from a *bodhi* tree in Punjab.

Lucien forced down the images and faced Tahj. No one would ever suspect that beneath the monk's humble exterior beat the heart of a dragon, that such a slightly built man possessed enough strength in the palm of his hand to kill another human being.

"I'll ring for someone to see you to your room," Lucien said.

"I have my pallet. I need nothing else."

"Fine. As long as you're not snoring at my feet."

"As you rarely find yourself in your own bed, one can only wonder how you would know my sleeping habits." Regarding Lucien with that penetrating stare, he added, "Your desires will only lead you further down the path of destruction."

"I have no interest in spending my life in meditation and shunning sin. I happen to like sin."

"As well I know. Each year you acquire more wealth and more possessions, and you need none of it."

"Wealth is power." The Earl of Redding had taught him that lesson.

"It is the evil of that power which you seek. It shall bring you nothing in the end."

Lucien glanced back out the window and watched the only woman who had ever bested him disappear into a copse of trees like a woodland sprite. He wondered what would impress Miss Mary Purdy. Something told him neither wealth nor power would do the trick.

"Tomorrow, we practice," Tahj said as he walked away.

"Tomorrow," Lucien idly repeated.

Today, however, he would indulge his desires.

Seven

Fancy followed her cat at a distance, stepping lightly over the loose stones along the landing wall that had been built centuries earlier, perhaps by some Celtic ancestor. The wall minimized the tall plumes of sea spray that crashed into the cliff and kept them from pouring over the edge toward the house.

She needed this escape, and was using Sassy as an excuse to accomplish it. For the past few days, her mischievous tabby had been disappearing. Today she would find out why.

Following the elusive feline gave Fancy something to occupy her mind and keep it off her reckless guardian. She hated to admit that she had been impressed by his fighting skills. She had never seen such a method before. He moved with the grace of a panther, each blow fluid and calculated, each strike effective. It was clear that the two men had played out that scene numerous times before.

Fancy wondered who Tahj was to Lucien. It seemed an odd pairing, considering there was no love lost between the people of Britain and India.

Had they met during the Rebellion? Could Tahj have fought against his own people? Fancy had never agreed with England's role in Indian government, dictating laws and pressuring religious sects to convert to Christianity, making English the language the Indians were to speak. Her country had in effect enslaved a people, and it had never felt right for George to fight for such a cause.

Fancy paused and gazed at the diamond-peaked waves of the ocean, inhaling a deep breath of the sea-scented air. The day was temperate, the sandy shores washed clean from last night's rain.

Birds that had taken shelter before the storm were now out in force. A group of gulls piloted a fishing boat to shore, diving in to snatch an occasional morsel, and oystercatchers swooped toward the mud banks in a flash of black and white, while small redshanks and sanderlings scurried to probe the slate.

Upriver, where a thick branch lay fallen from the gale, a heron stalked, picking its way along like a spindle-legged man before it stopped and stood broodingly, its wings humped, its head buried in its feathers.

An echoing meow stirred Fancy, and she resumed walking along the stone wall. Jumping off at the end, she followed the mewling sounds until she found what she had been looking for.

Sassy glanced up at Fancy with her mismatched eyes and purred a greeting. She lay on her side, four squirming kittens suckling hungrily.

"Oh, my." Fancy knelt down and took a black kitten, one eye ringed in white, into her palm. "You are precious," she said softly, stroking the kit between its ears, its fur soft and warm. It was so tiny, she doubted it was more than a week or two old.

The kitten needled her palm, impatient with Fancy for interrupting its meal. With a soft laugh, Fancy returned the kitten to Sassy's belly, where it nudged aside its brothers and sister.

"Who would have thought you had a motherly instinct in you?" Fancy murmured, tickling her cat under the chin. "So where did you get these kittens?" Sassy had not been pregnant, so the babies did not belong to her. But she had been lactating when Fancy found her, discarded and starving, two months earlier.

Pushing to her feet, Fancy glanced around for the mother cat, but deep down, she did not have a good feeling. Her suspicion was confirmed a moment later when she found the feline's lifeless body beside a rock, its neck broken. Who or what had killed it? This was the second dead animal she had found in a week.

A tear coursed down Fancy's cheek. She wiped it away. Crouching down next to the dead cat, she saw the little hollow beneath the rock where the tabby had probably given birth to her kittens and sheltered them.

The poor babies had most likely tried to nurse from their mother's lifeless body. If Sassy hadn't come along, Fancy knew she would be burying more than just the mother cat today.

She dug into the soft ground. When the hole was deep enough, she gently laid the cat into it, saying a silent prayer before shifting the dirt over its body.

Standing, she stared down at the newly turned earth. Dappled light filtered through the canopy of leaves overhead onto the grave. She laid several weighty stones over the top to keep the scavengers at bay.

A plaintive mewling brought Fancy's gaze over her shoulder. Sassy was on her feet, trying to corral the restless kits now that they had eaten their fill. Fancy counted three. The black one was missing.

A quivering meow brought her head up, her gaze scanning the trees until she spotted the kitten perched in the crevice of a limb, frozen in fear. A large, menacing hawk, which must have swooped in and grabbed the kitten, now stalked it. Either the hawk or a tumble from that precarious position would kill the little creature.

"Stay there, love," Fancy gently crooned, keeping her eyes on the kitten as she cautiously proceeded to a spot beneath the tree, afraid a sudden movement might startle the frightened animal.

Fancy had climbed many trees during her child-hood, hiding among the leafy branches in fun as her brother searched high and low for her. Though her body was no longer as wiry as it had once been, she managed to scale the trunk nimbly before grabbing hold of the nearest limb, prompting the hawk into flight and unnerving the kitten, who recoiled into the crook of the tree.

Fancy glanced down. The ground was farther away than she had expected. If she fell and hit the outcropping of rocks bordering the tree, she could easily break her leg.

She shut out the thought and anchored herself more firmly on her perch. She was not as light as she once was, and the branch beneath her was not as steady as she would have liked.

The black kitten watched her from its limb several feet away, a scattering of twigs jutting between them. The distance was farther than Fancy would have liked, but there was no way to get any closer.

Bracing one hand around the shaft, she leaned forward, stretching as far as she could, her fingers barely making contact. The kit batted a paw at her, its mewling growing more insistent.

"Come on, love," Fancy softly coaxed, extending a few more inches, her fingers brushing the kitten's fur. "I won't hurt you."

Tremulously, the kit scooted around to the very edge of the limb, its young legs still wobbly. Fancy watched in horror as the little feline teetered and then tumbled into the air.

"No!" Fancy lunged in a desperate attempt to catch the kitten, and the branch beneath her suddenly cracked.

• • •

Lucien glanced around the shadowed woods he'd seen the girl enter and swore. He had lost her again, damn it, even though he had dressed with lightning speed and practically vaulted down the stairs two at a time, the pain in his ankle blotted out.

He wasn't quite sure why he was so eager to see her. Perhaps he simply wanted to discover if what he had felt the night before had been more than a sexual craving that any woman could fill. He knew he should stay away from this particular woman, but he had never met a female with such fire. He needed that fire. He needed her to take the coldness from him.

He moved farther into the woods, but stopped when he heard a faint crooning. He listened, frowning. Was the girl with a lover? Would he catch them in a delicate situation?

Lucien stalked toward the sound, elbowing aside a wildly growing shrub until he came to an abrupt halt. The mangy-looking cat he'd seen that morning was nudging a litter of kittens with her nose, trying to get them to behave.

From somewhere above Lucien's head came Mary's voice. He narrowed his eyes and glanced up, catching a glimpse of a small, booted foot before his gaze moved farther up to a shapely leg.

He had just stepped beneath the tree to get a better look when he heard her cry of alarm and saw a tiny ball of black fur plummeting toward him. He thrust out his arms, catching the squirming creature in his cupped hands.

He could feel the kitten's heart racing. Chocolate eyes, too big for its small face, stared unblinkingly up at him. Lucien absently stroked the little beast between its tiny ears as he returned the kitten to the warm circle of its siblings. He had just straightened when he heard the tree branch snap, then a scream as Mary tumbled from the sky. She landed on top of him, sending them both hurtling to the ground, his side bashing against a protruding rock, knocking the breath from his lungs.

Fancy opened her eyes to find blackness all around her. It took her a moment to realize that her hair covered her face, veiling her in a dark cocoon.

It took considerably less time to realize that she was uninjured—and that what she was lying on was not the grass, but a very big, very solid man. The prickling sensation on the back of her neck told her exactly *which* man had broken her fall.

Swallowing, she parted the curtain of her hair and found herself face to face with her beleaguered custodian, his aquamarine eyes tinged with equal parts amusement and annoyance.

The feel of his body cradled snugly against hers prompted traitorous memories of the last time he had been this close.

And what he had done.

She opened her mouth, but he laid a finger against her lips, silencing her. "I appreciate you so much more when you don't talk, for I know I will only hear some chastisement about what I did to make you fall from the tree, or how it was my fault you had to take a rock to my skull, or most heinous of all, threaten my manly parts."

"*That* you deserved."

He gave her a crooked grin and brushed a length of hair from her face, smoothing it behind her ear, where his fingers lingered, lightly tracing the outer curve of her ear before skimming slowly down her jaw.

Fancy prayed he couldn't feel her trembling, even as her gaze dropped to his mouth, wondering if he would try to kiss her again.

"You are a troublesome baggage, Miss Purdy. Dare I hope to survive my stay here?"

"Perhaps if you stopped following me, you wouldn't have to be in fear for your life."

"But who would have saved you from the tree, dear girl?"

Drat the man. He did have a point.

"I thought you were having a rendezvous with a lover," he said.

"A lover?" Fancy scoffed. "You must be delirious."

"Why?" He fanned the ends of her hair through his fingertips. "You're a desirable woman." He regarded her intently. "Is it true that you haven't had a lover yet? Are you really as pure as you appear to be?"

His husky voice and the simmering heat in his eyes were mesmerizing. "That's none of your concern, Mr. Kendall."

"Lucien," he told her, softly teasing her neck with her hair. "We're too close for such formality."

The reminder that she lay on top of him, hip to hip,

chest to chest, jolted Fancy. She tried to scramble away, but his arm snaked around her waist, not painfully, but not allowing her an escape.

"I think we have some unfinished business," he said.

Fancy struggled against his hold. "We have no unfinished business, you great lumbering ox."

"I beg to differ. And if you stopped squirming, you might realize that you want me to kiss you as much as I want to kiss you."

She did. Oh, how she did. "You've hit your head one too many times."

"If my brain is scrambled, I owe it all to you, my lovely tree pixie." He lifted his head to whisper in her ear, "Your nipples are hard, love. I can feel them against my chest. But," he murmured, his breath grazing her cheek, "I'd much rather feel them in my mouth."

Fancy bit her bottom lip to contain her gasp and closed her eyes, trying to block out the images his words had created.

"You are far more stoic in your resistance than I could ever hope to be," he said.

Fancy fought to remain utterly still as her gaze met and held his. "You'll release me, please."

"You're a hard-hearted woman, Miss Purdy. I've come to your rescue twice, now. In days of yore, a man received a token of gratitude for such things."

"You'll receive something far more memorable if you don't let go of me this instant."

He chuckled and kissed her nose. "I'll take you at

your word, since I know how eager you are to hurry me along to my final reward." He opened his arms. "You're free. For the moment," he added pointedly.

Fancy hastened off him and pushed to her feet. The longer she had lain on top of him, the more his body began to feel like a hot brand. She could still feel his heat marking her skin.

With a lazy smile, he remained on the ground, regarding her as he laced his hands behind his head and crossed his ankles. "Do you often scale trees to save kittens?"

Fancy scowled at him as she dusted herself off. "Shouldn't you be nursing your wounded ankle, Mr. Faker?"

"The deception was necessary. I needed to evince some sympathy from you. Consider it a test to see if you possessed any. Besides, I have other things to nurse at this moment." The glint in his eyes was devilish and instinctively drew Fancy's gaze down to his lap, where indecently snug trousers gloved the manly parts he so prided. She struggled not to blush.

His luggage had obviously arrived with his manservant. His attire, a loose-fitting white shirt and dove-colored trousers, had been crisp until she toppled him. Now the shirt sported a tear along one side, which showed a tempting view of his torso, quite well formed and entirely distracting.

The picture he made became even more irresistible when the black kitten he had saved clawed its way over his shoulder to plop on his chest like an ink stain. Fancy knew then that she had to escape before she succumbed to the desire to do the same thing.

She swung on her heel, heading in whatever direction her feet took her.

"Where are you going?" Lucien called out. She didn't answer or stop. She barely maintained a dignified retreat when what she really wanted to do was run.

She knew the moment he was on his feet and trailing after her. She resisted the urge to glance over her shoulder, though she felt distinctly like a doe trapped in a hunter's sights. The urge to seek shelter was palpable.

As she exited the shadowed protection of the woods, the blasted man fell into step beside her. She suddenly remembered the kittens and stopped.

As though reading her thoughts, he said, "They're all fast asleep under the watchful eye of that scruffy tabby."

Fancy relaxed, but made a mental note to return and collect them. She wanted them inside where it was safe.

"So have you lived here all your life?" he asked after a few moments of silence.

She glanced up at him. The breeze was toying with his hair, running through it with invisible fingers. No matter how hard she tried, she could not dispel the image of the kit curled up so trustingly on his chest. She had almost envied the feline.

"Yes," she replied, not quite untruthfully. She felt as if she had lived in Cornwall all her life. She could barely remember the life she had known before, just faint images of an endless series of nursemaids and countless country homes that were too lovely to despoil with the antics of two rambunctious children.

"Don't you get lonely, so far from civilization?" he queried, plucking a wildflower and tucking it behind her ear.

"Everything I know is here," she said, removing the wildflower and putting it behind his ear.

With a scoundrel's smile, he caught her around the waist, pinning her arms to her sides while he slipped the flower slowly down the front of her shirt, teasing it into her cleavage, making her squirm with need and anger, before releasing her and jumping out of the way of her slap, leaving her to either root around for the bloom while he watched—he could rot first!—or let it remain for the time being.

When she marched away from him he persisted, "So have you ever wanted to live somewhere else? Perhaps go to London and get the feel of the city?"

No, she never had. Heath had traveled to London a few times for materials and additional labor to tend his father's fields. Next to Calder Westcott, the Courtenays were the wealthiest landowners in the district.

"A friend of mine told me London was loud and crowded, that hawkers scream their wares from nearly every street corner, and that there are so many people, almost every space is occupied." Fancy darted a glance at Lucien before adding, "He even said that in some places, scantily dressed women offer themselves to men for money. Is that true?"

He shrugged. "London can be a cesspit. But other areas are entirely different. There is a definite class distinction."

"And what class do you fall into?"

He looked down at her. "I suspect you and I are of the same breed."

"And what breed is that?"

"Working class."

"You don't strike me as a man who works." Though he had been in the military, his clothing and attitude radiated gentry. But she also knew that part of his wealth came from gambling. It seemed her guardian was quite the cardsharp.

She knew nothing about his background, where he had grown up, if he had any family, or what he had done with his life since leaving the service.

"Is London where you've spent most of your life?" she inquired.

"A good part of it."

"And your family?"

He seemed to miss a beat before replying, "Yes."

"Is that where they are now?"

"No."

"Where are they?"

"You ask too many questions."

"How does one get answers if not by asking questions?" He remained closemouthed, but she was not ready to give up yet. "Have they left England?"

A muscle worked in his jaw as his gaze dropped to hers. "My family is gone, Miss Purdy. Now desist."

Gone? What did that mean? Disappeared? Or dead? And how many family members were they talking about? Parents only? Or parents and siblings?

She filed her questions away as they came to the edge of the village. A straggle of cob-walled cottages, washed yellow and ivory like the color of clotted cream, were strewn haphazardly along a winding dirt lane that was heavily rutted by cart wheels.

Tall hedges rose on either side, bordered by elms. Many of her youthful days had been spent with the other children of the village, hiding among those hedges and jumping out at each other. Here she had always been Fancy. Not Lady Francine.

"Look!" she said, pointing toward the mouth of the harbor. "The krill have come in!"

Long crimson slashes painted the water as thousands upon thousands of the small, red-coated crustaceans made their annual journey around the cape.

Without thought, she took hold of Lucien's hand and tugged him through the meadow to the cliff's edge. The first sighting of the krill was always exciting.

Fancy waved to a group of fishermen who had gathered around the dock below, checking their nets. She knew all of them well, having grown up with their children and eaten at their tables. She couldn't envision such comfortable familiarity in the teeming city of London.

Fancy felt a feather-light sensation on her hand and turned to see Lucien brushing his lips over her knuckles. "If only you would blossom for me with such passion," he murmured, "I'd count myself a lucky man."

She watched him in a daze before reality rushed in and she snatched her hand back. "I'm going to dig for oysters," she said a bit breathlessly.

Not waiting for his reply, she started down a steep path that led to a grouping of rocks near a secluded inlet where large beds of the delicacy could be found.

Fancy removed her shoes, rolled up her breeches, and waded into the shallow pool of water, sand shifting through her toes as minnows skimmed along her ankles.

Squatting down, she began to probe the seabed, fishing out her first oyster a moment later and placing it on top of a flat rock beside her.

A shadow fell over her, and her heart missed a beat. She had thought he wouldn't want to dirty his clothing, but he hunkered down next to her, far too close for comfort.

"I haven't done this in years," he said.

She cast a furtive sideways glance at him. At that moment, he didn't seem the imposing man who took delight in overwhelming her senses. In the sleek line of his profile, she glimpsed the boy he might have once been.

He looked over and caught her questioning expression. "My father was a fisherman," he explained, pulling up a handful of the rough, gray shells and tossing them onto the rock next to hers.

"Where is your father now?" She framed her question in a conversational tone, hoping he would let his guard down.

"You don't give up, do you?"

She returned his steady gaze. "Do you?"

He smiled slightly and shook his head. "Not when I want something."

Fancy had no illusions about what he meant. He wanted her. Each time she allowed that realization to sink in, her heart did crazy things. He was so beautiful, so incredibly captivating, with those penetrating color-shifting eyes and that wicked mouth. And his body—pure sin. Just remembering how hard it had felt beneath hers, how massive his arms, a strange weakness came over her.

"How long has Tahj been with you?" she asked, forcing her thoughts back to the present.

"Too long," he replied in a suffering tone, his fingers grazing her foot as he continued his search, leaning closer, his bare forearm brushing over her calf. He glanced up at her, and Fancy held her breath, thinking he meant to kiss her. Then he lifted his hand, showing her a crab. "He was going for your big toe." He winked at her and then tossed the crab onto the wet sand, where it scuttled away into the surf.

Fancy felt oddly disappointed as she probed among the seaweed. "So where did you and Tahj meet?"

"Punjab."

Fancy caught the tense note in his voice and wondered at it. She ached to ask him questions about George, but knew she would have to wait until after her last shipment from Bodie, when she could finally reveal herself and accept the consequences.

"Were you in India long?"

"I was stationed there three years."

"Was there a lot of fighting?"

"There were skirmishes. But the situation was volatile. The Indians were not going to accept English rule for long. They were fiercely opposed to any and all changes, especially those that dictated their religion."

George's letters had not relayed much about what he was going through in India. Fancy knew he had not wanted to worry her, but the lack of information had concerned her far more. To this day, she still didn't completely understand the circumstances surrounding his death.

"Did you ever have to kill anyone?"

"Yes," he said, staring at his hands through the murky water.

Fancy felt at a loss. What did she truly know of war? She considered herself more educated than most women, but she could not begin to comprehend men's reasons for taking up arms.

"Does it bother you?" he quietly asked.

Fancy blinked and turned to find Lucien regarding her steadily. "Does what bother me?"

"That I've killed men."

The way he looked at her told Fancy her answer was important to him. But could she condone death? "You must have had your reasons."

"What if I said I didn't? What if I said I just wanted the bastards to die?"

A chill breeze swept across her shoulder blades. "I . . ." She shook her head. "I don't know."

He nodded and shifted his gaze. Strained minutes of silence followed while Fancy thought about what he seemed to be telling her, that he had killed people without just cause. She couldn't reconcile that in her mind.

She slid her hands back into the cool water and searched for a neutral topic. "Why does Tahj dress in those orange robes?"

"He's a Buddhist monk. It's part of his culture."

"Aren't monks generally sequestered in monasteries?"

"Most of them are. But to my great misfortune, Tahj has appointed himself my keeper."

Though he tried to sound aggrieved, Fancy was coming to see that he just enjoyed grumbling.

"He must think you need a keeper." She glanced sideways at him. "Do you?"

She was half joking, but the look on his face as he raised his head to pin her with his gaze was far from amused. "No." He sounded deadly serious. "What I need, Miss Purdy, is to be left the hell alone. My life is what I make of it, and nobody's damn business but mine."

Fancy didn't know why the warning stung so much, but it did. "I'll leave you to it then." She made to rise, but his fingers coiled around her wrist, a challenging light in his eyes as he stared up at her.

"I didn't take you as a girl who ran away. Are you frightened?"

"Of you? Of course not," she scoffed. Not physically, for she knew he wouldn't hurt her. She had given him plenty of reasons to raise a hand to her, and he hadn't.

But he had ignited something in her, a feeling that spread each time he smiled, and it was even worse when he touched her.

"Then stay, and maybe you'll learn something," he said, his words a challenge, as though he understood what compelled her. Every moment he became more of a puzzle to her, and that only made her desire to know more about him that much stronger.

"And what might you know that I would care to learn?" Even as she asked, she sank back down to her knees beside him.

The deviltry had returned to his eyes as he replied, "How to kiss a man properly, to begin with."

Eight

He laughed when she gasped in outrage, drawing her into his arms. "Retract your claws, hellion. I was merely goading you." He leaned close, his lips a whisper away from hers as he added, "I love the way you kiss me. You hold nothing back, and those soft whimpers you make in the back of your throat drive me wild."

"I do not—"

His mouth closed over hers, silencing her protest, and Fancy melted in a second. Mercy, how wonderfully he kissed, gentle yet fierce, hot and wicked, making her forget her vow to keep her distance.

He drew back and tilted her face up to his. "Better?" he murmured, and all she could do was nod when she should have railed at him for taking liberties. Again. "Friends?"

"Why?" she asked, her voice little more than a croak.

"Why would I want to be your friend, you mean?"

She nodded.

"Because you make me smile. And you make life a damn sight more interesting by being a part of it. But mostly, you keep me on my toes. I don't know if you'll shoot me or kiss me so sweetly that my heart might stop. If you only knew how much I want to lay you down in the grass and taste every inch of you. The images I have of you at this moment are not gentlemanly."

Her own images were also less than pure. She envisioned taking him by the hand and leading him to the bank, waiting in trembling anticipation as he came over her like a glorious dark angel. She had needs and desires, and never had she felt them as strongly as she did at that moment.

She closed her eyes as his fingers skimmed her neck, tilting her head. "I'd start here," he rumbled in a husky tone, the barest sensation of his lips touching her throat. "I'd slowly work my way along your collarbone, then down between the valley of your breasts, tasting every silky piece of flesh . . . until I reached your sweet, hard nipples." He breathed into her ear. "I'd seduce them with my mouth and tongue until they were so sensitive I could blow across them and you'd shatter for me. But instead I'd trail kisses over your stomach and down between your thighs, where I'd linger, tasting you, until I had licked off every drop of sweetness."

His erotic words made Fancy shiver, heat blossoming between her thighs where she throbbed . . . and he hadn't laid a single finger on her.

He released her, and she stared up at into his smoldering eyes. She didn't know what to do. She couldn't touch him; it would be an invitation into her bed.

He took a deep breath and turned away, his hands clenching at his sides before he plunged them into the water to unearth more oysters.

Fancy watched him for a moment, trying to still the riotous feelings inside her. His shirtsleeves were rolled up to his elbows, his strong, corded forearms glistening with water. His hands were so very large, and she wanted them on her.

She shook her head and shut out the thought, allowing the breeze from the ocean to cool her flushed skin and the boom of the surf to soothe her until she was herself again.

"Where did you learn to fight?" she asked.

"Growing up on the streets, you had to know how to fight, or take a lot of beatings. But it was Tahj who taught me Shaolin."

"Did you get beaten up very often when you were young?" She had a hard time envisioning anyone getting the better of him.

"Once or twice."

"Do you remember why?"

"Just looking at someone the wrong way was enough of a reason to get the shi— To come to blows."

Fancy perched on the corner of a rock, letting the

sun warm her chilled legs. "Sounds like you grew up in a very tough place."

He skipped a smooth stone across the surface of the water. "No worse than most."

What had happened to make him keep the past so close to him? "Were you poor?"

His arm paused in the act of pitching another stone, his profile stark. "Yes."

"How poor?"

"Is there a measure for poor?"

"I guess not." Until this past year, Fancy hadn't thought about money. Though her grandmother was not rich, she and George had never gone without. There were things they might have had if they had never lost their parents, but they didn't miss them, whatever they were. They had each other, and they had the land, with all its mysteries and beauty, and they were content.

"What about you?" he asked, scooping a minnow out of the water and releasing the small, squirming fish into her hands. She watched it swim in circles until the water drained away and it flopped on its side.

"What about me?" Opening her hand, she freed the minnow back into the water, where its tail furiously propelled it into the murky undergrowth.

"Where is your family?"

The question brought an instant rush of pain to Fancy's heart. The ache had only dulled with time; she doubted it would ever truly go away.

"Gone," she said, repeating the answer he had given

to her, realizing how true it was. Her family was gone to her forever. Tears stung the back of her eyes, and she looked away.

Lucien's hand wrapped around her ankle, and he gently rubbed her foot. "Seems we're both alone."

Emotions welled in Fancy's throat. "Yes," she whispered, feeling an odd kinship burgeoning between them, one she had not expected to feel. In that moment she hated her lie, knowing that whatever tentative bond existed between them would crumble like the walls of Jericho with her revelation.

But she had to think of her future, as well as the danger hovering just out of sight. Being without her family made her want to hold on that much tighter to the people who remained. She shouldn't even be allowing herself this time with Lucien while Rosalyn's life was in danger. But he made her forget herself. Just a few more minutes, she vowed. Then she would go.

Idly, she plucked a blade of seaweed, the idea that had formulated earlier in the day returning to prod her. She darted a glance at Lucien, trying to gauge how receptive he might be to her request.

"Would you do something for me?" she asked.

"Somehow I suspect I would." He graced her with a lopsided grin. "What is it you'd like?"

Gathering her resolve, she replied, "I want to learn how to fight."

"Fight?" He frowned. "Why?"

She shrugged. "I'd just like to learn how to defend

myself." Then men like Calder and his thugs wouldn't have the upper hand.

"Defend yourself from whom?"

"No one in particular," she said, averting her gaze from his probing one, almost wishing she could confide in him. She was fairly certain he would understand. Perhaps he would even help.

But then he'd know the truth, and she couldn't take the chance that he would interfere with her plans. When she met Bodie, she would make arrangements to increase the shipments. Once she had secured payment, she could breathe again. Perhaps then she could come up with a strategy to thwart Calder.

She didn't know what they were going to do. Leaving Moor's End seemed the only solution. But traveling by coach took the chance of being waylaid along the road, and Calder's hirelings would undoubtedly be waiting for them. Where would they go, anyway? With money in short supply, how would they live?

If only she had the money being held in trust for her—but her father's will stipulated that it could only be dispersed when she got married. Until then, her guardian had control of her finances.

Perhaps she could talk Lucien into giving it to her. But would he be so angry over her deception that he would deny her? Could she even convince him of Calder's plot? If not, would he coldheartedly return Rosalyn to her stepbrother?

Or worse, would he demand Fancy marry? Perhaps

she was being foolish, but she had always envisioned that her marriage would be a grand affair of the heart, like Iseult waiting for her Tristan.

Fancy sighed.

"Stand up." Lucien's deep voice shook her from her musings as he rose to his feet and held out his hand to her.

Fancy blinked up at him. "Where are we going?"

"You wanted to learn how to fight." He took her hand and hauled her up in front of him. "I'll teach you, as long as you don't use any moves on me," he added, amusement in his eyes.

"I won't."

"Good." He turned her so that her back was flush against his chest, one large hand pressed against her belly, holding her firmly; the feel of him an aphrodisiac to her senses. "Shaolin is a secret martial art," he said, "passed down from master to student, but never to outsiders."

"Weren't you an outsider?"

"Yes, but Tahj considered me an exception."

"Why?"

He laid a finger against her lips, his warm breath blowing tendrils of her hair. "A closed mouth opens the mind to listening." He brushed a light kiss across her temple before going on.

"There are hundreds of moves, but they are represented by five styles." He molded his arms around hers and cradled her hands, making small motions with them, rhythmical and fluid. "Dragon, Tiger, Leopard,

Snake, and Crane, which complement the five essences. Dragon cultivates the spirit. Tiger represents the training of the bones. Leopard develops strength. Crane works the sinew. And Snake promotes ch'i."

"What's ch'i?"

"Intrinsic energy, a state where life and death lose the quality of fear and you become a true master of your self.

"Buddhists adhere to the doctrine of *samsara,* that all beings pass through a continual cycle of birth, death, and rebirth until liberated. They reject the notion of an unchanging entity that transmigrates from one incarnation to the next."

"You mean they don't believe people have souls?"

"They prefer the notion that a person is a collection of elements. The physical body. The senses. Mental disposition. And consciousness that arises when the mind and body come in contact with the outside world."

"It's very complex, isn't it?"

"It takes years of studying to understand the intricacies. Some of the doctrines are thought-provoking, but I don't agree with the basic principle."

"Which is?"

"That suffering is necessary to reach enlightenment, and that we need to spend our lives atoning for past sins. I don't want to have to be that good."

"Why?"

"Because," he murmured, his jaw brushing against her neck, his fingers tracing hers, "being good would mean I couldn't touch you. For desire, in all its forms, will doom the sinner to an endless cycle of hell on earth."

Fancy could barely think with his caressing her that way. If desire would doom her, she would take the punishment. Any other way was a life deprived.

"Pleasure is to be shunned," he went on, his lips feathering along her jaw, "because it is only temporary. Desire," he whispered, turning her face up to his, his lips a breath away, "is bondage."

Fancy closed her eyes and tried to breathe as he turned her head back around.

He widened her stance, controlling her actions, making her body thrum. "Draw your energy inside. Calm your mind so that each movement becomes graceful and harmonious. Concentrate on your breathing. Inhale slowly. Now exhale. From here." He flattened his palm against her diaphragm.

Fancy felt weak, heady with every light stroke of his hands across her body.

"Focus on the attacking point." He straightened her arm, thrusting forward, palm up. "Use your enemy's strength to defeat him. If he's strong, attack laterally." He made a sweeping downward motion. "If he's weak, strike from the front." He brought her arm across her body. "If he grabs you from behind"—he wrapped his arm tighter around her waist, one large hand precariously close to her breasts—"bring your head back against his nose, or work your arms loose"—he gave her room to do so—"and elbow his solar plexus." He showed her how. "If that doesn't work"—he moved closer, a tantalizing heat and hardness cushioned against her buttocks—"then bring your heel up into his groin."

Fancy closed her eyes, her breath rasping through her lungs as she instinctively moved against him, his deep-throated groan raising the heat to a new level.

He sucked in a breath and turned her around to face him. "The simpler the method," he instructed, his eyes heavy-lidded as he stared down at her, "the better it is." Then he released her, leaving her feeling oddly bereft.

"Why did Tahj teach you Shaolin if it was only supposed to be passed down to other monks?"

"Because he considered me a pathetic specimen of manhood and took pity on me."

Fancy laughed at such a preposterous claim. "Be serious."

"I am serious. The little bastard knocked me flat on my arse during our first go-round. A humbling experience, I assure you."

If Fancy hadn't seen a display of Tahj's skill, she would never have believed Lucien's story. "What compelled Tahj to perform this good deed?"

"He believes a strong body can overcome the deficiencies of the mind."

Lucien definitely had a strong body. Her gaze traveled shamelessly over the solid width of his chest, the bulging of his arms, and lower.

"And what deficiencies of the mind do you possess?" she asked, her body tingling from his nearness.

He reached out and pushed back a lock of hair that

had tumbled over her cheek. "Far too many for an innocent like you to comprehend."

"I'm not innocent."

"God, I hope not," he uttered in a ragged voice as he leaned down and brushed a feather-light kiss over her lips. The caress was over before she had a moment to savor it. Each time he touched her, it became more natural, more needed.

When she found her breath, she asked, "Why did Tahj teach you these secret techniques?"

He shrugged and bent down to run his fingers through the water, pressing them against the back of his neck. "I had time on my hands."

"Why?"

"Can't a man be idle?"

"I can't picture you being idle."

He glanced over his shoulder at her. "Should I take that as a compliment?"

"An observation."

"I suspect you have plenty of those."

She did, which was another reason she would never fit into the posh and polished realm of London society. She had a tendency to be unerringly straightforward and speak her mind. Heath had told her that coyness and demure flirtation were considered the height of desirability for women in London.

It all seemed silly and meaningless to Fancy. She'd much rather read an engaging novel and discuss its merits than attend functions where the most interesting topic of conversation was the latest fashion. She would suffocate in such a constricting atmosphere. How could people exist in a place where they couldn't see the ocean or smell the sea-scented air every day?

"Woolgathering?"

Fancy turned to find Lucien regarding her with a curious expression. "I'm sorry. My mind wandered."

"Am I boring you?"

He had given her an opening to depart, and yet all she said was, "No."

"Good, because I've collected you a week's supply of oysters."

Fancy's gaze followed his to the rock where she had placed her first oyster. A small mountain of them were now piled there. She smiled. "You have been industrious, sir."

"Indeed, but I have my reasons. I intend to ply you with each and every one of them."

"I couldn't eat even a third. I'll have to come back later with a bucket."

"I'll send Tahj for them. I don't want you going down that slope alone; you could fall and break your neck."

For a moment, Fancy could only stare at him, then she laughed. "That's absurd. I've explored these cliffs since I was a child."

"And someone should have taken you in hand. Perhaps you would not be so reckless."

"Are you proposing to be my father?" she asked incredulously, her humor having fled at his dictatorial attitude.

"You will not come back here without me, and that is the end of the discussion. Do you understand?"

How dare he be so highhanded! Who did he think he was, dictating to her? Her lord and master, it appeared. And in her role as servant, she had to comply.

Nodding brusquely, she pivoted away from him, intent on leaving him where he stood. She gasped as he came up behind her, as silent as a wraith.

She stiffened in his embrace. "Do you make a habit of dallying with the servants?"

"Only the ones who hit me," he said, his lips brushing her hair.

"That explains why you are utterly witless."

His laughter was unexpected. "You are a handful, my little Valkyrie."

Fancy hated the way he could so easily melt her. "Leave me alone."

"You're put out with me because I don't want you getting hurt?"

"Yes," she replied stiffly.

"You are an odd female, Miss Purdy."

His comment stung. She already knew she was an oddity. "If you don't like how I am—"

"Oh, but I do like how you are," he countered, the words a caress against her skin. "You make a man want to tame you and capture your fire for his own."

"I'm not some wild horse you can bring to the bit. I'm—"

"Hell and damnation," he swore, the heat at her back suddenly gone.

Concerned, Fancy whirled around. "What's the matter?"

He dropped down onto a rock and wrapped a hand around his foot. "I think something bit me."

Fancy lowered herself to her knees in front of him. "Let me see." When he wouldn't remove his hand, she chided, "Don't be a baby." He raised an eyebrow, but she ignored him and gently pried his fingers away one by one. She smoothed her thumb over the sole of his foot and frowned. "I don't see anything." When she looked up, she found an amused glimmer in his eyes and knew she had been duped. "Why, you horrid man!"

He laughed, and she splashed him with water, dousing the front of his shirt, which sobered her immediately as her gaze followed a bead of water down his chest until it disappeared behind the material.

He cupped her chin and raised her gaze to his. "I had to do something to bring you back into charity with me."

"You don't play fair."

"I know. But you are so damned tempting." His gaze lowered. "Your shirt is wet."

Fancy glanced down and heat sprung to her cheeks. Her splashing had not only wet his shirt but her own, showing the dark outline of her nipples and their pebbled peaks.

"Dare I hope I affect you as much as you affect me?" he asked.

Fancy knew she should move, do something, but

her limbs wouldn't obey. All she could do was shake her head. "This isn't right."

"It sure as hell feels right," he murmured in a husky voice that made her shiver, his fingers wrapping around her arm and pulling her between his thighs.

He opened his palm and showed her a buttercup. He trailed it along her jaw before tucking it behind her ear. Then he took her hand and uncurled her fingers, revealing several oysters, clutched and forgotten.

He stuck his hand in his pocket and pulled out a small folding knife. He pressed along the seam of the shell, popping open its hardened casing. Tipping his head back, he let the oyster slide into his mouth, taking an almost sinful delight in it.

His eyes were sultry as he looked down at her and scooped another oyster from her palm and cracked the shell. This time he held it out to her. "Open up."

She did as he asked, and he placed the wet shell against her lips and watched as she sucked the oyster down. The act felt intimate, and the way he regarded her made her chest tight.

"They say oysters are an aphrodisiac," he murmured, holding another up to her lips, which she obediently swallowed, her breath locking in her throat as he leaned down and whispered in her ear, "They remind a man of a woman's most intimate parts. Do you know what part I speak of, sweet?"

Fancy's mouth went dry, and she could only shake her head, riveted, as he tipped his head back once more and gently lapped another oyster into his mouth, the picture shockingly erotic, as was the slight smile that curled the corners of his lips when he looked at her.

He laid his palm against her cheek, his thumb smoothing over her bottom lip. "You do know that I want to make love to you, don't you?"

"Yes," she said, barely audible, the world seeming to conspire against her as a soft breeze washed over her skin, the trickle of water running down a crevice in the stones lulling her senses.

She was drawn to him and could not dredge up a single protest when his arm came around her waist and pulled her to him. They were both wet from the chest down, and the water lapping around them only heightened the moment.

He kissed her, his mouth insistent. She understood desire, and knew that was what she felt for him, as much as she knew she had to deny it. He was her guardian, the man her brother had entrusted with her care. Her virtue. If he knew who she was, he wouldn't want her. When she finally told him, he would hate her.

But all those things seemed leagues away as he cupped her breast, his tongue curling against hers as his thumb caressed her nipple.

She felt dizzy, her mind whirling in heady delight while her body turned languorous. She didn't want the sensations to stop. And when Lucien cupped her other breast, so that he held both in his palms, gently squeezing, she pressed into him, wanting more.

He trailed kisses down her neck, and she shivered.

"Let me teach you pleasure, Angel. I promise I'll go slow. But I need to touch you."

He lifted her, and she instinctively wrapped her legs around his waist as he moved them deeper into the rocky gorge and into a secluded overhang, where he laid her down on the soft sand, a light trickle of water moving against her back.

"Have you ever been pleasured, love?" he asked as he slowly undid the buttons on her shirt, nothing but a girlish camisole barring her naked breasts from his view. "Has any man ever tasted you?"

Fancy shook her head.

He smiled and braced his hands on either side of her head, his big body blocking out the sun, leaving the golden rays to backlight him as he stared down at her, his long, dark hair tumbling forward, the soft strands whispering across her chest as he pulled apart the laces of her camisole and kissed each piece of skin he exposed, until . . .

She moaned and arched up as he drew her nipple into his mouth and suckled deeply. She could feel every tug, every teasing lick of his tongue, down below.

"You're so untutored," he crooned against her skin, looking up at her as his tongue circled her nipple, her labored breathing lifting her breasts up and down as he toyed with her, licking her each time her breast rose, so that she never wanted to exhale. "This is all I'm going to do. For now. But each time you come to me, I'll teach you a bit more. Do you want that?" He asked the question as he tugged her nipple into his warm, wet mouth, and all Fancy could do was move restlessly against him. "Do you like what I'm doing?"

Fancy fought for air. "Yes," she breathed, the word a haunting whisper of sound.

He rolled her nipples between his thumb and forefinger, pulling them lightly before soothing them with his mouth. "You are full of passion you can barely contain." He groaned low in his throat as she pushed her hips up against his. "You know, don't you? Instinctively you understand. Soon, sweet. When you're ready for me. For now, all I want you to do is live and breathe the pleasure I can give you."

He traced her lips with his tongue. He tasted of the sea, and of hunger. Their mouths mated with carnal abandon, separating only to find a new angle, each labored breath beginning and ending with the other's mouth.

He cupped her breasts and pushed them high and tight so that his mouth and tongue left a wet path between her sensitive tips, all the sensation arrowing down to the core of her, heat flushing her body.

"My sea goddess." His breath bathed her in fiery pants, a tremor moving through him as she clutched his shoulders. "I love tasting you." He flicked his tongue over one taut peak while his fingers played with the other.

Fancy arched up against him as he kissed one nipple, then the other.

"Please," she moaned.

He pressed down against her, his hard length branding her, rocking against her as he opened her legs wider, his hands and mouth relentless on her.

Fancy threw her head back as a shattering climax speared through her body, pulses throbbing from deep inside, moist where Lucien's body was cradled tightly against her as the pleasure rolled over her, leaving her limp and sated.

And all too aware of the man who lay heavily on top of her, gently stroking the hair from her face.

Nine

What was it about passion that could completely obliterate a person's common sense?

Fancy stared up into the mid-afternoon sky, clouds like cotton tufts floating on the breeze as Lucien gently righted her clothes and then shifted her so that her head was nestled against his shoulder.

All the subtle touches and caresses had led to an irreversible mistake. It wasn't that she hadn't wanted him; she had. And had he not seduced her, she very well may have seduced him.

Once more, her rashness had mired her in trouble.

"What are you thinking?" Lucien asked, his fingers absently stroking her upper arm.

"That I need to get back to the house," she replied, which was the truth, but not what consumed her thoughts at that moment. "My absence will have been noted." And she could only imagine the earful she would have to listen to if anyone got wind that she had been alone with Lucien. Olinda would neuter Lucien, then hold him at sword-point until he said, "I do." The repercussions were too awful to contemplate.

He nudged her chin up. "I hope I didn't get you in trouble with your mistress. If she is upset with you, I'll take the blame."

Fancy hadn't expected him to care about the consequences that might befall a common servant.

"And what will you say to her?" she asked.

"That I wanted a tour of the property," he said, softly sliding his thumb across her bottom lip. "I won't let anything happen to you. I promise."

Fancy averted her gaze. He was making her like him more than she could allow; she needed to hold on to the image of him as a gamester and womanizer. Both were his stock-in-trade, and she could not forget that.

Pulling away, she rose to her feet. Without a word, she started back up the path, thinking about how every decision, even the simplest one, could easily lead to disaster.

"Hello!" a distant voice called out as Fancy mounted the rise, bringing her head out of the clouds and her gaze snapping up.

She caught sight of a figure approaching. A man. Her mind raced. Could it be Calder? Lord, how could she have forgotten about him for a moment? His treachery had been what had driven her to the tavern and into a fateful first meeting with Lucien.

But it was not Calder, she realized with relief as the man drew closer, but Heath. His tall, rangy body materialized from the reedy grass, moving in that familiar loping stride, his sandy brown hair glimmering in the late-day sun.

The Courtenays claimed to be descendants of Cornish kings, and everyone had always treated them with a certain level of respect. Every eligible young girl in the area hoped to snare Heath and become the woman fortunate enough to earn a place in such an illustrious family.

He waved, and Fancy instinctively waved back. Then she stopped abruptly, her heart missing a beat. Today she was not Lady Francine Fitz Hugh, but an impostor, and she had to warn Heath before he said something to Lucien that would ruin all her plans.

"I'll be right back," she told Lucien hastily, praying he wouldn't follow her as she moved to head off Heath.

As they met in the middle of the field, Heath suddenly grabbed her around the waist and swung her about before giving her a brotherly kiss on the mouth, his brown eyes alight with mischief as he returned her to her feet and backed up a step to look at her.

"Good Lord, Fancy, girl, you fill out those breeches quite stunningly. Turn around and let us have a look." Before she could protest, he caught her shoulders and swiveled her around, whistling low in appreciation. "You'll have all the young bucks falling at your feet if you keep dressing this way." With a laugh, he tapped her on her behind as though she were still a little girl.

Fancy slapped his hands away and faced him with a scowl. "Stop that."

"Stop what?" he returned, all innocence. "I was just having a little fun."

"This is no time for fun. I have something to discuss with you." Fancy darted a glance at Lucien, who now stood atop the rise, a glower on his face. At any moment he would walk over, which left her not a second to spare.

Unfortunately, Heath had followed her gaze and frowned. "Who's that?" he demanded.

Fancy sighed. "That's my guardian. Lucien Kendall."

Heath stared at her for a stunned second. "Colonel Lucien Kendall? George's commanding officer?"

Heath knew all about Lucien. Fancy had been so sure the man would never deign to step foot in Cornwall that she had confided everything. Until yesterday, she would never have thought she had anything to worry about.

"The same," she said.

"What is he doing here? I thought his concern only went so far as to hire another keeper for you?"

"I guess I chased off one too many." And her heedless behavior might very well be the gust that toppled her precarious house of cards. "I don't have time to explain everything now, except that he doesn't know who I am."

A frown pulled at Heath's brows. "Doesn't know?"

"Please, just listen. I couldn't tell him the truth. He said he intends to marry me off."

Heath regarded her reflectively. "That wouldn't be the worst thing," he said, his tone gentling as he lightly touched her cheek. "You can always marry me, you know. I'll take care of you."

"Yes, I know." And she also knew they would make each other miserable. Heath didn't love her, and she didn't love him. "But I have to do this on my own. I can't lose Moor's End."

"I don't know about this, puss. I think your guardian should be made aware of the trouble you're going through."

"No." Fancy shook her head vigorously. "Moor's End has been in my family for more than a century. I won't be the one who loses it. It belongs to future generations."

"What future generations?" Heath asked, not unkindly, and yet his words brought a pang of hurt to her heart.

There would be no future without children. Without a husband. It wasn't that she didn't want to marry; she did. But in her own time. To a man who loved her.

"I'm sorry," he murmured, drawing her into his arms. "I know all this hurts you terribly. If you would just let me take care of you."

For a moment, Fancy allowed him to comfort her. Then she drew back, casting a glance at Lucien to find his scowl bordering on fury. He started toward them, and Fancy panicked.

"Oh, Lord, he's coming. Please, Heath, don't tell him who I am."

"Fancy . . ."

"He thinks I'm Mary Purdy, a servant," she rushed on. "I promise I'll tell him the truth. But not now. Please, Heath. Help me."

"There's something I have to tell you."

"Fine. Just not now."

"When?"

"I'll meet you tonight at Mariner's Nook. You can tell me then. For now, I beg you not to reveal me."

Then her time ran out as Lucien stopped beside her, the possessive light in his eyes revealing far more than Fancy would have liked. There was nothing she could do but pray.

"Heath," she said, hoping she didn't sound as nervous as she felt, "this is Lucien Kendall, Lady Francine's guardian. He just arrived yesterday from London. Mr. Kendall, may I introduce you to Heath Courtenay, a close neighbor of Lady Francine's."

Lucien inclined his head. "Courtenay," he said stiffly.

Heath returned the gesture. "Kendall."

Fancy's palms grew clammy as she watched the two men size each other up. Heath was a few years younger than Lucien, but her guardian had several inches on Heath, as well as an additional stone's worth of solidly packed muscle.

Anxious, Fancy hooked her hand around Lucien's arm and tugged. "Mr. Kendall was just seeing me home."

Lucien glanced down at her beneath tightly drawn brows. He did not look pleased. "Indeed," he murmured gruffly.

The tension was palpable, and Fancy wanted only to retreat. "Good day, Mr. Courtenay," she said, not missing Heath's stony look, displeasure vibrating from him.

"Good day, Miss Purdy. Perhaps we will run into each other again soon." His glance communicated exactly what he meant.

"I'm sure we will."

He nodded to both of them and turned on his heel. Her gaze followed him until he was out of sight. As soon as he had disappeared down the path that led to his home, Fancy exhaled a sigh of relief.

She realized then that her fingers were clutching Lucien's sleeve. She immediately let go. But he clamped his hand over hers. "Not so fast."

"We really should be getting back to the house."

"Who is he?"

Lord, had she been that obvious? Could he tell she was hiding something? She managed to return his gaze calmly. "A neighbor, as I said."

"You know damn well what I'm asking. Who is he to you?"

"A friend."

"How close a friend?"

For a moment, Fancy could only stare, then anger swept over her at his implication. She wrenched her arm from his. "That's none of your concern."

She turned to walk away, but he blocked her path. "It's my concern as long as I'm here."

"Well, leave. No one asked you to come in the first place." She nudged him in the chest and brushed past him.

He caught up to her in two strides, gripping her arm and twirling her around. "I don't share what's mine, and until I leave, you're mine."

Fancy gasped angrily. "You arrogant, bullheaded giant. I don't belong to any man." But even as she said the words, the idea of belonging to Lucien, of stepping into his protective embrace and staying there, was tempting. Would he be so possessive once he knew the truth?

His arms came around her, his body a warm, solid wall, calming her, and she felt the strongest desire to lay her head against his shoulder. She understood what he was doing, that he was staking claim, but she couldn't coerce her limbs into doing a thing about it.

More strongly than ever, she realized that she had to tell him the truth, sooner rather than later. She had already found herself wanting to be around him, and wondering when he would kiss her again. It was all too dangerous.

She had only one option for getting the money she owed more quickly, something she had steadfastly avoided doing. But she had no choice now. She would give Bodie the antique mother-of-pearl brooch her grandmother had given her shortly before she died, and have him sell it for her. Just the thought brought tears to her eyes, and she averted her gaze.

Lucien caught her chin and forced her to look at him. "Don't cry." He smoothed the pad of his thumb across the path of a lone tear. "I didn't mean to yell," he said, mistaking the cause of her tears. "I just want you. I don't know how you've bewitched me so thoroughly, but you have." His head lowered, and Fancy could not find the strength to deny him.

Her eyes closed on a sigh as his mouth pressed against hers, gently shaping her lips, the kiss a communion of mutual desire. Her body tingled in remembrance of his touch.

He broke the kiss, and Fancy uttered a sound of protest. Then her gaze followed his, and she realized why he had stopped. They were not alone. She smiled. The black kit had wandered off from Sassy again and was now plunked at the edge of Lucien's boot, staring up at him.

"What is it with this bloody fur ball?" Lucien groused, scowling down at the kitten, who was completely unconcerned about his ferocious mien.

"I believe it thinks you're its mother."

Lucien's head jerked up, and he glowered at her. Fancy had to bite her lip to keep from laughing. "You find this amusing, do you?"

She nodded. "You did save it, after all. And they say if you save a life, your destinies are forever entwined."

"I saved you," he murmured, gently cupping her cheek. "Does that make us forever entwined?"

Fancy could barely look at him for the dart of longing that went through her. "We had better gather up the kittens. It's too dangerous for them out here." She leaned down and scooped up the sleeping baby beside his boot. "Hold out your hand."

"Hell, you aren't going to make me hold that thing, are you?"

"Yes." She promptly laid the kitten in his palm, the difference in size between man and feline endearing.

He looked incredibly uncomfortable, especially when the kitten began licking his thumb with a raspy pink tongue. He frowned, and Fancy enjoyed every minute of it as she rounded up the remaining three kittens, the squirming bundles of fur keeping him occupied as they made their way back to the house.

They had just stepped out of the woods when she heard Lucien say, "Come out from behind there."

Fancy turned to see a shrub rustling. A moment later, a curly head and a pair of frightened brown eyes appeared. "Jimmy?" she said.

He moved out from his hiding place. "Aye, mum."

"What are you doing?" Then a terrible thought struck her. "Has your mother taken a turn?"

He gave a quick shake of his head. "No, mum. She's doin' much better now with the poultice y' gave her, I just come to . . . well . . ." He swallowed and looked at Lucien, an intimidating monument, even with kittens crawling up his shirt. "I had to see if y' was all right."

"I don't understand."

"I do," Lucien remarked, bringing Fancy's gaze to him. "We've met before, Jimmy and I."

"Met?"

"Last night."

It only took Fancy a second to figure out where. The tavern.

"So you know her, do you, lad?" There was no rancor in Lucien's voice, only humor. "Were you worried she would come to harm?"

Jimmy stared down at his hands, nervously twisting his cap. "I didn't mean to be dishonest with y', sir. I told y' most of the truth."

"But you needed the money."

He nodded, appearing utterly dejected as he peered up at Fancy with eyes that had seen too much sorrow. "I'm sorry, miss. I din't mean to rat y' out."

Fancy's heart went out to him. His parents had brought Jimmy and his sister, Lisbeth, to Cornwall from London, hoping for a better life. But his father had died in a mining accident at Wheal Rose six months earlier, and their mother had contracted a lung infection last month. She was improving, but slowly, leaving a grave burden on her children. Fancy did as much as she could, bringing supper and reading the children a bedtime story, but often it felt like too little.

"Come here, Jimmy." He shuffled over to her, his head bowed as he stopped before her. Fancy stroked his hair. "Olinda is making sweet buns this morning. Why don't you go inside and see if they're done?"

"Y' forgive me, then?" he asked in a small voice.

"Of course," she assured him, kissing his forehead. "Now go and get yourself a bun while it's hot. And bring some home with you," she called after him as he dashed toward the kitchen door.

When he was gone, Fancy faced Lucien, who was trying to capture a white-pawed kitten as it worked its way up over his shoulder.

"What's that look for?" he grumbled, clearly disgruntled as his chest got little claw punctures for his efforts.

"Did you bribe that poor child for information?"

He frowned. "No. He offered it."

"Jimmy is the most honest-hearted boy I've ever known."

"So I'm dishonest, you mean?"

She gave him a look that conveyed her opinion and swung on her heel.

"Now wait just one damn minute." But she didn't, blast her, and he was stuck juggling kittens as he followed.

Sadie came trotting up to him the minute he stepped through the kitchen door, nearly toppling him. "Down, you confounded mutt." Like her mistress, the dog ignored him, sniffing the kittens, who batted at Sadie's nose. "Just wait until I put them down," Lucien muttered. "Then you'll be shivering in the hall closet."

He bent over, intending to fulfill his threat, when he heard, "For goodness sake, not there! They'll get trampled. Over here. I've made a bed."

Grumbling beneath his breath, Lucien glanced up to see the housekeeper stifling a chuckle, while Jimmy ate his treat, too absorbed to care about Lucien's plight. Lady Imperious stood impatiently across the room, pointing to a crate turned on its side, lined with a fluffy blanket.

Lucien stalked over to the crate, dropped to his haunches, and one by one deposited his burden, more than ready to be done with this exercise in futility.

Standing, he glared down into the girl's haughty, upturned face, and knew the strongest desire to kiss her. God save him, she had put a spell on him. "Satisfied?"

"Yes."

"Fine."

"Good."

They exchanged scowls, and then Lucien strode out of the room. Fancy wanted to kick herself for allowing her gaze to follow his retreat, that magnificent form a thing of beauty even when he was angry.

"Good afternoon, Mr. Kendall," Rosalyn chirped in a sunny tone as she came down the hallway, which earned her a grunt in reply. Entering the kitchen with a puzzled expression, she asked, "What's the matter with him?"

Fancy watched Lucien until he disappeared into a hazy patch of late sunlight in the front hall. Then she snapped, "He's a man."

As she marched off in the other direction, Olinda and Rosalyn exchanged confused looks.

Ten

The house caged Lucien like a tomb. The four walls seemed to close in on him as he stood in the middle of the library, the smell of old leather and disuse surrounding him as he tried not to think about his escalating restlessness or an insufferable chit with a hair-trigger temper and a smile more radiant than the sun.

He curled a hand around the worn mantel above the fireplace, the clock tolling out the quarter hour before midnight. He stared down at the burning wood crackling on the dulled andirons in the grate, fighting the ache building deep within him, knowing tremors would soon rack his body if his need was not appeased. He reached out a hand toward the flames, but he didn't feel the heat, only a terrible, growing cold.

He struggled to concentrate on the rattle of the rain against the windowpanes, the howl of the wind that cursed a shutter to rap against the house.

Restlessly, he paced to the liquor cabinet and took down an aged bottle of brandy, his stride not yet marked by the feeble swaying of a drunk, though he was definitely well-liquored, having already finished what remained of a bottle of bourbon.

Why had he come to this godforsaken place? He should be back in London, doing what he did best, gambling and remaining free of entanglements—and accepting responsibility for Lady Francine Fitz Hugh was a huge entanglement. Most days his life hung together by only the barest thread.

But what awaited him in London? An empty town house? Memories that had begun to stalk his mind, leaving him with fewer places to hide?

He glanced over his shoulder at the slim black box on a table in front of the sofa, perched there like a bird of prey, just waiting for him to lift the lid. He had thought himself strong enough to conquer the yawning void inside him, and had initially left the box under lock and key at Charring House. But he had barely traveled an hour's distance before he had been forced to go back and retrieve it. His life was tethered to that box, body and soul.

Lucien finished off his glass of brandy and poured another, walking past the table once more and bracing his hand above the window to look out at the storm-tossed night, thunder rolling through black clouds, lightning illuminating the headlands, desolate and bleak, leaves shivering in the chilled gust.

With each passing moment, the guillotine dug deeper into his neck.

He needed Mary. Needed her almost as much as he needed the contents of that box. Something about her soothed him, made him temporarily forget the images of a young man who had taken three days to die from a bullet that had been meant for Lucien, and the cries of a woman whose only mistake lay in loving him, and his mother's frightened eyes as she submitted to her husband's brutality—and a shame no one could speak of.

God, how he hated the night.

Fancy stood at the window, watching the rain run over the panes in a thick sheet. Storms came frequently during the fall nights, sweeping in with a flourish and abating before dawn.

There was a time when she used to love the rain, when she would sit at this very window, her nose pressed to the glass, watching fat raindrops plunk down onto the road like silver shillings, turning it into a murky lake.

If only the raindrops really were shillings, her problems would be solved. But even that wouldn't change the fact that storms now left her with night terrors.

Her parents had died in a storm at sea. Her grandmother had passed away on a rain-lashed night. The news of her brother's death had arrived during an unexpected gale.

She would never forget the somber-faced young military officer who had told her of George's valiant struggle to survive, of his heroic deeds for his country. Of his love and devotion to her. For the first several moments, all Fancy had been able to think, selfishly, was that she was alone. Then she had grieved, and for months afterward, she had barely functioned.

Sadie bumped against her thigh, and Fancy glanced down, seeing those big brown eyes fixed on her and understanding the sorrow.

She patted the dog's head. "I know," she consoled. "But we must be brave. It'll be over soon."

Turning from the window, Fancy stared at her bed. Lucien had vacated her room that morning, having been relegated to a chamber down the hall by Olinda. And yet an imprint of him remained, images of his body sprawled across her coverlet, his full lips shaped into a taunting grin as his gaze caressed her.

Fancy closed her eyes and laid a hand upon her breast, lightly sweeping a finger over her nipple, feeling it respond. Lucien had awakened something inside her, and it could not simply be put back or locked away again.

She dropped her hand and blocked out the thought, thinking instead of Heath. What did he want to tell her that was so important they must meet in seclusion at midnight? Would he be waiting for her at the cove in this weather?

Fancy's rational mind told her that nothing bad would befall her; she knew the terrain well. It was the storm that left her immobile.

She decided she would check on the kittens, make sure Sassy hadn't gotten tired of her new duties and left the babies to fend for themselves. One kitten in particular was smaller than the rest, a little calico who had refused to nurse. It wouldn't survive if it didn't eat soon.

Leaving her room, Fancy moved down the darkened hallway, the howl of the wind and creak of the house surrounding her. How many nights had she heard those same sounds and been lulled by them? And how often had she crawled into her grandmother's bed and listened to her tales of Cornwall's legend-filled past and of growing up the only girl in a family of five older brothers, lifelong tinners and miners, all of whom had eventually died of poisoned lungs? Times had been hard, but their love had been strong. There were moments, late at night, when Fancy thought she could hear their laughter and the sound of running feet. The sounds of a house that had a soul.

She entered the kitchen from the servant's corridor, Sadie's nails clicking against the hardwood floor. Setting her candleholder down on top of a flour bin, Fancy knelt in front of the crate.

She smiled at the sight that greeted her. The kittens were curled against Sassy's belly, fast asleep, rumbling purrs of contentment filling the quiet room. She had named three of them Winkin', Blinkin', and Nod. The black, which she thought of as Lucien's, she called Inkwell.

Fancy frowned as her gaze ran over the kittens once

more. She counted only three. Inkwell was missing. She knew the little feline had wanderlust, but at midnight? There were many nooks and crannies in the house for it to get into, and places where it could fall and hurt itself.

Lifting the candle, Fancy set out to find the kitten, though locating a black cat in the dark would prove difficult. She could only hope little Inkwell had curled up somewhere for the night.

In the middle of the hall that ran along the stairwell, a sound stopped Fancy in her tracks. A single mournful note drifted through the air, followed a moment later by a slightly off-key chord.

Someone was playing the pianoforte in the library.

As she moved nearer, Fancy spotted a thin beam of light sliding out from underneath the closed door. Her mind dismissed an intruder. Calder's thugs would not stop to stroke the keys, or produce a sound of longing that struck at Fancy's very heart.

The knob made only a slight click as she turned it, inching the door open to peer inside. In the shadowed interior, all that was clear was the sharp angles of Lucien's profile and his dark hair brushing his shoulders, faintly tinted by firelight.

There was a bruised look about him, a vulnerability etched in that stark pose. She felt as if she was finally seeing all of him. Beneath the mien of the charming rogue, a pain seemed to reside deep within him, in a place that had not or could not heal.

Cradled against his chest he held Inkwell, gently

stroking the sleeping cat, an anguish on his face that nearly broke her heart. He had protested so loudly at being keeper of the kittens that afternoon, but now his actions belied his disgruntled behavior.

Spotting her new friend, Sadie's tail began to wag in earnest, thwapping against the wall before Fancy could back out of the room.

Lucien's head jerked up, his gaze impaling her where she stood. His eyes were glazed, and she could tell he had been drinking. He seemed on the edge of volatility; not the man who had hunted for oysters with her that afternoon.

"I'm sorry," she murmured. "I didn't mean to disturb you." She saw the empty bottle of bourbon and the half-empty bottle of brandy.

Then she noted other things, like his shirt, which was undone and pulled free of his waistband, leaving his chest bared to her gaze, the top button on his low-slung trousers negligently undone.

His torso was smooth, hard, with not a single hair to mar its perfection—just solid, rigid muscle framed by taut, sun-glazed skin.

"You've been disturbing me since I met you," he said in a low voice, a slight roughness to his words. "Why should now be any different?" He deposited the kitten on a worn wing chair and beckoned Fancy. "Come in, Miss Purdy."

"I was just looking for the kitten."

"Well, now you've found it." His gaze never left Fancy as he lifted his drink to his lips.

Something about the look in his eyes made her shiver. "I should take it back to Sassy."

"Ah, but you can't."

Fancy halted in her tracks. "Why?"

"Because I'm holding it hostage. The price of its release is your company. Have a drink with me."

"I think you've had enough to drink."

"Do you? I'll take it under advisement. Now, what would you like?" He moved to the cabinet and took down another glass. "Sherry? Port, perhaps?"

Fancy hesitated, her inner voice sending out a warning, which for once she almost heeded. "Sherry," she said, vowing only to stay a few minutes.

Drink poured, he turned and leaned back against the edge of the cabinet. "Don't hover there in the doorway, my girl. Come get your drink."

There was something taunting in the way he studied her as she walked toward him, a certain feral gleam she couldn't comprehend as he held the glass out to her with a hand that trembled.

"Thank you," she murmured, trying not to stare at his chest, even as her fingers itched to mold her palms against its sculpted beauty.

"Couldn't sleep?" he asked.

Her fingers tightened on the glass. "The storm . . . it kept me awake. And you?"

"A variety of things." None of which he intended to share, it seemed. "I guess we are both among the ranks of the sleepless tonight."

Fancy could only wonder what his reasons were.

Then she noted an odd black box on the table behind him. "What's that?"

"You are inquisitive, aren't you?" He shifted his body slightly so that he blocked all but a corner of the box. "Drink up." He tipped the glass to her lips.

With only a slight pause, she took a sip. The liquor was aged and smooth, and it warmed her as it went down, taking away some of the chill. Her gaze slipped to the box again.

Fancy started as Lucien's hand wrapped around her wrist and pulled her forward until she stood between his thighs. "What is it about you, Miss Purdy, that can make a man so crazy?" His voice was whisper soft and incredibly seductive.

"You seem to be the only man I have that effect on."

"Somehow I find that hard to believe."

"Undoubtedly. Otherwise, it would put a taint on your own outrageous behavior."

The smile he suddenly leveled on her was devastating. "If memory serves, I was the white knight, charging in to save you."

"You kissed me."

"I beg to differ. We made a business arrangement: I kissed you with your consent."

"You blackmailed me into it!"

"Blackmail is such a harsh word. I prefer to think of it as collateral for future assistance."

"Meaning you'll expect a kiss each time I need your help?"

"A kiss—or whatever else you'd like to throw into

the bargain." He stroked a finger down her arm, raising goose bumps as he went. "You'll find I'm a very conciliatory fellow."

Heat began to swim in Fancy, and had he kissed her at that moment, she would have melted into him. Raising her chin, she said, "You'll get nothing else from me."

"No?" The glint in his eyes told her he felt obliged to try as he leaned down and pressed his lips to the crook of her neck.

Fancy instinctively tilted her head and closed her eyes, reveling in the warm pressure of his mouth as he trailed his lips down the column of her throat, dipped into the hollow at the base, and worked back up the center, feathering kisses over her chin until his mouth was but a breath from hers, his eyes liquid blue as he looked into hers.

"Your nipples are hard," he murmured in a husky tone.

Fancy gasped at his brazen remark and jerked back, but his hands manacled her wrists and tugged her forward.

"You may want to deny me, but your body can't."

"Stop this."

"Are they aching, love? Do they want my mouth again?"

Yes, Fancy wanted to cry, her treacherous body betraying her.

He ground his hips against her, letting her feel his arousal. "If you only knew how long it's been since I've felt this way."

Fancy tossed her head back and glared up at him, even as she pressed tighter to his hard length. "A week?"

"Try six months. Longer than that, if I want to be honest with myself. And now you come along." He softly stroked the inside of her wrist with his thumb. "What am I going to do?"

"Take a deep breath, perhaps?"

"I need you."

"You don't even know me."

"But I do. As loathe as I am to admit it, some of Tahj's teachings did sink in, and something in me knows you, understands you."

Fancy felt the same way. It was as if she had waited all her life for this man, and even though her mind fought it, her heart knew.

He kissed her then, in that soft yet unrelenting way that she was coming to crave. She tried, but the words that might put an end to the blissful torment would not come.

He was so intoxicating to her senses, so very hard to resist. He was a well-known womanizer, his exploits thoroughly documented. He was frequently seen in the company of other rogues and scoundrels. Yet she believed him when he said she had bewitched him, for he had certainly put her under a similar spell.

Summoning up her will, Fancy stepped out of his embrace. His scent, that unique blend of sandalwood and musk, clung to her as she walked over to the wing chair and stroked Inkwell's soft fur.

She knew Lucien followed her. She sensed him

behind her, could almost feel his breath on the back of her neck, and knew what she had tempted when she stepped into his lair.

A spear of lightning blazed through the night with a flash of stark white, and the boom of thunder shook the entire house. She hugged herself tightly.

"Are you afraid of the storm?"

She whirled around, having momentarily forgotten Lucien was there. He stood a scant foot away, one hand sunk into the pocket of his trousers, the tail of his shirt draped behind it, showing his lean waist.

"Do you always walk around half dressed in a woman's presence?" she asked, sounding frightfully self-righteous.

"Are your senses offended, Miss Purdy?"

They were outraged, but only because he made her want to touch him. "It's not proper."

"Just as it wasn't proper for me to worship your body on the beach?"

Fancy blanched, shocked at his bold remark. "A gentleman would not bring that up." She sounded like a pious maiden rather than a servant, but it was too late to retract her words.

"I've never laid claim to being a gentleman." He took a step toward her, and Fancy darted behind the chair, which only seemed to amuse him. "Am I to pursue you about this room? I will, you know."

"And would you force yourself on me?"

A glint of anger briefly sparked in his eyes. "Did I force myself on you this afternoon?"

It certainly would have given her ammunition if he had, but he hadn't. "No," she said. "But it isn't right."

"Why? Is there someone else?" He slowly worked his way toward her. "That fool from this afternoon, perhaps?"

"Heath is not a fool!" she fumed. "He's a good friend."

"And he wants you. You're blind if you can't see it."

"We're friends, no more. But even if we weren't, it's none of your concern."

"I'm making it my concern."

He was the most infuriating, highhanded churl she had ever met. And yet he had opened up a door she boldly intended to walk through.

"Then I expect equal courtesy from you."

He palmed his glass. "What exactly are you thinking to get, sweetheart?"

She raised her chin. "I want you to tell me about your family."

He went still, his gaze narrowing on her face. Then he shook his head. "What's between us has nothing to do with my family."

"If you are going to intrude on my life, then you must be willing to give something up in return."

"Is that what I'm doing? Intruding on your life?"

"You are being deliberately difficult."

"It's what I do best."

"I won't make this easy on you."

"Somehow I doubted you would." He regarded her

for a long moment, and then said, "So what will you give me for sharing these confidences?"

"Give you?"

"What piece of yourself?" At her shocked expression, he smiled. "I intend to exploit this opportunity, love, make no mistake about it."

"That's sinful and deplorable!"

He laughed. "Between fire pokers and that chastising tongue of yours, I can understand why you are still a maiden. I suspect most men are too afraid to get close."

"But not you."

"No. Not me. You're like this fire." He reached a hand out toward the flames, inching nearer until she thought his flesh would surely be singed. "You allow people to look, but not touch. You crackle and hiss and warn away the unwary, but introduce something volatile into the mix"—he tossed the remainder of his drink on the fire, igniting a searing burst of heat, driving the flames higher—"and you burn out of control. I, my dear girl, am that volatile element." He moved to stand in front of the chair she had taken refuge behind. "And you will burn for me. So the question remains, what will you give me?"

The prospect was both heady and frightening. "What do you want?"

"Equal compensation for each revelation."

"That is too vague." Hearing the sound of capitulation in her voice, she added, "And unscrupulous."

"It is, isn't it?" His smile was wicked. "Now that

we've come to an agreement, where should we begin?"

"I haven't agreed to anything."

"But you will. You have an innate curiosity that needs to be appeased; you can't help yourself."

Was she that transparent? "Perhaps I do, but you will name your price first."

"Fine. What is it that you want to know?"

Fancy pondered his question for a moment, then said, "I want you to tell me something about your life and family."

An odd tension settled over him as he glanced down at Inkwell, who stretched in her sleep and flopped to her other side. Fancy was alarmed at how ashen his face had suddenly become.

"Are you unwell?" she asked, worried that his wound was worse than he had let on.

"What?" His gaze cut to hers, a look of confusion in his eyes before they cleared, making her wonder if the shadows were playing tricks on her. "I'm fine," he said, a gruff edge to his voice. "And I have come to a determination on a price."

"And that is?"

"To hold you."

Fancy blinked, surprised by his request. "That's all you want? Just to hold me?" She had feared he would want far more—and that she might consent to the terms.

"Yes. That's all I want. Are we in agreement?"

Fancy hesitated, then slowly nodded.

His gaze slid away from her, and he moved back to

the liquor cabinet, grabbing his empty glass and tip-ping the brandy bottle to it.

"Don't drink any more," she heard herself say, not quite sure why she made the request, only that she wanted him sober. She could tell something was both-ering him, and he was using the liquor as a balm.

He stared down at the bottle, then returned the glass stopper to the top and pushed the decanter away. Silence invaded the room, and Fancy wondered if he was regretting the bargain he had made.

Then he began to speak.

"I have a vivid memory of Church Lane in St. Giles. My father took me to a brothel there when I was thir-teen years old. He thought it was time I became a man, so he made me watch while he screwed a prostitute named Blythe."

Everything inside Fancy grew still and cold. "But you were just a boy."

He remained staring at the wall. "In the rookery, thirteen is old enough to father a bastard, let alone for-nicate with a doxy. It wasn't surprising to see a young girl, scarcely more than a child herself, carting a wail-ing baby on her hip. The East End is a world unto itself, and what would be considered unconscionable to most of society did not reach those within its con-fines."

Fancy could not have imagined such deplorable actions by a parent. While hers may not have been the most attentive, they had never subjected her to depraved acts.

"Was your mother no longer alive?" she asked, knowing by the tensing on his shoulders what the answer would be.

"She was very much alive. I never told her."

"I'm sorry."

He turned to face her. "I didn't tell you the story so you'd feel sorry for me. But if you do, all the better. Perhaps you'll take pity on me."

"I don't think pity is what you want."

"You know me so well, do you?"

She met his scrutiny unflinchingly. "Why did you tell me the story?"

He shrugged. "It was the first thing that came to mind."

"It's a very curious thing to be thinking about all these years later."

"I have a long memory."

Fancy wondered if those memories were what kept him up at night. "So what did you do?"

"Do? About what?"

"About the prostitute? Did you share her with your father?"

His eyes turned flat and his expression stony. "That's all the questions."

"But your story is not complete," she protested. "I cannot honor our agreement without hearing the beginning and end of the tale."

He took a step toward her, his countenance like a thundercloud. "You think to play me, do you?"

"I wish to know what happened. It couldn't be any

more shocking than it already was. The worst is over, I would say."

Fancy waited, wondering what he would do next. She pushed him, but perhaps someone needed to do so. She sensed he wanted to talk, but couldn't find the words.

"No," he said.

"No what?"

"No, I didn't touch her."

"I didn't think so."

His gaze captured hers, and he asked belligerently, "Do you think I was afraid?"

"I think you were terrified, and you had every right to be. You were just a boy."

"You know a lot for being an innocent."

"One need not be worldly wise to have an understanding of human nature. What your father did was reprehensible. Were he standing before me now, I would flog him."

Lucien rubbed his chin and regarded her, a reluctant half-grin working its way over his lips. "Have you always had this violent streak?"

Fancy straightened her spine. "If violence entails protecting myself and my family, then yes. I won't allow anything I love to be harmed."

"Such devotion is admirable."

Fancy heard the bitterness in his voice, and something else—longing, perhaps. Had no one ever been devoted to him? Had he never felt that way for someone? Again, she wondered who Sanji was, and why just hearing the name caused him such anguish.

"Please go on with your story."

"I've put a period on that story, if you haven't noticed, and now I expect my payment." He moved around the sofa and sat down. "Come here, Miss Purdy."

Fancy's heart skipped a beat. It was shameful how much she wanted to feel his arms around her. "You've only told me about one family member, and I know nothing about your life."

"I've given you both, and you well know it. Now stop hiding behind that chair."

Technically, he had answered her question, but she wanted more. "I will do as you ask, if—"

"There are no ifs, love. Now come here."

Fancy sighed and accepted her fate. It really wasn't such a bad one. Yet the niggling of her conscience trailed her as she came to a stop in front of Lucien. She had to tell him the truth. What had transpired between them the previous afternoon was proof of that.

Yet she wanted to steal this time with him. She could only pray he would understand her plight when she confessed, and maybe if they shared some kind of connection, he would allow her to do what she must to save her grandmother's home.

Taking a deep breath, she sat beside him, then let out a startled gasp as he lifted her across his lap. "What are you—"

"Holding you. You didn't say how or where. You're not the only one who can play this game."

Fancy stared into his fiery eyes and felt a hitch in her

breath as he reached up and started unpinning her hair. "Ssh," he murmured when she began to protest. "I just want to see you with it down. You've got it coiled so tightly, I'm surprised you have any left." With deft fingers, he undid the topknot and let her tresses spill over her shoulders. He picked up a length and fanned it through his fingers. "The contrast is striking."

"What contrast?"

"Between the chaste girl you appear when it's up, and the seductress you look like when it's down. I nearly fell over when I first saw you at the stables."

"You must be mad. I was dressed like the worst guttersnipe."

"Boy's togs could never have camouflaged your beauty."

"Do you practice complimenting women?"

"Rarely, though most women expect it."

"And you, being a man, are immune to compliments, I presume?"

"Why?" he asked with a devilish twinkle in his eye. "Have you some compliment you wish to bestow upon me? Do you find my eyes beguiling, perhaps? My body too irresistible not to touch?"

Yes. "Do you take nothing seriously?"

"I try not to. Life is bloody hard enough without complicating matters."

"And do you find the guardianship of your ward one of those complications?" As soon as the words had left her mouth, Fancy cursed her tongue.

"It does present problems," he said, his demeanor sobering.

"Why did you accept the responsibility, then?"

"Because I owed it to the lady's brother."

The way he stared straight ahead, as though forgetting she was there, told her he was remembering those last days with George. He tried so hard to make people think he didn't care, but somewhere beneath his smooth exterior beat a heart.

"Did he suffer terribly?" she heard herself ask in a quiet voice. She knew George had lived for nearly three days after taking a bullet to his belly, and there had been times when they had thought he would pull through. But in the end, he had succumbed.

Lucien's hand lay unmoving on her thigh, and he stared at it. "He told me he didn't feel a thing, but he had always been stronger than the rest of us. I just never knew it until then. He was a damn fine officer."

Tears pricked the back of Fancy's eyes, and she struggled to keep them at bay. "I'm sure he would be happy to know you thought highly of him."

"Fitz was the one who kept us all going. He never had anything but a kind word to say. He was always coming up with some bad joke or outrageous tale to make us laugh."

A bittersweet poignancy flowed through Fancy's veins. "That was George," she murmured.

"Did you know him well?" Lucien asked.

"As well as anyone."

He glanced up at her and then looked away, his gaze focused on her shoulder. "Was his sister . . . did she take his death hard?"

"She was devastated," Fancy replied honestly, all the

months of coming to grips with George's death surfacing, threatening to free all the pain she had thought exorcised in her grieving.

"I think that's part of the reason I stayed away," he said, absently smoothing the material of her dress between his fingers. "I couldn't bear to face her."

His soft confession wrenched at her heart. All this time she had thought he didn't care, that he was too busy gambling and having a good time to give her a second thought.

She could see now that he, too, had been devastated by George's death. She sensed that guilt weighed heavily on his shoulders. Did he grieve for all the men he had lost? Feel that somehow he could have prevented their deaths? Perhaps that was where the sadness in him emanated from.

"I'm sure she would have understood, had she known," Fancy told him gently, the wood from the fire crackling softly in the grate behind them.

He shook his head. "I couldn't. I've never been good with words." He sighed and rubbed the back of his neck. "I wrote her."

"I know."

When he looked at her, she could see the pain in his eyes. "She showed you the letter?"

"Yes." Fancy wanted to wrap her arms around his neck and comfort him. She would tell him the truth. He was not the uncaring man she had once labeled him; he had simply not known what to do. "Lucien, I have to—"

"Say it again."

"What?"

"My name. Say it again."

Not quite understanding the feelings whirling inside her, Fancy boldly laid a hand on his cheek and whispered, "Lucien."

His fingers framed her jaw, holding her immobile as he planted his mouth on hers, his lips moving insistently in a breath-stealing kiss, the air around them suddenly charged.

He smelled like warm brandy and carnal heat. Fancy pressed closer to him, clutching the front of his shirt, hard planes and flexing muscle moving as he cupped the back of her head, holding her as though he never meant to let her go.

His hands skimmed down her neck, his fingers sweeping across her skin in a gentle caress. Fancy held her breath as he continued to move down until the lacey edge of her blouse hindered his sensual exploration. She knew she should stop him, knew she should take hold of the hand that slowly worked the buttons free, but she couldn't.

Instead she closed her eyes and moaned as his callused palms slid across her heated flesh and cradled her breasts, his thumbs flicking with deliberate seduction across her sensitive nipples until she could barely think. And when he leaned forward and closed his lips around one delicate peak, her world focused on the sweet pressure against her breast, the delicious sucking on her nipple, the fingers expertly massaging her.

She gripped his hair and held him to her as his tongue trailed a wet path between the aching tips, flicking, circling, lapping until the room was filled with the sound of her ragged breath.

Against the backdrop of the rain, Fancy felt like she was drowning, immersed in her own need, the sound of Lucien's voice pulling her from the pleasure-filled haze.

"Look at me."

Fancy struggled to open her eyes, watching as Lucien reached into a small silver bucket on the side table and scooped out a cube of ice. He licked it and, holding her gaze captive, ran the cube across her nipple, making it pucker tightly and sending a shiver down her spine.

Then he put his mouth over the turgid peak, and the sensation was heightened, hot to cold, the process repeated, back and forth until Fancy thought she would faint from the sweet torment.

Then she felt his hand beneath her skirt and tensed.

"I won't hurt you," he murmured, his palm sliding up her thigh, his fingers squeezing gently as he nudged her legs apart. "I just want to touch you." His fingers lightly feathered over her mound. "If you want me to stop, I will. I won't do anything you don't want me to." He stilled and looked into her eyes. "Should I stop?"

Fancy knew she should say yes, but the hunger inside her, coupled with her desire for Lucien, made her shake her head. She wanted this new experience, and yet she instinctively tried to close her thighs as his fingers found the opening in her pantalets and boldly stroked the hot nub nestled there.

His expert caress quickly soothed her, and she opened her legs wider for him, moaning and writhing as he sucked and laved her nipple while the finger between her nether lips worked her toward ecstasy until her body went rigid, deep pulses crashing through her, leaving her in a sated heap against his chest, where he held her tight, pressing his lips to her hair.

Fancy stayed in his arms for long minutes, not wanting to open her eyes as reality seeped back into her brain to chide her. The first time Lucien had touched her, she might have been able to justify her actions as a mistake that would never happen again. But twice?

When she was brave enough to look up at him, she nearly dissolved beneath the languorous eyes staring down at her. She opened her mouth, but he spoke first.

"I don't know why I can't keep my hands off you. I think I'm strong enough to resist, but then I see you, and my resolve becomes nonexistent."

In the face of his honesty, Fancy knew she could no longer keep the truth from him. "Lucien, there is something I have to—"

A sudden splintering crash rent the air, jerking them both upright.

Lucien gripped her arms, his expression intent as he ordered, "Stay here." Then he was up and moving toward the door, listening for a moment, his body alert, the military man in him showing in full measure.

Fancy could scarcely breathe as he turned the knob, not making a sound. The corridor beyond was pitch-black, every object appearing sinister.

In the next moment, Lucien disappeared into the darkness.

A second later, Fancy followed after him, swallowed into the frightening morass of the unknown.

Eleven

"Lucien," Fancy called out in a hushed voice as she felt her way along the wall, the blackness around her complete.

A shiver trickled down her spine. It felt as if someone was breathing down her neck. She shook off the ridiculous thought, yet she reached down to lay her hand on Sadie's head, comforted by the big dog's company.

The crash had sounded like a window breaking—and the thought that had been stirring in the back of her mind came to the fore.

Calder. Or his thugs. Or both.

Why had she assumed he would not come after Rosalyn at the first opportunity? He couldn't yet know that her guardian had arrived, which would leave him to assume that it was only two old retainers and two women. Not even odds by any measure.

Fancy heard the creaking floorboard behind her a moment too late. Fear tightened her muscles, slowing her movements as she swung around, a hand clamping down over her mouth.

"Don't make a move," a voice hissed in her ear, which she instantly recognized. Calder.

Sadie began to bark uproariously at her side. "Shut up, mutt," he growled, and Sadie yelped.

Fancy reacted with fury, slamming her booted heel down into Calder's foot, reveling in his grunt of pain. "Bitch," he spat, his grip tightening around her waist so that she could hardly breath.

She tried to scream, but all that came out was a muted shriek that worked its way through the meaty fingers pressed bruisingly against her face.

"Now I've got you, you interfering little witch. Where is my darling stepsister?"

Fancy's heart raced. He was suffocating her! Dizziness swam at the back of her head, threatening to take her under. But she refused to go down without a fight.

Lucien's instruction still fresh in her mind, Fancy snapped her head back against Calder's face, hearing his yowl as she took him by surprise.

She used the opportunity provided by his slackened hold to lean forward and thrust her heel up into his groin, doubling him over and freeing herself.

"Sadie, run!" Fancy raced behind the dog as they

tore down the hallway, her progress abruptly halted as she slammed into something solid. Oh, God, how many were there? "Let me go!" She struggled wildly against the stranger's fierce hold, kicking out and hitting his shin.

"Damn it," he grunted. "That was my bloody injured ankle."

"Lucien? Thank God!" She wrapped her arms tightly around his neck, just as his arms came around her to hold her close.

"I heard Sadie barking."

"The intruder attacked me—"

"Where is he?" Lucien demanded.

"At the end of the hallway. I think I broke his nose."

"I'll tan your hide if you move this time." Once more, he disappeared into the darkness.

"Fancy?" It was Rosalyn, coming toward her from the opposite direction.

"Here," Fancy replied.

A single beam of moonlight slanting in through a side window illuminated Rosalyn's pale face, her tall, slim body garbed in only a night rail, confirming she had just jumped out of bed. Two familiar figures appeared behind her.

"Och, lass," Olinda scolded, "what in heaven's name is going on down here?"

"There's been a break-in."

"Oh, my God," Rosalyn gasped. "Are you all right?"

"I'm fine. Sadie took a blow."

"Sweet, brave Sadie," Rosalyn murmured, stroking

the dog's fur before turning those concerned eyes on Fancy. "It was Calder, wasn't it?"

"Yes."

Rosalyn put her hands to her stricken face. "This is all my fault. I never should have involved you in my problem."

"*Our* problem," Fancy stressed. "You're my friend, and as long as I have a breath in my body, I won't let anything happen to you."

"Did he hurt you, miss?" Jaines asked.

"No." Just frightened her a bit. Lucien's lesson had given her the power to defend herself, and she glowed with the accomplishment.

"Whoever it was, he's gone now," Lucien remarked as he materialized from the shadowed corridor, taking in all four faces staring back at him. "You definitely landed a blow," he said to Fancy. "There was a smear of blood on the floor."

"You fought him?" Rosalyn exclaimed, her eyes wide. "Oh, how foolish of you! You know Calder's temper. He'll never forgive you now."

Fancy winced, feeling the impact of Rosalyn's statement before anyone else did.

Lucien's brows drew tightly together. "Who the hell is Calder?" Narrowing his gaze solely on Fancy, he demanded, "Did you know the person who attacked you?"

Fancy sighed, recognizing the end of the road. She had planned to tell Lucien the truth, but not like this, surrounded by people who had only been doing what she had asked them to do. If somewhere deep down she had thought she might possibly muddle out of this, the time had come and gone.

"Yes," she said, resignation in her tone. "I knew him."

The thunderous look on Lucien's face grew as he regarded her. "And who is he, that he would break into the house in the middle of the night?"

"A neighbor."

Lucien's jaw locked. "Another neighbor. Is he in love with you, too?"

"Who's in love with her?" Rosalyn asked, and then turned to Fancy. "Is someone in love with you?"

Fancy shot an exasperated look at Lucien before shifting her attention to Rosalyn. "No one is in love with me. He's talking about Heath."

"Oh. Well, Heath *is* in love with you, or at least he thinks he is."

Why, Fancy wondered, had she never imagined having this conversation in the middle of a corridor in the dead of night, after being attacked by a friend's crazed stepbrother? She should have expected it, considering her life had never followed a normal course.

"Hinny, ye know that lad has been mooning over ye since your body changed into a woman's," Olinda interjected.

Fancy closed her eyes and flushed to her roots.

"He's a rapscallion," Jaines intoned, his wiry brows twitching.

"Ye'd say that about any mon who looked goose-eyed at our girl," his wife remonstrated.

"Heath is a bit of a wild card," Rosalyn put in, the three of them huddled together discussing Fancy's life as if she weren't there. "I'm not quite sure of his intentions."

"I'll give ye that," Olinda returned with a nod. "But he's a handsome lad, ye must admit."

"True enough," Rosalyn conceded. "And yet, I—"

"Enough!" Lucien barked, silencing them all with a glare that eventually landed on Fancy. "Now—I will ask this one time, and one time only. Who, in the name of Hades, is the man who attacked you?"

Fancy hesitated, but finally said, "Calder Westcott."

"And why would this Calder Westcott be after you?"

"He wasn't after her," Rosalyn corrected. "He was after me."

Lucien stared up at the ceiling. "Why did I think the answer would be a simple one?" Lowering his head, his intractable gaze skewered Rosalyn. "I hope you're about to tell me why this insane neighbor is after you."

Rosalyn blinked, her gaze sliding to Fancy with a questioning look before returning to Lucien's. "I . . . Well, you see . . . Calder is . . ."

Fancy took pity on her friend. Lucien's scowl was enough to intimidate the most stouthearted man, let alone a gently bred young woman. "Calder is her stepbrother."

Her answer brought that glowering mien to bear on her once more. "Lady Francine has no stepbrother."

"She's not Lady Francine."

"She's not Lady Francine," he repeated, a tic beginning in his jaw. "And who is she, dare I ask?"

Fancy took a deep breath and said, "Lucien Kendall, may I introduce you to Lady Rosalyn Carmichael."

"Lady Rosalyn—" The rest of his words seemed to back up in his throat, and she watched as a red flush of anger worked its way up his neck. Then he bellowed, *"Where the bloody hell is Lady Francine?"*

With a cold sweat making her palms clammy, Fancy clutched her skirt and dipped into a rather awkward curtsy. "At your service."

Before she could draw another breath, Fancy's wrist was clamped in Lucien's viselike hand, and she was dragged back down the hallway, the protests of the last people who would probably see her alive following in her wake.

He would kill her, Lucien thought as his boots struck the hardwood floor with punishing force, the real Lady Francine in tow and stumbling to keep up. He would wring her pale, slender neck with his bare hands, and then kill himself for his stupidity.

The lying little baggage.

Well, Christ, what had he expected? He had been amply warned about the minefield he was stepping into, hadn't he? He should have known something was afoot when he had been introduced to that ethereal blond creature who looked as though she had never raised her voice, let alone committed the outrageous acts his ward had been accused of.

None too gently, Lucien shoved the girl into the library, slammed the door, and pushed her down onto the sofa, where only a half hour earlier he had held her in his lap, confiding secrets he had never before revealed.

He couldn't even assuage his conscience by attributing his behavior to the alcohol. He'd never slipped before. No, she had done something to him, conjured up some sort of sorcery that held in him a crazed thrall.

Jesus, his ward. George's sister.

The lad was probably spinning in his grave, and Lucien couldn't blame him. George may have chosen him to be his sister's guardian, but he wouldn't have chosen Lucien to be his sister's lover. And damn it, he had come closer to making love to her tonight than she would ever know.

For over five months, he had thought his sexual instincts gone; his drive a thing of the past. But in one afternoon, Lady Francine Fitz Hugh had changed all that.

And he couldn't touch her again.

"I can explain," Fancy rushed out, her heart beating like a trip hammer as Lucien towered over her, his gaze black and furious as he stared down at her. He looked as though he was deciding her fate, and the scales were not tipping favorably.

"You can explain, madam? This I can't wait to hear."

"I had to deceive you."

"Oh? And did you have to continue deceiving me when you writhed in my arms *beneath your very roof*?"

Fancy flinched. She could have told him who she

was then. If nothing else, she could have denied him. But she had chosen silence instead.

"I didn't know things would go so far." Even to her own ears, her answer sounded pitiful.

"You may rest assured it never would have, had I known who you were."

His remark confirmed what Fancy had thought. He would not have laid a finger on her if he had known her true identity, and she had *so* wanted him to touch her. *Rash,* her inner voice chided.

"What a gifted liar you are," he went on, pacing two steps away and swinging back. "You can look a man dead in the eye and make him believe you are sincere and genuine."

"I *am* sincere and genuine!" she protested, then frowned, adding, "Most of the time. But you left me little choice!"

"So now I'm to blame? Somehow that doesn't surprise me. So tell me, *my lady,* should I number whoring along with your other talents?"

Fancy gasped. "How dare you blame me! You were the one who couldn't control your animal instincts."

"Yes, but I thought I was dallying with a servant." Leaning down face to face with her, he bit out, "What is *your* excuse?"

Mutiny rose in Fancy. "I don't wish to speak of this anymore."

"I suspect not, but you're not getting off that easily."

"I'm sorry. What more can I say?"

"You can start with the truth. Or is that beyond

your ability?" As though he could no longer bear to look at her, he stalked away and poured himself another drink.

Out of the corner of her eye, Fancy saw his hand hover over the black box she had noted earlier. Then he curled his fingers into his palms and faced her.

"Speak," he demanded.

Fancy itched to tell him to go to blazes, but that would not improve her situation. "Calder Westcott is an unscrupulous cur."

"Well, that tells me everything, doesn't it?" he drawled.

"He is trying to marry Rosalyn."

"If she's half as wild as you, perhaps she needs marrying."

Fancy glared at him. "Why should I expect any understanding from a man? You're all alike."

"Oh, no, my dear. Another man would not be contemplating the merits of wrapping his hands around your neck—or having you facedown across his lap for the thrashing you so richly deserve."

"I'd fight you to my last breath."

"So I heard previously." He pushed away from the edge of the cabinet and prowled toward her.

Fancy scooted back on the sofa. "If you lay a hand on me—"

"Nothing could be further from my mind," he said tersely, dropping down into a peeling leather wing chair. "Now, why is this Calder person trying to marry his stepsister?"

"Because Rosalyn's stepfather, Lord Westcott, left her a substantial fortune when he died a few weeks ago."

"And the unscrupulous Calder wants to get his hands on it, I presume?"

Fancy nodded. "He was left quite a bit of his own money, but Rosalyn discovered her stepbrother had acquired a hefty debt, much of it owed to fellows even more contemptuous than he is. Rosalyn overheard Calder telling one of his hired thugs that he intended to wed her, then do away with her. She slipped out of the house that night and came here. I didn't know what to do, where to go. Calder's the new magistrate, and he owns the land the village sits on. Few would go against him, and even if some were willing to help us, I didn't want to bring his wrath down on them."

"Quite a quandary," Lucien murmured, his face partially obscured by shadows.

"I thought if I could find some proof of his misdeeds, he would leave Rosalyn alone."

"Doubtful," he said. "Once a man's mind is set upon a woman, his noose has been sufficiently knotted." He took a swig of his drink, leaving Fancy to wonder if Lucien's mind had ever been set upon a woman.

She recalled the nightmare that had plagued him, and of the name he had called out. Sanji. Was Sanji a woman? Had he met her while in India? Perhaps Tahj would know. Tomorrow she would ask him.

Her guardian regarded her steadily for a moment, his demeanor cool, a reserved stranger.

"I'm afraid to ask, but what were you doing at the tavern?"

"Two of Calder's men tried to kidnap Rosalyn yesterday while we were out riding. We had assumed that Calder would not attempt anything now that Rosalyn was with me, and certainly not during the day, with potential witnesses. We were wrong."

Lucien's fingers tightened around his glass. "Let me guess—you managed to track down these men and followed them to the tavern."

"Yes," Fancy replied, impressed. "How did you know?"

His jaw knotted. "Because you're a harebrained female who takes moronic risks with her life."

Fancy bristled. "And I suppose *you* would have had a better plan?"

"Yes. I would have sent for me."

"Ha! To which brothel or gaming hell should I have directed my attention?" The look on his face could have frozen water, but Fancy didn't care. "You've thought nothing about what went on here for the last year. You were too busy with your harem, or waving your imperious finger at some pinched-mouthed, hunchbacked governess to relieve you of your duty. I cannot fathom what George was thinking when he put you in charge of my life."

"Nor can I. You, my dear Lady Francine, are pure trouble."

"Fancy."

"What?"

"No one calls me Lady Francine."

"Well, you had best get used to it. Tomorrow we leave for London."

"London?" Fancy shot up from the sofa. "But I can't!"

"You can, and you will, even if I have to bind you hand and foot and throw you over my shoulder." He sounded as if he relished the idea of carting her about like a sack.

"You *cannot* dictate my life. I have responsibilities here."

"They are my responsibilities now. Your only responsibility is to smile and look pretty. Perhaps if you don't speak, a man might even offer for your hand."

Fancy stared at him, incredulous. "That's why you're taking me to London? To marry me off?"

"What did you think, my dear? That I intended to have you tied around my neck for the remainder of my life? I am a bachelor, need I remind you."

"And of course you must get back to your mistresses," she retorted scathingly, hating that the image bothered her.

He just regarded her with those unfathomable eyes.

"You don't care at all, do you?" she accused. The realization hurt.

"I care about getting you wed. Then you will become your husband's burden rather than mine."

"So you'd toss me off to the first man who comes along?"

"Don't be absurd. I'll find someone who is your social equal, and who can provide for you. All the better if you feel some affection for the poor fool."

Frustration simmered beneath Fancy's skin. "I must stay here."

"No."

"*Please.*"

"The discussion is over."

Desperation swelled in Fancy. "Heath will marry me."

"Courtenay is out of the question."

"Why?"

"Because I say so."

"You're being unreasonable."

"That is my prerogative."

Before she thought better of it, Fancy lifted the small glass vase from the table beside her and hurled it at him. Her aim, being rotten, made the vase sail right past the chair. But she didn't have time to either curse missing him or find another object to throw as he came out of the chair in a blur of movement and swung around the sofa.

Fancy backed up as he stalked her. "Don't you touch me. I'm warning you."

A muscle worked in his jaw. "It's past time someone taught you the consequences of your actions, you selfish little brat."

"If you lay a hand on me, I'll—"

"You'll what?" he taunted as he kept coming.

Fancy's gaze darted left and right. He had her caged.

Either way she went, he would be on her in a flash. She continued to back away until her spine was pressed up against the wall, her chest tight and breathing shallow as he came to a stop in front of her.

Lifting her chin, Fancy glared at him. She trembled as he reached out and framed her face with his fingers, keeping her gaze locked to his.

"You are an impetuous chit," he said, but the words were softly spoken, his thumb lightly stroking her jaw.

An ache began to burn inside her, a need he had awakened. It must have shown in her eyes, for he dropped his hand away, his regard dispassionate once more.

"I'll leave your husband to bring you to heel." He stepped away from her. "But you will heed my word and do as you're told. Should you feel compelled to disobey, I will lock you in your room."

"I am not a child!"

"Then don't act like one. You are excused."

Excused! How dare he! "I'll leave, but only because I wish to be out of your odious presence."

His eyes glinted. "You had best get used to my odious presence and work diligently to keep me happy. Else the four walls of your bedroom will begin to resemble a prison."

"No more of a prison than you've seen fit to trap me in!"

"It's past time you grew up, my lady. You cannot spend your life running wild like some ill-bred hoyden; you're the daughter of an earl. And were your parents still alive, you would have had your season at least three years ago. You very well could have been married with a child by now. Consider that."

Fancy remembered enough about her parents to know that she would never have been allowed to gallivant about the countryside in men's breeches. She would have been living a very proper life in the country, attending tea parties and routs and local balls. She would have been primped and prodded and coiffed by maids and modistes to within an inch of her life. How would she have ever survived a life that didn't include the moors and the coves and the cliffs?

How would she survive a life without it now?

She glanced up at Lucien's face, still implacable, and knew that he would not be moved by anything she said. Heaviness settled on her heart. She couldn't lose Moor's End; she *wouldn't*. If she must play his game, she would at least walk away with something of her own. If she had to marry, she would find a man who would let her return to Cornwall and give her as much freedom as she wished. A kind man. A gentle man.

A man who was not at all like her guardian.

"Fine," she said. "I'll go willingly to London. But Rosalyn must come with me—as well as Jaines and Olinda."

He studied her, something almost sad in his eyes. "They may come, but if they should aid you in any ill-advised scheme, they will be held accountable. Do you understand?"

His warning was clear. Her friends would feel his

wrath should they go against him. Never had Fancy felt more alone. "I understand."

"Good. Then I'll see you in the morning." He turned his back on her and stalked to the window to look out. The rain had slowed to a trickle, the dark shapes of trees bowed with water visible through the panes.

Fancy remained for another moment, staring at Lucien's solitary figure, afraid, for the first time, of the future and what it held for her.

She forced her feet to move. She had just opened the door when Lucien's words stopped her. "I expect you to stay in your room," he said, not looking at her. "Do not come down here again."

Fancy quietly let herself out.

Lucien stood immobile, listening to her footfalls until they died away. Then he dropped his head into his hand and closed his eyes, self-disgust churning inside him, threatening to boil over at any moment. If she had stayed one more minute . . .

He pivoted sharply, stalked across the room, and yanked the black box from the table. Sinking down onto the sofa, he sat it on his lap, his hands shaking.

The image of her sad eyes would haunt him through the night. Fancy—the name suited her. She was as incorrigible as the governesses had proclaimed and acted nothing like the lady she was supposed to be.

And yet Lucien felt the loss of her. He wanted the breeches-clad thief who rescued kittens and threatened lechers with bodily injury. Damn her for being the one woman in the world he couldn't have.

He would forget whatever he felt for her, banish whatever guilt laid heavily on him, for he had learned long ago that a conscience was an encumbrance. He had managed to pass most of his life remembering little of the possible goodness of the human heart, and he didn't want to start now.

With sweat-dampened hands, he opened the lid of the box. Inside was the panacea for all sorrow, a short-lived joy that could be bought for as little as a shilling and carried blithely in a waistcoat pocket.

He stared down into a familiar pit of hell, a hell he had lived with for nearly ten years, since his early days in India.

During the ensuing years, he had only succeeded in escaping the torment for short periods. But specters from his past would seep through his careful constructed wall and obliterate his willpower.

He was owned by his addiction to opium.

Lucien reached into the box and took hold of the long metal spike, turning it over and over in his palm, trying to fight the need, to drop the needle and slam the lid closed. But he had been through this routine many times before, and it played out by rote.

Opening a small packet, he impaled one of the pills on the end of the needle. It was too moist and would have to be dried. Extracting a small spirit lamp, he lit it, which produced a fierce hot spot above the roughened glass cowl.

When the desired consistency had been achieved, he spread the pill around the base of the bowl. Then he inverted the lamp until the pill melted and vaporized, the air becoming rich with the scent.

He closed his eyes and prayed for salvation, but it never came. So he took a deep breath, inhaling the drug's rich fumes through the main tube of the bamboo pipe, hating himself and everything he had become.

"You let the demon in, I see."

Through the hazy euphoria that seeped into his bloodstream, Lucien recognized the voice. "Get out," he told Tahj. He couldn't bear when his friend saw him like this, when he stood there like a sentinel to a failed life.

But as was always the case, Tahj did not leave. "You have suffered a setback. We will see it righted."

"I haven't suffered a damn setback!" Lucien growled, his hand tightening around the hookah, a part of him wanting to break free while another part said *never.* "This is my life; when will you begin to understand that?" He gritted his teeth and stared up at the ceiling. "Jesus, just go back to India. Nobody asked you to follow me in the first place."

"Buddha asked. And I do as Buddha wills."

The drug was numbing Lucien, taking away his ability to fight. He sucked in another breath and waited. Waited for peace. Waited for an illumination that would never come.

He remembered all the months he had spent in Limehouse, London's East End Chinatown, upon his return from India, where he would sometimes spend an entire week at an opium den, surrounded by a nimbus of smoke, heavy and sensuous, which rose and fell like the wave of an ocean, little lamps scattered about to dispel the gloom. Vice reveled in gloom; it went hand and hand with the darkness people sought.

"In order to live a life that is free from pain and suffering, one must eliminate attachments to worldly goods," Tahj recited, the refrain sickeningly familiar. "They must rid themselves of greed, hatred, and ignorance. Only then will they attain peace and happiness." Then Tahj said, far too astutely, "You have let the girl affect you."

"The only thing she has affected is my temper. She's an accomplished liar."

"You have discovered her deception."

The flat statement made Lucien glance up. "You knew?"

Tahj inclined his head. "Had your eyes not been so full of lust, you would have seen the truth for yourself."

Lucien gritted his teeth, knowing he had been blinded by the desire the girl brought out in him. "Why didn't you tell me, damn you?"

"Because you wanted her, and you would not have heeded me. You still want her," he observed, regarding Lucien in that all-knowing way of his. "Perhaps she is what you need."

"She is the last thing I need. God, she's George's bloody sister!" Lucien dragged a hand through his hair.

"She is a woman, first. And you are a man in need of someone to help you heal."

Lucien pressed a hand to his head and slid down onto the arm of the sofa. "Christ, I almost told her everything."

"You should have. It would be one less burden on your soul. You cannot continue to blame yourself for that which was beyond your control."

Lucien rocked his head back and forth. "I was in charge, and I wasn't prepared. I'm the only one who can be held accountable."

"Tell her what happened. Speak from the heart and trust her to listen."

Lucien jammed his eyes shut. "I can't." He forced himself to put the hookah down on the table. "Tomorrow we're leaving for London. Be ready to go."

"You shouldn't go back yet. Resolve this problem first."

"There's nothing to resolve. I'm going to do my duty by the lady, and that'll be the end of it."

"Will it?"

God, he hoped so. "She will be happily forgotten," Lucien stated, knowing that forgetting Fancy would not be so easy. "Now just get out and leave me in peace. Lock the bloody door behind you."

"The peace you seek will never be found in that pipe. You need to look within yourself."

Then, like the phantom Lucien had always labeled him, Tahj slipped out the door, the whisper of the key in the lock all-consuming in the silence.

Twelve

The ocean stirred in gentle agitation as Fancy looked out the coach window, about to begin her first journey away from Cornwall since her parents had deposited her and George with their grandmother years ago.

A dovelike calm had settled over the landscape, which belied the nerves tightening her stomach. This might very well be the last time she saw Moor's End, and she could barely contain her despair. She wanted to rail that she couldn't go, that it wasn't right. This was her home, and no one would make her leave it; and yet Lucien had managed the task with savage aplomb. She could have told him about the taxes that were owed on the property, but pride and stubbornness had kept her mum. It was her problem, and she would solve it—even if it meant marrying to do so.

The very thought made her heart ache, and in that moment, she hated him.

She watched him through a part in the curtain. The sun streaked his raven hair and outlined his body as he stood talking to Rosalyn, who had been anxiously awaiting Fancy in her bedroom the night before.

As soon as Fancy had stepped over the threshold, Rosalyn rushed toward her. "Did he beat you?" she asked, inspecting Fancy from head to toe.

"No, he didn't beat me. He's ordered us all to London. We leave in the morning."

Rosalyn's face lost some of its color. "Oh."

"You're to come with us," Fancy hastened to add. "Lucien can amply protect you, and it would be foolish of Calder to go up against him."

"I don't know," Rosalyn said hesitantly. "I don't want to put any of you in harm's way."

Fancy snorted. "As though I didn't put you in precarious situations every other day when we were children. But you stayed with me, didn't you?" Fancy wrapped her arms around her friend's shoulders. "We will get through this together. Have faith. Everything will be all right."

Now, as Fancy watched a smiling Rosalyn glide toward the carriage, she hoped her prediction would prove true.

"You look happy," Fancy said as she opened the coach door for her friend, who climbed in beside her and arranged her skirts.

"My mood is significantly lighter, I'll confess,"

Rosalyn replied, looking more relaxed than she had in a long while. "Mr. Kendall really is a wonderful man— though simply dreadful for taking you away from home," she promptly added, ever the friend.

"What did he do?" Fancy asked.

"He went over to Westcott Manor this morning to confront Calder."

For a moment, Fancy was speechless. While confronting Calder was exactly what Lucien should have done, a twinge of jealousy goaded her. He had done something very gentlemanly for Rosalyn, and Fancy felt horrible for feeling the way she did. Rosalyn needed a protector, and Lucien had come to her rescue. It was certainly not Rosalyn's fault that men were drawn to her like wolves to moonlight.

"Not surprisingly, Calder wasn't there," Rosalyn went on. "Poor Harold," she sighed, speaking of the Westcotts' longtime butler. "He was treated to Calder's wrath and then ordered to pack a bag. My stepbrother left last night."

"Coward," Fancy said with distaste. "He's only brave when he's terrorizing women and the elderly." Although Jaines and Olinda, who were supervising the packing of the last few bags onto the boot of the coach, would balk at being thought of as beyond their prime.

"I wonder where he went?" Rosalyn mused, renewed worry in her eyes.

"Hopefully to the devil."

Lucien appeared at the doorway then. "Are you ladies comfortable?"

Still furious with him, Fancy didn't reply. But he

didn't appear to care, as his question seemed to be directed to Rosalyn.

"Quite comfortable," her friend responded, treating him to a brilliant smile, which he returned. "Would either of you mind if I rode on the box with Tahj for a while?" She darted a glance between them. "He really is the most interesting man. He was telling me about the six realms of being. Truly fascinating."

Fancy nearly begged Rosalyn to stay. She didn't want to be trapped in the coach with Lucien and his brooding presence—but Olinda and Jaines would be traveling with them, so she could ignore him to her heart's content.

"Go ahead," Fancy said, "but be careful up there."

"I will," Rosalyn chirped, alighting from the coach with Lucien's help, which earned him another smile.

The gentlemanly expression melted from his face when he turned to look at Fancy. "Seems it will be just you and me."

Panic spurted through Fancy's veins. "Olinda and Jaines will be traveling with us too, of course."

"They will be riding in a separate conveyance."

Panic blossomed. "Separate? But why?"

"They believe servants should ride apart from their employer."

"That's utterly ridiculous." She had never treated them like servants. What were they up to?

"I told them that, but they were adamant."

"I'll speak to them." Fancy rose from her seat and moved toward the door, but Lucien was in her way.

"Let them be. We have to get under way." He

entered, forcing her back until her bottom plunked down on the velvet squabs.

"But—"

"I don't like the situation any more than you, but it's best gotten used to."

"Sadie—"

"Is perfectly happy with Jaines." He rapped on the roof, and the coach jolted forward.

Fancy opened her mouth, but closed it at the warning look he gave her. Fine. She would ignore him, as planned. She would not worry about Jaines being licked for hours so that his skin looked like parchment paper by the end of the trip. And she would not worry about poor Sassy and the kittens, who had to be left behind, though Lucien had hired a woman recommended by Olinda to take care of them. But it didn't allay Fancy's fear about their fate, nor her own. What would London hold for her? Would she really leave with a husband?

It was all too much to contemplate. Perhaps she would take a nap; it would be a long trip. Besides, her traveling companion didn't appear inclined to speak to her, anyway. Did he intend to glare the entire way to London?

Fancy had just settled herself firmly into the corner, which didn't seem to keep Lucien's long legs from brushing her skirts, when she glimpsed a horse and rider out of the corner of her eye.

"Heath!" She sat bolt upright as she spotted her last hope for salvation. If only she had accepted his marriage proposal, she would not be in this predicament. But even as the thought came to her, she knew she could never have married him for such selfish reasons.

Fancy scooted forward to open the window, but Lucien gripped her wrist. "Sit back, madam," he said in a dark growl. "Courtenay will be of no help to you."

"But you must let me speak to him! He doesn't know where I'm going."

"All the better. I don't want some lovesick swain panting on my doorstep."

Fancy glanced out the window and saw Heath still riding toward them, confusion etched on his face, and then anger as the coach continued on its way.

"Please," she said, even as she vowed she would not beg. "At least let me tell him to check on Jimmy and his sister."

"I've already taken care of that."

His answer stole the protest from her lips. He'd had the foresight to see to a suffering family's welfare as well as champion Rosalyn? Once again, he surprised her. Still, she needed to talk to Heath.

"But what if Jimmy's mother worsens?"

"She knows how to get in touch with me. Relax, madam, the boy and his family will be seen to."

Fancy cast a longing glance at Heath and then flopped back against the well-sprung squabs and crossed her arms over her chest, surging with impotent fury.

"You've thought of everything, haven't you?"

"Almost everything."

Fancy forced back the tears stinging her eyes as she watched Heath fade into the distance. "Almost? What detail could you have possibly missed?"

"You," he answered simply, regarding her in a way that made her heart slow to a dull thud.

"Me?"

"You've turned out to be a broken cog in the forward momentum of my life."

Fancy snorted. Why had she expected him to say anything conciliatory? "As though you are Prince Charming."

Her remark wrung a reluctant grin out of him, which lifted his dark look and made a traitorous yearning spark to life inside her. Why did he have to be so blasted handsome? It wasn't fair, especially when he had turned out to be every bit the ogre she had originally dreaded.

"It seems neither of us is very high on the other's list." He shifted, and his knee brushed her thigh again, leaving a warm tingle in its wake. "You made a fetching servant, though," he murmured, a hot glint in his eyes that was gone in an instant.

"I'm no different than I was yesterday." But she was. Yesterday she had not known this man's touch, or yearned to know it again. She almost wished she could go back and simply be Mary rather than Lady Francine.

"You are worlds different," he said. "And it would be wise not to forget that again."

Before she could tell him he was wrong, he closed

his eyes and tipped his head back against the top of the seat, leaving Fancy to either stare or look away.

She stared. He was just too big to shut out, his masculinity too powerful to ignore. He had the thickest lashes she had ever seen on a man, a stunning frame for those unusual eyes that no mere mortal should have been blessed with.

His expression in repose was youthful yet rugged, wiped clean of scorn, his lips full and soft, making Fancy want to lean over and place her mouth against his. He was an exquisite kisser, and the things he could do with his tongue . . .

"If you're thinking of ramming a dagger into my heart," he said in a deep tone, popping one eye open and looking at her, "think again. I'm prepared for you today. I've donned a metal vest beneath my clothing."

How had he known she was looking at him? Well, she would not give him the satisfaction of knowing he had riled her.

She focused her gaze out the window. It was hard to believe that winter was fast approaching. Christmas, once Fancy's favorite time of the year, would all too soon be upon them, her first without her family.

The lonely image sent a deep pang of despair through her. How her grandmother had loved Christmas, decorating the house with bright baubles, inviting the villagers in for hot cider.

Bittersweet memories swelled, and Fancy forced herself to think only of the good times as the coach rattled down a steep, narrow lane toward Loe Bar. The sudden appearance of the sea roused her spirits. A wide sweep of bay drifted into the dark, still waters of an inland lake, a broad ridge of sand serving as a bridge between the two.

The effect of the clear blue sky and a golden sun upon the water was dazzling. Rippling cobalt waves broke one on top of the next on the bar, which gleamed white. On the other side, the freshwater lake lapped gently against the shifting sand.

Fancy could almost picture Moses standing upon the strand when the tide overflowed after a heavy rain, sending water over the bar, lake and ocean becoming one, then receding like the Red Sea as the pharaoh's chariots closed in.

As her eyes drifted shut, Fancy imagined it was she who stood at the divide, and that the fierce warrior thundering toward her, garbed in little more than a dark strip of material knotted tightly about his waist and serpentine bands coiled around his muscular upper arms, was Lucien—preparing for battle.

Lucien knew the moment Fancy had drifted off to sleep, just as he had known she had been watching him. He wanted her as much today as he had yesterday. Perhaps more.

He had studied her while she stared out the window, the wistful expression on her beautiful face tugging relentlessly at his heart. He was taking her away from everything she knew, and he doubted she would ever forgive him. He could tally up one more mistake to add to a lifetime of them.

She needed a protector. Ironic, really; the very thing George had wished to shield her from now resided under the same roof with her.

But that would all change in London. He would stay at Blackthorne Manor and twist the knife in the Earl of Redding's side, while Fancy and the rest of her entourage resided with Lady Dane.

Clarisse was not only well respected, but also had connections into a world Lucien had neither been a part of, nor would ever be accepted into.

He may have accumulated a great deal of wealth, but that would never buy lineage. It had never bothered him before—not until he had discovered the identity of a brazen, skull-cracking female. Now he almost wished he had been born into that world, that he had not grown up on the streets or known the tragedy of ignorance.

Lucien jammed his eyes shut, but he could not escape the memories: the sound of his mother's muffled cries, beseeching him with her eyes to do nothing and vowing him to silence afterward, and the screams of a woman whose only mistake had been to love him when doing so would bring her disgrace.

He had ever been a woman's curse. He had vowed to protect them—his mother, his sisters, Sanji—yet he had failed them all. What had he been thinking, to take on the guardianship of a young woman? Jesus, he couldn't do it.

A palm gently pressed against his cheek, jolting Lucien upright. He lunged out to capture the person, a response born of long nights spent in the Indian desert, waiting for a faceless enemy.

But the face now staring at him, eyes wide, was no stranger but his ward, regarding him with a mixture of fear and concern.

"Are you all right?" she softly asked.

Lucien knew he should release her, but he didn't want to let her go just yet. "What happened?" he said, sitting up straighter, his brain foggy.

"You were having a bad dream."

Lucien frowned. He hadn't realized he had fallen asleep. Christ, had he said anything? He had never worried about it before because he always slept alone, always kept his guard up. He was slipping.

He dropped his hands from her arms and raked his fingers through his hair. "I'm sorry." He had to get away from her before he revealed all his darkest secrets; any of them would make her despise him forever.

He glanced out the window, his tension easing as he saw they were within a half hour of London.

"Are you sure you're all right?"

Lucien's gaze cut back to those mossy green eyes a man could get lost in. "Fine," he said more forcefully than he intended, which made her retreat into her seat. "We'll be there soon," he added, moderating his tone.

He could see she was frightened about what awaited her in a new city. Soon she would be attired in fashionable gowns and attending lavish balls, and men would be panting at her feet. That was where he would be, if given the chance, but he had no right. She had given him a gift, allowed him a taste of her lush body—a body another man would someday claim, to touch the way Lucien had touched her, to be burned by her fire in a way that he had not.

She darted a look at him and then glanced away, nibbling the corner of her mouth as she stared down at her hands, which were clutched nervously in her lap.

"Where will we be staying?"

"I've made arrangements for you to visit with Lady Dane, a good friend of mine. Clarisse is a widow, though not much older than you. Her husband died in a duel last year."

"How tragic," Fancy murmured.

Lucien snorted. "He was a bloody idiot. He left a good woman behind."

Fancy wondered at his feelings for this Clarisse. Could she be the woman who had crawled beneath his skin and owned his heart? Was she his mistress, perhaps?

She started as Lucien's fingers cupped her chin, turning her face to him. "Don't worry," he said in a gentle tone that almost undid all of her good intentions not to cry. "You'll be fine. I think you and Clarisse will have a great deal in common."

Fancy looked into his eyes and saw the reassurance there, and something else. Something heart-wrenching. She desperately wished he would kiss her.

As though discerning her thoughts, he leaned

toward her, his light, warm scent surrounding her. His silky hair tumbled across his forehead, making her itch to push it back.

Then the coach lurched in a rut, jarring both of them back to reality, and the hot look in Lucien's eyes was gone. This was not the time to ask him anything, yet questions rose in her mind, questions that needed to be answered but had remained unasked because too much turmoil had been swirling around them both. This might be the last opportunity she would have.

"Lucien?"

His chilly gaze slid to hers. "Yes?" His tone advised her to think twice, but if she backed down now, he would know he had succeeded in intimidating her.

"Would you tell me about George?"

His body seemed to tense beneath his finely tailored navy jacket. "What is it you'd like to know?"

Fancy plucked at her skirt. "Was he afraid?"

"No," he replied quietly. "At least, I never saw it. He was a soldier until the very end. His only concern was leaving you."

The tears she had so valiantly tried to contain spilled over her lashes and down her cheeks. "George was still so young when we lost our parents, but he was forced to grow up quickly. It seemed as though overnight the joy of our youth had been abandoned.

"He had just received his commission a few weeks before our parents died. My father had been a career military man, and he wanted George to follow in his footsteps. I don't think he wanted to go, yet he accepted his duty, just as my father expected. He told me in one of his letters that he wanted me to be proud of him. He never understood that I would have been just as proud of him if he had become a sheep farmer. As long as he was still here."

Fancy closed her eyes tight, but the tears seeped through. She heard Lucien shift and felt a handkerchief gently wiping away her tears.

"He adored you, you know," he murmured, his touch making Fancy want to lean her cheek into his palm. "I think half the men in my outfit wanted to be the one to take care of you. They were all jealous when I was given the honor."

Fancy sniffled and opened her eyes. "They were?"

He nodded. "Every man wanted to set eyes on George's little sister, the angelic Fancy. We were all certain that you had stardust for freckles and heaven in your eyes. We were sure that you could redeem us all."

"But you said—"

"I say a lot of things when I'm angry. I don't always mean them."

In his own way he was apologizing, and Fancy's heart softened another bit toward him. "Thank you," she whispered. "I needed to hear that." Her gaze dropped to where his hand rested near hers, the tips of their fingers touching. "I missed him so terribly for so long. I didn't think I'd ever pull through. He was all I had left, and I . . . I was so alone."

"You're not alone anymore," Lucien vowed softly.

Without thought, Fancy leaned forward and

pressed her lips against his. He stiffened, and she realized her mistake, pulling away, but he grabbed her
arms and held her there, a fierce growl rumbling up in
his throat as his mouth slanted over hers, teasing and
nipping until she opened for him and he could slip his
tongue inside.

Fancy clung to him, her hands gripping the lapels of
his jacket, tugging him closer until he was practically on
top of her. She didn't care how wanton her behavior was,
or that a proper lady wouldn't kiss a gentleman first.

Impetuous, her mind whispered. *Reckless,* it said
even louder. But she paid no heed as his body began to
press her down against the seat.

Abruptly, he stopped and closed his eyes, a muscle
working in his jaw. When he opened his eyes, the fire
was gone. He regarded her steadily for a long moment,
the current running between them too palpable to will
away, but she could see the regret in his eyes.

He sat back, his expression resolute. "We're here," he
said, pulling her upright, his touch impersonal as the
coach began to slow, rumbling down a cobblestone
road dappled with the dim light of early evening.

Fancy tried to focus on her new surroundings
rather than on what had just transpired. She told herself it was a mistake and that it would never happen
again, but the thought did not console her.

"Where are we?" she asked, pretending fascination at
the quaint homes they passed, some very stately with
their perfectly trimmed hedges and large, leafy trees.

"Mayfair," he replied as the coach rolled to a stop in

front of a lovely gabled town house of red brick with an ornately carved black metal fence enclosing a well-tended courtyard.

Fancy glanced at him. "Are you sure we won't be intruding on Lady Dane? Perhaps she'll be frightened of Sadie."

"Very little frightens Clarisse," he said with familiarity and warmth, stirring up a jealousy inside Fancy that she tried to squash.

As she stared out at the town house, nerves took over. Had she once really lived in this city? She had no memories of it, just a sense of being overwhelmed and landlocked. Already, she missed the wide-open space of Cornwall.

"Coming?"

Fancy blinked and realized Lucien now stood outside on the walkway, holding a hand out to her and waiting patiently.

Tentatively, she placed her palm in his, captured by the look in his eyes as he helped her down, his gaze drifting over her in a sensuous appraisal that made warmth run down her spine.

She had donned her best dress for the trip, a pale rose tulle with a lace-trimmed hem, and a high-waisted bodice that was edged with primroses and undercut with a thin satin ribbon of darker rose. A pendant her mother had given her dangled in the hollow of her neck, becoming a prism for the dying sun, whose crimson-gold rays waned into a burning copper as it descended into the horizon.

As she stood before Lucien, Fancy understood the true meaning of feeling overwhelmed.

Until today, she had only seen him dressed in casual attire. Now he looked like an aristocrat in his blue-gray jacket and slate trousers, a white lawn shirt beneath and a white silk cravat around his neck, accentuating the angle of his jaw and the dark hue of his skin. They were in his territory, the world he understood, and Fancy knew that things had irrevocably changed.

Thirteen

$\mathcal{F}$ancy wished Rosalyn was there with her, but the other coach lagged behind.

"Nice to have you back, Mr. Kendall," a voice intoned, shaking Fancy from her thoughts.

She turned to find the man she presumed was the butler standing before them. His appearance made her blink, for he was an eyeful, with his jet black hair and gem-green eyes, his body amply matching Lucien's height and width.

"Thank you, Pierce," Lucien said. "It's nice to be back. Is Lady Dane at home?"

"Yes, sir. She has been awaiting your arrival. If you and the young lady would please follow me."

Fancy started as Lucien touched his hand to her elbow. "Don't gape, my dear," he said as they followed

Pierce up the front steps, an underlying gruffness in his tone. "It's not polite."

Fancy flushed. "I'm sorry. I was just a bit surprised."

"Pierce is well used to it. Lady Dane is the envy of every female of the ton. For the last two years, all the matrons have endeavored to steal him away, but Pierce is devoted to her."

Fancy darted a glance at Lucien. "Are they . . ."

"No, they aren't," he replied, a hint of censure in his voice. "Lady Dane is very circumspect, and as you may have noticed, Pierce is far beneath her socially. Any relationship between them would be out of the question."

Fancy sighed. "I never could understand why rank is so important, especially if two people truly care for each other. It seems ridiculous to me."

"It's simply the way things are."

Hearing the bitterness in Lucien's words, Fancy glanced up at him, but he was not looking at her. He stared straight ahead, the front doors opening before them as if drawn by an invisible hand.

As he guided her into the marble-lined foyer of Lady Dane's town home, Fancy marveled at the opulence. A painted ceiling soared above her head, and gilded artwork lined the wall going up the stairs, where a beautiful oriental carpet in shades of burgundy, green, and gold flowed down, gleaming brass rods pining it in place.

Fancy peeked around Lucien's broad form and into the formal drawing room to her left, catching a glimpse of its green flocked walls and silk moire draperies, heavily carved furniture dotting the vast space, a fireplace of green marble as its centerpiece.

"Lucien!" a voice rang out, bringing Fancy's gaze to the landing at the top of the stairs where a statuesque woman stood in a cream silk day dress.

Clarisse Templeton was everything that Fancy had feared she would be, and her heart sank as she watched the woman glide elegantly down the stairs, her smile warm and welcoming, her eyes showing her joy at seeing Lucien.

"Lady Dane." He reached out to take her proffered hand and placed a delicate kiss on its back. "You're looking lovely, as always."

She laid her hand atop his. "I'm so glad to see you. I hope you fared well on your trip?"

"Very well." Their gazes held for a moment, and Fancy felt like an intruder.

Then Lady Dane turned to Fancy with a bright smile. "You must be Lady Francine. My, you are lovely, just as Lucien described in his letter."

Surprised that Lucien had made more than a passing comment about her, Fancy turned to him. His smile had been replaced by a fierce scowl, directed at Lady Dane, who seemed to be trying not to laugh.

She tucked her arm in Fancy's and walked her away from Lucien. "I'm overjoyed that you've come to stay with me. I have many events planned for us, and I'm certain we will have the best time together. It has been far too long since I've had an acquaintance closer to my age. May I call you Francine?"

The good humor in her hostess's eyes made it difficult for Fancy to find a single thing to dislike about her. Clarisse Templeton appeared to be as friendly as she sounded, and it certainly would be nice to have a friend who could guide her and Rosalyn through London society.

"My friends call me Fancy," she answered with a smile of her own.

"How lovely! It suits you." With a brief flick over her shoulder, she said to Lucien, "Don't just stand there, darling, pour yourself a drink in the study, if you care to stay. I will be showing my guest to her bedroom."

Sounding as disgruntled as he looked, Lucien replied, "Lady Rosalyn should be arriving shortly."

"Marvelous!" Clarisse gave Fancy's arm a little squeeze as they started up the stairs. "It shall be just us girls. We have so much to discuss. I'll need your advice on the ball I'm hosting in your honor."

"A ball? Oh, but you mustn't."

Lady Dane stopped in the middle of the staircase and stared at her. "Whyever not, my dear? All the men will be eager to make your acquaintance. The season is just getting into full swing. Your debut will be spectacular."

"What she is saying," Lucien interceded from the bottom of the steps, his arm propped negligently on the banister, "is that it's time you were thrown into the pool of piranhas ironically known as polite society."

"Good heavens, Lucien," Clarisse scolded, hands on hips as she faced him. "Just because you are jaded about society does not mean it is all bad."

"So says the queen of society."

"I don't know what has gotten into you today, but that remark was uncalled-for."

Lucien held her gaze for a moment and then let it drop. "You're right. Forgive me. Perhaps it's best if I leave. I have things to get in order at Blackthorne."

"I imagine you do," she returned, displeasure in her tone. "You realize there is still a great deal of rumbling going on about your game against Redding, though the earl himself has said not a word."

"Let them rumble. I won the damn house fairly." Turning sharply on his heel, he headed for the door, slamming it behind him.

Clarisse sighed deeply and turned to Fancy. "Men," she said, then hooked her arm through Fancy's to continue up the stairs.

"Who is Redding?" Fancy asked. "And why does Lucien have such an aversion to him?"

"I'm not quite sure what the tension is between the earl and Lucien. It just is. Whenever I try to get Lucien to talk about it, he seals his lips together. As for your first question, I'm referring to Christian Slade, the Earl of Redding. A more attractive and eligible specimen of manhood, a woman could not find." A glimmer of mischief sparkled in her quicksilver eyes as she added, "And that is why he was first gentleman on the invitation list to your soiree."

"But if Lucien doesn't like him—"

"All the better for the scoundrel. He deserves a bit of comeuppance." Clarisse ushered her into a bedroom. "Will this be all right?" her hostess asked.

"It's lovely," Fancy said, noting the contrast between her spartan bedroom back at Moor's End and the lush counterpoint before her now.

Sheer curtains framed with burgundy velvet drapes hung from the window rods and matched the canopy on the huge four-poster bed, which was held to the posts by gold tassels. The counterpane was jade silk with gold and crimson threads woven through it in an intricate floral pattern.

On the far wall, a beautiful limestone fireplace contrasted perfectly with the other colors splashed about the room, accompanied by a lovely grouping of chairs and tables, a perfect place to enjoy a book or a quiet meal alone.

Beside her, Lady Dane chuckled. "You are so wonderfully fresh, Fancy. Every thought and emotion plays on your face." She took hold of Fancy's hands. "I really am glad you're here. It won't be so bad. Trust me."

"I do. It's just that Lucien"—she blushed—"I mean, Mr. Kendall, expects me to marry."

"And you don't want to, I presume?"

"I would someday, but other things are more important to me right now."

"If I'm not being too forward, may I ask if there is someone you left behind in Cornwall? A man who has captured your interest?"

"No." Fancy briefly imagined Heath. "No one."

"Well, Lucien seemed in a great hurry to get you here. I've known him a long time, and I've never seen him quite so fired up over a cause. He is bound and determined to see you wed. Has he expressed any of his reasons to you?"

He had expressed himself quite eloquently, Fancy thought. He wanted to be rid of her, and as quickly as was possible. She was a burden he did not want to bear a moment longer than he must.

Suppressing a sigh, she proceeded farther into the room so that Clarisse would not see her nervousness and wistful longing for home and familiar places. "I think my guardian believes me to be too wild, and that marriage will tame me."

"But it won't, of course."

Fancy strolled about the room, idly running her fingers over the tops of the furniture. "My rashness seems to frustrate my guardian's sensibilities."

"How surprising," Lady Dane mused, an odd lilt to her voice. "Not your impetuous nature, but Lucien's reaction to it. He rarely lets anything ruffle him. It has been suggested by a number of females that he is not in possession of a heart."

Had Fancy not been a witness to Lucien's gently cradling a kitten, and saving her from a tumble out of a tree, and the anguish he felt over George's death, she might have agreed.

Yet the man who had presented himself since her revelation seemed cold and remote, as though he truly didn't possess any feelings. If only she didn't know better, perhaps she could safeguard her heart more readily.

Fancy jumped as Clarisse touched her lightly on the shoulder.

"Forgive me. I didn't mean to startle you." She paused, and then asked, "Is something the matter?"

"I have much on my mind."

"Is there anything I could help you with?" Clarisse asked, sitting down on the edge of the bed. "I'm a very good listener."

Fancy wanted to confide, but she could not involve the marchioness in her problems. She did not want to bring Lucien's wrath down on someone else.

"Thank you, but I must work things out myself. I hope you understand."

"I understand perfectly well. You remind me a great deal of myself. But you know you can talk to me or Lucien about anything that is troubling you. It is his responsibility as your guardian to give you assistance in all areas."

What if he was part of the problem? Fancy almost wished she could go back and have them simply be two people getting to know one another.

"My guardian has other matters with which to concern himself." And Fancy couldn't help wondering if he was currently concerning himself with a mistress, as he seemed to have been in a hurry to leave.

With no preamble, Clarisse asked, "Do you have feelings for Lucien, Fancy?"

Fancy quickly said, "No," but her denial was a bit too abrupt. "Of course not."

"I suspect he has been tempted a great deal by you. There is an innocence about you that Lucien would be attracted to. I mean no disrespect. In fact, I quite envy that alluring freshness that seems so much a part of you. It reminds me of what I lost."

Was she thinking about her husband? Fancy wondered. It appeared that Clarisse had fallen in love with a gamester and a rogue, very much like Lucien. Would heartbreak have been Fancy's fate had she allowed herself to have feelings for Lucien? Would he ever find someone who could heal the wounds of his youth?

"I imagine even the most jaded men of the ton would be stirred by you," Clarisse continued. "I have little doubt that you will have your pick of men and will be walking down the aisle before the season is through."

That was exactly what Fancy feared. And yet her thoughts continued to focus on Lucien. She sat down next to Clarisse on the bed. "Has Lucien ever confided anything of his life to you? I'm just curious, you see. He shuts down any time I approach the topic."

"I guess you wouldn't know, would you?"

"Wouldn't know what?"

Clarisse looked at her with sad eyes. "Lucien lost his entire family."

Fancy stared, her mind going back to the day Lucien had told her his family was gone. "You mean they're dead?"

"Presumably. No one quite knows. Most people are not privy to this information. I know because my curiosity, like yours, got the better of me, and I hired a Bow Street runner to find out what I could. Some of the things he told me . . ." She shook her head. "No child should have to live as Lucien did."

"I know he was poor."

"He was worse than poor. He lived in a small cottage on the Thames, at the edge of the marketplace, where the stench of sewage and rotting fish permeated everything. His father was a hauler, carting in the day's catch, and Lucien and his brothers and sisters had to gut the fish and hawk it to those who had little more than they did. The rich rarely set foot in that part of London.

"His father was out of work more often than not. He drank heavily and beat his children regularly. Lucien never went to school, Fancy."

"You mean he never learned to read and write?"

"He learned eventually. I think Tahj taught him. But for all intents and purposes he was ignorant. It's a wonder that he has come so far in his life. He's extremely wealthy now, mainly due to his innate business sense and savvy dealings. And never was there a man who could read a deck of cards like Lucien. But more importantly, he can read people."

Fancy felt numbed by what she had learned. Lucien would hate it if he knew she felt sorry for him. "What happened to his family?"

"I don't know," Clarisse replied with a sigh. "Everyone seemed to disappear when Lucien was around seventeen. I'm not sure how he ended up in India; there is something about that part of his life he also keeps locked away. The man is carrying around heavy burdens, but he refuses to speak of them. I'm telling you this, Fancy, because I sense you care for him, and though Lucien would rather not care for anyone, I believe he harbors feelings for you, too. I saw the way he stared at you when you weren't looking. You've opened something up inside of him, something he locked away a long time ago, and I think you could be exactly what he needs. I once wished I would be that person, but as much as Lucien squawks at being called a gentleman, he is one."

Fancy cast a sideways glance at her hostess. "Did you and . . . ?"

"No." Clarisse shook her head. "But not for lack of trying on my part. He's always been a good friend, though. He was there for me when Charles died."

"I was sorry to hear about the loss of your husband."

"Thank you, but I was no more than a convenience to Charles. My husband preferred men, you see."

Fancy tried to hide the astonished look on her face.

"No need to be polite. I knew when I married Charles that he didn't love me, but my confidence still suffered when he showed no interest in touching me. I took it quite to heart when I learned of his predilection."

"But that had nothing to do with you."

"I know, but oftentimes the truth is not a salve. I'm not proud of my behavior after I learned of Charles's secret. It was during those wild days that I first encountered Lucien. I owe him quite a bit." She lifted her chin. "But enough of this. We have a ball to prepare for. And I promise you, my dear, your debut will be the talk of the season."

Fourteen

〜⟡〜

By sheer dint of will, Lucien managed to stay away from Fancy for the entire week before the ball.

Perhaps that was why he had been sitting up late every evening, images of Fancy with another man plaguing his mind.

God help him, he missed her. She had such passion, such joy for life. Far too many times over the past week, he had pictured her animated face as she played with the kittens or imagined Sadie loping faithfully by her side.

Or thought about the way she had responded to his touch.

As he watched her descend the staircase in a pale yellow silk gown with a bodice more demure than most, but which accentuated the fullness of her breasts and the slender curve of her waist, making a man itch to wrap his hands around it and pull her close, he nearly forgot his good intentions. He wanted to cover her up and throw her over his shoulder, take her back to Cornwall and the secluded cove where they had dug for oysters. He wanted her to be someone else—Fancy without the title and trappings, without the brother who died because of Lucien.

"Why the grim look, my friend?"

Lucien turned from the object of his obsession and glanced over to find his friend and fellow Pleasure Seeker, Derek Hardwicke, standing next to him, urbane and impeccable as always.

Looking at him, no one would guess at the dangerous man who lurked beneath the perfectly tailored clothes, both an English lord and a Highland laird, who ruled with an iron fist. "Heathen" was the nickname Derek had acquired, and it was well earned.

"Jesus, if you aren't as ugly as ever." Lucien held out his hand to his friend, who laughed and gave him a slap on the back that would have snapped the spine of a lesser man. What Derek lacked in height, at a mere six-two, he made up for in brawn. He was a muscled brute.

He and Derek went way back to the time when Lucien had escaped from India, before he had returned to fight a battle that had nothing to do with England's desires to squash the Indian government underfoot. Derek understood the pull of two countries. His mother had been an heiress to a great English estate and his father the laird of one of the fiercest Highland clans.

"I wouldn't talk, my friend," Derek returned good-naturedly, inclining his head to a petite redhead batting her eyelashes at him in blatant invitation. "Your face looks like it's been pummeled one too many times. Perhaps one of these days someone will break your nose so that it looks normal again. If I wasn't otherwise engaged this evening, I might be tempted to give it a go."

"Stand in line."

"Still working your charm on the masses, I see," Derek drawled, directing Lucien's attention to the glowers pointed in his direction, most from men whom he had separated from their money at one time or another. "You never were one for tact."

"You don't need tact when you win at cards as much as I do."

But Derek's gaze, like everyone else's, had been diverted to the vision in pale yellow who had reached the receiving line where her guests eagerly awaited an introduction.

A glint of deviltry danced in his friend's eyes as he glanced back at Lucien. "Your ward, I presume?"

Lucien didn't like the look on the man's face. "In the flesh," he muttered.

"And what lovely flesh. Could she be as innocent as she appears?"

Lucien remembered exactly how innocent Fancy was. "Yes, and I expect her to stay that way."

Derek cocked a black brow. "You're sounding awfully proprietary, lad."

Damn it, what had come over him? His goal was to find Fancy a husband, and Derek was as eligible as they came. Yet something about the idea of Fancy and his friend rubbed Lucien the wrong way.

"Nothing of the sort," he replied, taking a sip of his drink. "But I made a promise to her brother to watch out for her."

Derek sobered. "You still haven't forgiven yourself for that, have you?"

Lucien's chest tightened. "I was his commanding officer."

"You're human, first."

It seemed as though he had lost his humanity a long time ago. Some days he forgot what it had been like to care, but as he watched Fancy smile at one person after the next, her warmth genuine, her laughter infectious, he wished he could find his way back to the man he could have been.

"So are you going to introduce me to her?" Derek asked. "Or are we just going to stare at her the rest of the night?"

"Try not to drool on her, if possible," Lucien said as he started across the room.

Derek laughed. "I wouldn't dream of it, unless I want to rile you. Which is tempting, of course, but my brawling days are waning."

"If you were even lucky enough to land a blow," Lucien countered.

Derek clapped him on the shoulder. "Luck has nothing to do with it, lad."

• • •

Out of the corner of her eye, Fancy glimpsed Lucien and another man approaching. She had wondered if he would be attending her party, as he hadn't bothered with her for the entire week.

While Clarisse had stuck to the letter of her word and kept Fancy and Rosalyn busy with fittings and tea parties, Fancy had not been able to completely shut out thoughts of Lucien. It seemed as though his family had vanished without a trace. At least she knew the fate of her own family. What must it be like to go through life always wondering?

Fancy felt a tap on her shoulder and turned to find Rosalyn standing behind her, a warm smile on her face. Her friend had declined to come down the stairs with her, claiming it was Fancy's night to shine, though the party had been intended for the two of them. Fancy wished she could convince Rosalyn that she was not a burden, but with each passing day, her friend seemed to withdraw more.

"You look stunning," Rosalyn murmured, her eyes alight with sincerity as she took in Fancy's dress, which Fancy had balked at buying as it was so expensive, as well as too daring in the neckline. But Clarisse had insisted, taking delight in spending Lucien's money.

"The rascal deserves it," she repeated throughout the endless rounds of shopping, her eyes glinting mischievously as she wandered off to find other fripperies for Fancy's growing wardrobe.

"You look rather stunning yourself," Fancy told her

friend. "That color is marvelous on you." The gown was peach satin with matching lace ruching around the collar and sleeves that hung off her friend's smooth, pale shoulders. Rosalyn's golden mane had been swept up on top of her head, with soft curls framing her face, the style emphasizing the swanlike grace of her neck.

"Who is that with Mr. Kendall?" Rosalyn queried, drawing Fancy's attention back to the men striding purposefully toward them, both of them taller than most of the gentlemen present and devastatingly handsome, every female eye in the room tracking them.

To look at Lucien, Fancy would never have believed he had not grown up an aristocrat. His bearing exuded a self-confident arrogance, and people moved out of his path almost deferentially. He was also hard to miss, dressed in formal black attire that fit his muscular frame to perfection.

"My lady?"

The deep voice barely registered until a nudge from Clarisse, followed by a nod of her head, shifted Fancy's focus to the man standing before her in the receiving line.

"Pardon me," she murmured as her gaze lifted to a pair of stunning amber eyes.

The man smiled warmly down at her. "No apology necessary. I imagine this is all a bit overwhelming."

"Yes," she confessed, returning his smile. "I do feel somewhat like a fish out of water."

"No one would know it to look at you." Taking her hand in his, he added, "And if you don't mind my saying so, I have looked at you quite a bit this evening."

Fancy blushed. "Your honesty is refreshing . . ."

"Goodness, I've been remiss," interjected Clarisse, stunning in a dark rose, off-the-shoulder gown. "Lady Francine Fitz Hugh, may I introduce his lordship, Christian Slade, the Earl of Redding, and his lovely sister, Lady Diana."

Fancy hadn't noticed the young woman standing a bit behind the earl, a petite brunette with an ethereal quality about her. Her heart had missed a beat at discovering who she was talking to. Her gaze cut to Lucien, who now wore a fierce scowl on his face.

The earl had followed her gaze, and the look that transformed his expression was not a pleasant one. "It appears your guardian disapproves of the current company."

Lucien's anger was blazingly obvious, and Fancy feared blows would be exchanged. Glancing up at the earl, she hastened to ask, "Perhaps we could acquaint ourselves at another time, my lord?"

"Your concern for my welfare is appreciated, my lady, but I never bow out of a confrontation, which this particular hothead is clearly itching for. I hope you won't think ill of me?"

"I won't think ill of you, but I don't wish for a fight."

"I promise not to raise a hand to your guardian. The last thing I want is to ruin your party; then you might never forgive me." Lifting her hand to his lips, he lightly kissed the back. "I would hate to lose the opportunity to get to know you better."

"Get your hands off her, Redding," came Lucien's growled warning.

Straightening slowly, the earl greeted her guardian with indifference. "Why, Kendall," he drawled. "What an unpleasant surprise. I thought you disdained parties?"

Lucien's eyes glinted dangerously. "Not when the party is for my ward, you bloody sod."

"Lucien!" Clarisse scolded. "The earl is my guest. I won't have you insulting him."

Lucien's fiery gaze narrowed on Lady Dane. "You knew I wouldn't want him here, yet you invited him anyway."

"This is about Fancy. Not you."

"You won Blackthorne Manor, Kendall," the earl interjected. "You should be crowing, yet here you are, still snorting like an angry bull. Have you nothing better to do?"

"Think twice about patronizing me, Redding. I have no compunction about pounding your face into the floor."

Only a tightening of his jaw gave away the earl's anger. "I promised Lady Francine I wouldn't turn her ball into a fighting match. But if you'd care to take this outside, I'd be happy to oblige you."

"Fine." Lucien took a step, but the large man standing at his side grabbed hold of his arm.

"Think, man," he said tersely. "This is neither the time nor the place."

Fancy prayed Lucien would listen to his friend. He looked brittle, and there was a wildness in the eyes that he fixed on his friend, who did not so much as blink.

Tense moments passed, and then Lucien wrenched his arm away. As he did so, the back of his hand connected with Fancy's chin, the blow sending her tumbling back, but the earl's arms came around her to keep her from falling to the floor.

"My God, Lucien!" Lady Dane exclaimed, rushing to Fancy's side. "What has come over you?"

Pressing her hand to her lip, where a dab of blood dotted her fingers, Fancy glanced up in time to see the stricken look on Lucien's face. The blow had been unintentional, but the guilt in his eyes was awful to see.

He backed away from her, and Fancy instinctively reached for him, but he swung on his heel, pushing his way through the crowd and disappearing out a side door.

"Don't worry," his friend said, the words barely registering in Fancy's mind. "He'll be fine. I'm Derek Hardwicke, by the way."

"The Marquis of Manchester," Clarisse hastened to fill in.

Derek looked moderately uncomfortable with the label. "I wish we could have met under better circumstances," he said with genuine sincerity.

It took Fancy a moment to realize he was speaking to her. "Yes," she said distractedly, her gaze returning to the empty doorway where Lucien had disappeared.

"And you are . . ." He looked inquiringly at Rosalyn.

Dropping into a curtsey, her friend replied, "Lady Rosalyn Carmichael, my lord."

He took hold of Rosalyn's hand. "A pleasure," he murmured, brushing his lips across her skin and lingering a moment longer than proper. "I look forward to furthering our acquaintance. At present, however, I must search for my hardheaded friend."

"Please tell Lucien that I'm all right," Fancy pleaded.

"I will," he said gently, giving her a reassuring smile. Then he inclined his head. "Redding," he said flatly. "Ladies." His gaze boldly drifted over Rosalyn before he turned and followed the path Lucien had taken moments before.

Lucien strode blindly down the dark and deserted streets of London, his mind replaying the scene in the ballroom, the blood on Fancy's lip caused by his actions. He had never hurt a woman before. His anger had eclipsed his common sense. And in that brief flash, he saw in himself the man his father was, and he had felt loathing and disgust.

And fear.

Fear of an uncontrollable rage. Of the jealousy that surely simmered in his blood. His father had possessed only one method for relieving himself of his jealousy.

And that was to beat his wife.

Lucien jammed his eyes shut. Christ, he knew better than to let his emotions get the better of him. He told himself it was Redding's presence that had set him off, not the bastard touching his Fancy.

He choked on a bitter laugh. *His* Fancy? She wasn't his, and never would be. And if he was being honest, Clarisse had done exactly as he had asked her to. Christian Slade was considered a catch. He was rich, handsome, and privileged. None of the things that Lucien had ever been.

He heard the clatter of hooves and wheels rumbling toward him. The hackney driver hesitated to slow when he spotted Lucien, who looked menacing in the dark, his coat and cravat discarded, his hair wild, but stepping out into the path of the conveyance made the man's decision for him.

The horses came to a noisy halt barely three feet in front of Lucien, the driver peering warily down at him from beneath a grimy cap. "Where to, guv'nor?"

"Limehouse," Lucien growled, climbing inside. "There's five pounds extra in it if you get me to the Grotto quickly."

With such incentive, the hackney lurched forward and Lucien dropped his head back against the squabs, trying to erase the image of Fancy.

Long after the ball had come to an end, Fancy was still awake and restless, staring out at the street where the fading lamplight created strange patterns on the ground. An alley cat sauntered down the walkway in front of the house, poking its nose among the crevices in search of an unwary rodent.

Fancy turned away and wrapped her arms around herself. Where was Lucien now? Had Lord Manchester been able to find him? If so, had he told Lucien that she didn't blame him for what happened?

She closed her eyes and sighed. The rest of the night had passed in a blur of faces and endless questions, most of which Fancy answered by rote. During that time, Christian Slade had stayed close at hand. She wasn't quite sure how it happened, but he had managed to wring a promise out of her to ride with him through the park the next morning. She decided to send him a note first thing and cordially decline. She couldn't hurt Lucien like that.

Fancy's eyes drifted open as the haunting sound of her name seemed to rise out of the darkness and whisper across the fine hairs at the back of her neck.

Her heart beat in thick strokes as she turned in a slow circle, her eyes sweeping every corner, each shadowed place. "No one is there," she chided herself.

Then someone called her name again, louder, more insistent, and she realized it was coming from outside.

She looked out into the windless night, her gaze drifting down into the courtyard below, where a figure emerged from behind a tree and stepped into a patch of moonlight.

"Lucien," she whispered, her gaze drinking him in. Then she saw the tears in his shirt and the smear of what looked to be blood staining a corner of his collar.

Fancy spun on her heel and dashed to her bedroom door, her dressing gown flying out behind her as she raced down the dimly lit corridor to the servant's stairs that led to the courtyard.

She burst out the door, her breath rasping in her lungs, the chilled air stinging her cheeks, then came to an abrupt halt. Lucien stood not more than twenty feet from her, yet she could not move another inch.

Before she could speak, he said, "I had to see you."

"What happened to you?"

He shook his head. "I don't know."

Fancy finally found the strength to walk to him, not realizing that the moon made her nightgown nearly transparent, outlining her body and the hint of her nipples as well as the dark delta between her thighs.

She stopped before Lucien and raised her hand to smooth back his hair and look at his wound, but he jerked away, barking at her in a foreign tongue and staring at her as if he didn't know her.

"Let me help you," she murmured, thinking the injury to his head had left him confused.

She reached out to turn his face and check the gash at his temple, but he clamped his fingers around her wrist, his hold bordering on painful. "Go home, Sanji."

Fancy froze. She knew then that Lucien was not with her, and as she met his gaze, she glimpsed the glazed look in his eyes, devoid of recognition and feeling.

"Lucien, it's me. Fancy."

"I told you not to come here. Don't you understand the risks? If your family found out what you were doing—"

Fancy realized he was reliving a past event, and though she didn't want to deceive him, something told her it was imperative to hear what came next.

"They won't find out."

With a muttered oath, he let go of her. "They watch me all the time. You can't free me. You can't help. So, dear God, just go." He turned away from her and laid his forearm against the tree, his head bowed.

Taking a deep breath, Fancy moved around him and stood where he could see her, waiting until his gaze rose to hers. "What have I done so horribly that you want me gone?"

His jaw hardened. "You loved me," he accused. "Don't you understand that I can't love you back? I can't love any woman."

The revelation seemed to tear at him, as it tore at Fancy. Sanji was a woman—and she had loved Lucien. "Why can't you love me?"

"Because we will both die if I do. And I'm not worth dying for."

"And if I think you are?"

His hands shot out so quickly that Fancy could barely blink as he roughly backed her up against the tree. "They've kept me in these shackles for four years," he snarled. "They'll kill me before they let me go. I have nothing." He closed his eyes, his face contorted in pain. "I won't have any more blood on my hands."

"Lucien," Fancy pleaded, fear pounding inside her. "Please, I want to help."

He looked at her, finally seeing her clearly through the sheen of moisture that might have been tears. He cupped her cheek. "Don't let me hurt you, Fancy. I don't want to."

She laid her palm over his hand and leaned her face against the warmth of his skin. "You won't hurt me. I don't think you could."

"I could. I have."

"No."

"They disfigured her," he said, the admission wrenched from him. "They cut her face."

"Dear God." Fancy was beginning to understand how deep his scars were. He had been a slave in India. A young woman had fallen in love with him—and she had paid dearly for it. "Who hurt her?"

"Her father and brothers."

"Why?"

"Because she had dishonored them."

"By loving you?"

"By touching me. By being seen with me. Just by breathing, I had defiled her worth as a woman." He paused and added in a barely audible voice, "And when I made love to her, I caused her death. I wasn't strong enough to send her away. I've never been strong enough when it counted."

The horror of what he had been forced to endure welled inside of Fancy.

"You were strong with me," she murmured, gently peeling his collar back and seeing the large welt on his shoulder. He had been beaten and couldn't remember where. There was something dreadfully wrong, but she couldn't put her finger on what it was.

"I'm afraid of you," he said in a raw voice. "Afraid of what you'll do to me."

"I won't do anything to you," she vowed, looking up into his eyes. "I never meant to hurt you with my lie."

"If all I'd ever done in my life was lie . . ." He shook his head. Then, without another word, he turned and walked away.

"Don't go," Fancy called after him, but all that came back to her was the sound of the metal gate clicking shut.

Fifteen

Two weeks passed without a word from Lucien.

Fancy thought he had understood she would be there for him, no matter what. But she should have remembered that he had erected the world's strongest barriers and would let no one slip by them.

The tragedies he had confided still left her shocked. The brutality of the life he had lived was something she could barely comprehend. She wanted to see him, speak to him, but her missives to Charring House had all been returned.

She had spotted him at Lady Chatterley's rout a few days earlier. He had been with Lord Manchester, who had flirted outrageously with Rosalyn, going so far as to steal a kiss. It had left the usually serene Rosalyn flustered, even more so when Derek's roguish brother,

Ethan, equally as handsome as his sibling, had shown up and begun to compete for Rosalyn's attention. That had set the brothers at odds, a place they seemed to have spent a good portion of their lives.

Fancy had tried to listen attentively to her friend's turmoil, but her gaze had continued to return to Lucien, and when he did not come to her, she made up her mind to go to him. But when she started across the room, a woman had walked up to him, and he had smiled at that woman in a way that made Fancy stop cold.

The woman had been Diana Slade.

Fancy had heard the rumors that he had started paying court to Lady Diana, but she had not paid heed, knowing how viciously Lucien hated the lady's brother. But in her brief acquaintance with Diana, Fancy could see what would attract a man like Lucien. The woman exuded a demure femininity, her every move a graceful choreography, her words soft, yet carefully considered. A woman like Diana would never cavort in breeches or shoot anyone.

Fancy sighed and turned to face her image in the mirror. Invitations had been pouring in since the day after her ball, and Clarisse seemed inclined to accept each and every one. Fancy had not complained. She would have done just about anything to keep her thoughts from Lucien.

A knock sounded at her door. "Come," she said, swiveling halfway around to see Rosalyn enter, the dark smudges under her friend's eyes the only thing that conveyed her night had been anything other than perfect.

"Are you ready to go?" she asked.

"As ready as I'll ever be," Fancy replied, smoothing out the skirt of the brocade and silk gown that Clarisse claimed would be the envy of every woman at the Fordhams' gala.

Rosalyn came to stand in front of her. "Is everything all right?"

"Yes," Fancy replied quickly. She didn't want to burden her friend, who still worried about Calder—with reason, it seemed.

Rosalyn had been certain she had seen him one night a week earlier. And then there had been a suspicious event after they had returned from Lady Chatterley's. The window in Rosalyn's bedroom had been broken, but the incident was labeled an accident, caused by the limbs of the tree next to the house and a strong gust of wind. Fancy was not convinced, and Rosalyn was terrified.

Since that night, Rosalyn had been moved to a different room, and all had been quiet, but Fancy would not feel at ease until Calder had been found. According to correspondence from the Westcotts' butler, who was devoted to Rosalyn, Calder had not been seen or heard from since he slunk away in the middle of the night all those weeks ago.

"Will Lord Manchester be in attendance tonight?" Fancy inquired, as she and Rosalyn made their way down the hall.

"I don't know, and I don't care."

Fancy turned at the stiffness in her friend's voice. "That doesn't sound promising. Has he tried anything untoward?"

"The man lives to be untoward."

"Is he bothering you? I can speak to Lucien about it." If she could pin him down.

A moue of displeasure settled over Rosalyn's face. "No, he's not bothering me, but he really does the most wicked things. I should be appalled, or standoffish at the very least. But he is so very . . ."

"Persuasive?" Fancy offered.

"Exactly!"

Fancy understood that. No matter how often her conscience prodded her, she couldn't seem to behave prudently when Lucien was around.

"I suspect the problem has something to do with his brother, Ethan?" Fancy guessed.

Rosalyn nodded. "The lummox has the nerve to think I'm inviting his brother's attention! He called me a flirt. Can you believe that? Me! When *he* smiles at any woman who passes in front of him." Her shoulders slumped. "I don't know why I'm so drawn to him. He's only toying with me. He's not even going to be here much longer. He merely came to settle some issues regarding his mother's estate before he goes back to Scotland.

"He's a real Highland chieftain, you know. He wears kilts, and I heard from Lady Treadwell"—she lowered her voice—"that Scottish men don't wear any undergarments beneath those kilts. I don't think that's true. I mean, imagine what would happen if the wind kicked up." Her brows pulled together, and she seemed to lose her train of thought for a moment. "Well, none of that matters, I suppose. He'll be gone, and that will be the end of that."

They had reached the foyer by then, and Clarisse turned to smile at them. "Don't you both look stunning! The gentlemen will be beside themselves this evening." Stepping between them, she looped her arms through theirs and guided them toward the front door. "I have a surprise."

The butler opened the door, and standing outside were Lucien and Derek, garbed in black evening wear.

The carriage ride to the Fordhams' town house in Grosvenor Square was torture. The interior of the coach shrank to the size of a snuffbox with the men's presence.

Derek sat beside Rosalyn; Lucien next to Fancy. Though he hadn't spoken more than two words to her, she was forced to feel his body bordering hers, his leg brushing her thigh, his shoulder a constant friction. His big hands rested squarely on his thighs, his blunt fingernails an inexplicable attraction.

The tension was thick as a Cornish fog.

Fancy sighed in relief as the carriage drew to a stop in front of the Fordhams' home, which was set back from the street and took up nearly a full block. Every window was ablaze with lights, and Fancy could see the crush inside. She did not relish another night of mixing and smiling.

She started as she felt a hand at her elbow. She turned to find Lucien regarding her, his expression unreadable. "Ready to go in?"

She wasn't, but she nodded and allowed him to help her alight from the coach. On Derek's arm, Rosalyn had already gone ahead and now stood at the doorway, the footman divesting her of her wrap, leaving Fancy alone with Lucien in an uncomfortable silence.

He took her hand and laid it in the crook of his arm, his sleeve smooth against her fingertips, the flesh beneath as firm as she remembered.

Before they had reached the door, he stopped and turned her to face him. "I'm sorry," he said.

"For what?" Fancy noted the leanness of his face, the pronounced angle of his features, his resigned gaze, an unhealthy tint in his eyes. Something was happening to him, and she could neither stop it nor get him to speak about it.

"It's a blanket apology. I've done more than my share of things to you that I shouldn't have, starting when I first kissed you."

"You're sorry for that?"

"Shouldn't I be?"

"Are you?"

He looked at her, a light breeze toying with his hair, the scent of beeswax floating through the open door, where the butler awaited their entrance.

"No," he finally admitted. "I'm not sorry. But it can't happen again. Whatever's between us is a mistake."

"Why?"

"There are too many reasons to count. I never intended any of this, I hope you know that."

Her fingers tightened around his sleeve. "Please talk to me, Lucien. Tell me what's happening to you."

But his features closed over, telling her it was too late. He ushered her up the steps and into the brightly lit foyer, fluted crystal glasses glinting like small torches on the myriad silver salvers crisscrossing the room.

As they stood at the top of the stairs leading to the ballroom, for one fleeting moment Fancy allowed herself to imagine what a life with Lucien would be like.

To believe he loved her.

The dream dissolved when he kissed her gently on the hand and walked away, her gaze following his retreating form until he disappeared into the card room.

"My lady."

Christian Slade stood two steps below her, resplendent in navy and dove gray, a rose in his hand, which he extended to her.

"Thank you," Fancy murmured, staring down at the rose as the ache widened in her heart.

"Will you honor me with the first dance?" He held out his hand, and Fancy hesitated before placing her palm in his.

The ballroom was a glittering diamond, the chandelier reflecting a hundred little pinpoints of light, the French doors thrown wide, a warm glow spilling out onto the balcony and beyond.

Christian whirled her into a waltz, the soft lights a misty gauze around them. In the earl there existed everything a woman should want in a potential mate. He was sincere, intelligent, charming, and incredibly handsome. But he was not Lucien. He would never need her the way Lucien did, and it wasn't until that moment that Fancy understood how much she had come to care about her guardian, to believe that she could help him through whatever he suffered.

It took Fancy several seconds to realize that the dance was over.

Christian asked, "Would you care for some refreshments?"

She nodded and allowed him to lead her to the table where a large bowl contained champagne punch with slices of orange floating on top.

He handed her a cup. "Are you enjoying yourself?"

"Certainly," Fancy replied, taking a sip.

She caught a glimpse of Rosalyn exchanging words with Lord Manchester across the room, then marching away only to be intercepted by the marquis's brother, who swept her out onto the dance floor, a move that would bring the men to fisticuffs, if the glower on Derek Hardwicke's face was any indication.

"Perhaps I should leave?" the earl said, snapping Fancy back to attention.

"What? Oh, no." She laid her hand on his arm. "I'm sorry. I've had a lot on my mind recently."

"I've noticed. Does your preoccupation have anything to do with Kendall?"

A denial rose to her lips, but the way the earl was looking at her cut it off. "Perhaps some," she confessed.

"Am I to blame? I know how much he dislikes me." A wry half-grin lifted a corner of his lips. "I suspect dislike is a rather mild word, in this case. He's been out to get me since he returned to London a year ago."

"Can you tell me why?" When he shifted uncomfortably, she added, "Please. I need to know."

He hesitated, then said, "Let's go somewhere private."

Fancy nodded, and followed him out of the ballroom.

Lucien stood in a shadowed corner and watched the couple across the room, their heads bent close to one another, looking perfect together. His ward and Christian Slade. A simmering volatility built inside him, like a furnace on the verge of an explosion.

He forced his mind to refocus. He had ample opportunity to ply his charm on Slade's sister. She stood near the stairs with two matrons and several gentleman admirers. Prime game.

He could feel her eyes on him and knew he should ask her to dance, then tell her more tales of his life in the infantry, glossing over the horrific elements of war to satisfy her need to think of him as a hero.

He had once imagined himself as a hero, saving his family from poverty and abuse. But when the time came, he had played the wrong card and lost the hand.

It was a pattern that had continued throughout his

life; he was always losing the things that were most important to him. He could never pull out the ace when he needed it. Now he was going to lose the only person left who meant anything to him.

Lucien told himself that it was just the idea of Slade winning Fancy's hand that brought out his rage. Any man's attention toward her would affect him, but Slade was Lucien's enemy. An enemy he had vowed to grind beneath his boot heel.

Yet nothing he'd done so far had made more than a dent in the bastard's armor. Until now. The man had kept his sister carefully tucked away at a girls' school in Switzerland, but he couldn't keep her there forever. She had come of age.

Lucien had found his weapon.

Yet none of that mattered as his gaze kept returning to Fancy and Slade. Only by the barest thread was he containing himself from smashing in the son of a bitch's face.

"As I live and breathe!" a voice suddenly called out in a jovial tone. "If it ain't Renegade."

Scowling, Lucien turned and found Derek's brother, Ethan, sauntering toward him. Despite the four years separating their births, the two brothers were uncannily similar in height, weight, and looks. The surprise lay in the fact that Ethan was a bastard, the product of a cheating mother. A fact he never let his half-brother forget, as though Derek was somehow to blame for his illegitimacy.

Ethan resented that his brother had gotten everything—the titles, both English and Scottish, the estates, and the money—while he had been relegated to a small stipend and living on Derek's largesse.

"Nobody's called me Renegade in a long time," Lucien informed him in a clipped tone as the man came to a stop in front of him, a tall glass of whiskey in his hand, already half empty, which would inevitably lead to a brawl or some other public display to humiliate his brother.

Sporting a cocky grin, Ethan replied, "Could be 'cause you've fallen off, old boy. Not quite up to your usual tricks, from what I hear. Hard to believe, considering you're one of the founding members of the Pleasure Seekers."

"Still holding a grudge against Caine because he wouldn't let you join?" Lucien asked, a mental countdown in motion in his head as he watched Slade maneuver closer to Fancy.

"Good old Caine," Ethan said in a mocking voice. "Hear he's gotten himself into a bit of a mess. A shame, though I'm not surprised. He was always too full of himself."

"That's something you understand well, don't you?"

"Don't mistake confidence for a bloated head." Ethan smirked as he tipped his glass to his lips and downed a hearty swallow. "By the by, old man, the ladies at Madame Fourche's send their love. Heard you haven't been there in a while. Something about your not being able to get it up? That true?"

At Lucien's silence, Ethan chuckled and saluted him

with his glass. "You always were a stone-faced bastard, Kendall. Guess it's what gives you such a winning edge at cards." He took another swig of his drink, then gestured toward the crowd. "Why, look who's coming. Dear big brother to the rescue. What took you so long, King Manchester?" he taunted as Derek came within hearing distance. "Still trying to corral that sweet filly? Damn unfortunate for you that the ladies like me better. That brooding countenance doesn't inspire amorous feelings in women. You might want to keep that in mind."

A muscle worked in Derek's jaw. "I thought I told you not to come here."

"And I thought I told you that I'd do as I damn well please. You might be a big deal with those sods in Scotland, brother, but you don't impress me."

"Don't you ever get tired of yourself?"

"As long as I've got my older brother to look up to, I have everything. Now you'll have to excuse me. I see Lady Rosalyn over there, and she looks as if she's in need of some company." With a mocking bow, Ethan walked away.

Lucien grabbed Derek by the arm, dragging him back as he lunged after his brother. "He's not worth it."

"Damn him," Derek growled through clenched teeth. "He's my brother, for God's sake."

"I know, but Ethan's angry, and you're the only one he can take it out on. It didn't help that your father barely acknowledged him."

"He had a bloody good reason. My mother was a faithless jade."

Lady Manchester had been well known for her scandalous affairs, tossing them in her husband's face, eventually making him a laughingstock because he never did anything about it.

Lucien recognized that in one area of his life, he had been fortunate. He may not have had all of the advantages Derek had—money, a title, a guaranteed place in life—but his mother had been a constant blessing.

Lucien would never understand what his mother had seen in a brutish fisherman with little education and even fewer prospects. She had once told Lucien that his father used to be different. That he had been kind and loving, but that the constant defeat had worn him down, and then the alcohol had changed him into another man entirely. She had made a vow to stand by him when they married, and no amount of pleading on Lucien's part would sway her, even when his father beat her and Lucien would stay up half the night tending another split lip and black eye. Sometimes worse.

He remembered the time he'd begged a local doctor to come and see her after a severe beating had left her with a broken arm. But the man would not venture forth without payment in advance, and Lucien had no money to give. He'd been forced to see to her injury himself, making a splint out of discarded wood spikes and anchoring them the best he could with torn pieces of a sheet. Her arm had healed, but never properly.

For the next three weeks she had slept in the room with Lucien and his brothers. On four occasions his father had come for her, wanting sex, but Lucien had stood up to the old man. He had been big enough by then to make the bastard think twice. After that, the swine hadn't laid a finger on her—unless Lucien was gone from the house, and he'd come back and find her huddled on the floor, crying.

Lucien couldn't remember how many times he had sworn that he would find solid work and take care of his mother and siblings. They could leave, go somewhere else. His mother would smile at him and make him believe it might happen someday, but deep down, they both knew it never would.

"Why don't you just go over there?" Derek said, reminding Lucien of his presence.

"What?"

"I said go over and talk to your ward. If you haven't noticed, nearly every eye in the room is on you. I suspect they're placing wagers to see how long it takes you to throw Redding through a window. Wasn't that the way it went the last time you two crossed paths?"

"It was a glass door, and the swine had it coming."

"Just because he was the Earl of Redding's son, I presume?"

"Does there have to be any other reason?"

"Don't you think it's time to let it go?"

Lucien slanted his friend a look. "Would you?"

Derek sighed and leaned his head back against the wall. "Probably not." He glanced sideways at Lucien. "So what are you going to do?"

"Dissect him one small piece at a time."

"Not about Slade, about your ward. You want her married, but I don't think there's one man here who'll dare go near her, with you glowering at anyone who does. Face it, my friend, you have feelings for her."

Lucien tensed. "You're mistaking my determination to make sure she arrives at her wedding bed a virgin."

"Unless the wedding bed is your own," his friend countered. "So what makes you so sure she's still a virgin?"

"I know."

Derek lifted a brow, amusement glinting in his eyes. "You do? How interesting. Want to fill me in on the method in which you ascertained this information?"

"Bugger off."

Derek laughed heartily, which turned more than a few heads to see what the infamous pair were up to, many of them females wishing they could attract the men's attention. But they were both preoccupied with different women, and those women were with other men—a fact that made Derek swear a moment later, diverting Lucien's attention to follow his friend's gaze.

"Damn that bloody pup," Derek muttered.

Ethan had maneuvered Lady Rosalyn away from the women she had been conversing with and was now guiding her toward the balcony, but not before shooting a triumphant look over his shoulder in Derek's direction.

"The sod is really beginning to annoy me," Lucien grumbled as he pushed away from the wall.

A hand clamped down on his shoulder, bringing

him to a halt. "This is my fight," Derek said, then headed toward his quarry.

When Lucien finally looked back to the spot where Fancy and Slade had been only a few minutes before, he found neither of them in sight.

Fancy glanced over her shoulder toward Lucien as Christian led her away, but her thunderous guardian was heading in the opposite direction, his attention focused on Rosalyn and Ethan Hardwicke.

Christian ushered her into a lovely conservatory filled with lush green plants and hothouse flowers, a water fountain with a frolicking sea nymph occupying the center of the room.

Fancy sat down on the edge of the fountain, idly dipping her fingers into the water to create small ripples.

Christian paced in front of her for a few seconds before facing her. "I've kept this information to myself for a long time. Not for Kendall's benefit, but for my father's. And now my sister. The scandal could very well ruin our family's name."

Fancy sat up straighter. "What scandal?"

"The one concerning your guardian and my mother."

His words struck something deep inside Fancy, and she stared up at him for long moments before finding her voice. "Lucien and your mother . . . had an affair?"

Christian pushed a hand through his hair. "It wasn't an affair. It was one night. One night that changed everyone's life. Kendall blames me for his loss. Well, I blame him for mine. My father banished my mother to our country home in Hampshire after he found out what had taken place, and I was barely allowed to see her for the next ten years. He had me away at one boarding school after the next.

"There were times when I think he wondered if I was his true heir, or a product of one of my mother's string of lovers." He dug his hands into his pockets. "There were times when I wondered, too."

Fancy didn't know what to say. "I'm sorry."

He glanced at her over his shoulder. "It all happened a long time ago."

"But the hurt hasn't lessened. Does your sister know?"

His expression grew hard. "No. Diana has no idea about what happened; she was still too young to understand. When she was old enough to miss having a mother around, our father told her that our mother was mentally ill and it was best if Diana didn't spend much time with her. Diana grew up dreading that she would inherit our mother's illness. It took a long time for me to help her through her fear. And by God, I won't have Kendall ruin it. I'll kill him first," he vowed through clenched teeth.

Alarmed, Fancy rose and moved to stand in front of him. "I understand your anger, but violence will not solve anything. How does your sister feel?"

"She fights me on the issue. She doesn't understand why I've put my foot down about her associating with him. But she'll listen."

"And if she doesn't?"

"Then Kendall will suffer the consequences," he said ominously. "He only wants her to get back at me. He knew that losing Blackthorne barely made a chink in my holdings." He sighed and shook his head. "I hoped that would put an end to all this."

"Did you lose on purpose?"

He shrugged. "I don't know. Kendall is a damn good card player; I'll give him that. But I'm not so bad myself. We were both deep in our cups and playing hard." He stared down at the floor. "I just want to put it all behind me and move on. Sometimes I hate my father for what he did, for all the lives that were destroyed. But there's nothing I can do to change it."

"What happened to Lucien after your father found out what was going on?"

Christian glanced out the window toward the street, where a string of coaches came and went. "I didn't know the truth for many years. Perhaps I might have done something had I been older, but my father had always been an intimidating figure—and I had been a coward."

Fancy placed her hand on his shoulder. "You and Lucien share the trait of blaming yourself. Some things are out of our control. No matter what your father may have done, you've grown into a wonderful man. Your sister adores you."

His eyes were warm as he looked at her. "She likes you quite a lot, you know. She thinks you and I would make a perfect couple." He held her gaze and said with feeling, "I've come to the conclusion that she's right."

Fancy realized the conversation had taken an unexpected turn. "My lord—"

"Christian," he murmured, gently wrapping his arms around her waist and pulling her closer. "I'm not so bad, you know. You said so yourself." When she opened her mouth to reply, he leaned down and pressed his lips to hers in a soft kiss. Lifting his head, he said, "Just think about it."

Before Fancy could tell him that she had already labeled him a friend, and that another man had crept into her heart, a sardonic voice drawled, "If you think that because you've compromised her, I'll allow you to marry her, Redding, you'd best think again."

Fancy's gaze jerked toward the doorway to find Lucien leaning a shoulder against the jamb, his casual pose belying the murder in his eyes.

Sixteen

Instead of releasing her, the earl trapped Fancy in his embrace. "You always did have the most inconvenient timing, Kendall."

Sensing a fight brewing, Fancy removed Christian's hands from her waist. "This isn't what it looks like," she told Lucien.

"Really?" he retorted. "What is it, then?"

The accusatory way he looked at her made Fancy angry. "His lordship and I were simply talking. Nothing more."

"You lie unconvincingly, love. I foolishly fell for those lies once. You'll have to forgive me if I don't intend to be so gullible again."

"Could it be your own guilty conscience that's lead-ing you to make accusations, Kendall?" Christian challenged. "Perhaps your feelings for the lady are not as pure as you'd like everyone to believe. So tell us, old man, are you lusting after your ward?"

"My lord!" Fancy gasped.

"Thank you, Redding," Lucien drawled.

"For what?"

"For giving me a reason to put my fist through your teeth." Lucien came away from the door like a bull, and Fancy placed herself squarely between the men, her hands pushing against Lucien's shoulders until he looked down at her. "Get out of the way," he bit out.

"No. I won't have the two of you putting me in the middle of your war. You'll not use me as a reason to fight."

A muscle worked in his jaw. "It's my responsibility to protect your honor."

"It's not my honor you're protecting. It's yours."

"She's right, old boy," Christian said in a taunting tone behind her. "You'll use any excuse to have a go at me. Not that I mind, but you do pick the most inopportune moments."

"Like when you're fondling my ward?"

The earl choked on a laugh. "Don't be absurd. Although I would have tried to kiss her again had you not interfered. I've developed rather strong feelings for the lady."

"Please, my lord," Fancy implored.

"Odd, that you bring up feelings," Lucien countered, "since your sister seems to have discovered some for me."

The jab hit its mark; Christian's hands fisted at his side. "You're to stay away from her. Do you understand?"

"That's for Diana to decide. Not you."

"Diana will do as I tell her."

"I'm a grown woman now, Christian," came a new voice, bringing all eyes to the doorway on the opposite side of the room where Diana Slade stood, looking young but determined, her chin tipped up in defiance as she stepped out of the shadows to confront her brother. "I appreciate how diligently you try to protect me, but you must start letting me make my own decisions."

"This is between Kendall and myself, Diana."

"You must stop thinking of me as a child, Christian."

"I don't think of you as a child."

"You do," she said vehemently, color staining her pale cheeks. "Do you think I don't know about Mother? I know. I also know that what Father did was despicable. Mr. Kendall was not to blame." She turned to Lucien, who had remained surprisingly silent. "I'm sorry. What happened to you was cruel and unconscionable."

"Diana!" her brother barked angrily. "We don't owe him any apologies."

"You're wrong, Christian. It's time for this feud to come to an end."

"But I enjoy hating your brother," Lucien remarked in a deceptively calm voice.

"You don't mean that," Diana refuted, and Fancy

could see that the young woman had found a cause in Lucien, believing she could save him from himself.

"Oh, but I do."

"You heard him, Diana," her brother interjected. "Can't you see he only wants you to get back at me?"

Lucien regarded Diana steadily. "He might be right, my lady. Perhaps you should turn tail and run."

Diana shook her head. "You won't hurt me, Lucien. I've given you several opportunities, and you've done nothing dishonorable."

"What are you saying, Diana?" her brother demanded, stepping away from Fancy to take his sister by the arm.

"I'm saying that I practically threw myself at Mr. Kendall. I even kissed him the other night in the gazebo. He could have taken advantage of me; I would have welcomed it. Yet he acted the gentleman."

The earl whirled around to face Lucien. "You bloody bastard," he swore viciously, taking a step toward his adversary.

Diana tugged at his arm. "Didn't you hear me, Christian? *I* was the one who behaved badly."

"He's corrupted you. He'll do anything to pay us back for what Father did."

Lucien glanced down at Fancy. "Are you getting all this, Lady Francine? I am a rogue and a scoundrel, completely unfit to be any young woman's protector. You could use this information to get the magistrate to assign you a new warden, my dear. You could be free of my tyranny once and for all."

"Is that what you'd like?" Fancy asked softly, knowing that Lucien had never wanted the responsibility for her.

His gaze narrowed on her face. "You still have that annoying propensity for asking questions rather than answering them."

"Is that what you'd like?" she persisted.

He glared at her and shoved his hands into his pockets. "I don't know, damn you."

"You don't want her, but you don't want anyone else to have her, do you?" the earl spat.

"Not at all. I just don't want *you* to have her."

"Please," Fancy begged, a strangled sob welling in her throat. "Stop this."

Lucien stared down at her, a spark of regret in his eyes. "Fancy—"

"No." She shook her head, tears stinging her eyes even as she tried to hold them back. "Don't say any more. All I wanted was to stay in Cornwall, to live a simple life with the people I love. I didn't want expensive gowns." She gripped the material of her skirt. "I didn't want tea parties and maids and empty flattery. I just—" Choking back tears, Fancy lifted her hem and fled the room.

Lucien's gaze followed her departure, a yawning void engulfing him as he fought every instinct that shouted to go after her.

"I hope you're proud of yourself, Kendall," the earl said caustically. "You don't have a single damn clue what you've got in Fancy. But I do. And if she'll still speak to me after all this, I will do whatever it takes to win her heart. I don't care anymore about your vendettas. There isn't a thing I can do to change the past—but I sure as hell don't intend to be like you, and spend my life living in it."

He took his sister by the arm and headed toward the door. As they passed, Diana laid a hand on Lucien's forearm.

Lucien slid her an impersonal glance. "Listen to your brother, my lady. Go home."

She bowed her head and nodded. He watched her walk away, knowing in his gut that he had lost his last chance to strike at the heart of the man who had ruined his life, a man long dead and buried, but who Lucien could never forgive. He'd had a golden opportunity to avenge his mother's pain, his family's ostracism, and he had opened his hand and let it fly away.

He had never handled anything in his life the right way. It was a curse, and he had afflicted Fancy with it, taken her down with him when he had never meant to hurt her. He should find her another guardian. He should walk away.

He turned and headed out the door.

Then he swung back and strode across the room, to the garden where Fancy had gone.

Fancy escaped out the French doors and hastened down the stairs into the deeply shadowed comfort of the Fordhams' garden. The scent of honeysuckle enveloped her as she moved along the rows of flowers and hedges, wanting only to be alone. She could not face another person.

But most of all, she could not face Lucien.

She didn't understand what had come over her. It was not like her to have such emotional outbursts; she had always prided herself on her calm sensibility. But Lucien had a way of shaking her very foundation. He was so tied up in his revenge against the ghosts from his past that he could not see what was right in front of him.

She now knew enough to piece together a part of his life, to envision the story of a young man seduced by a wealthy woman and sentenced to the worst of punishments by her cuckolded husband. A young man who hadn't possessed either money or influence to save himself.

Fancy didn't blame Lucien for the bitterness he felt, for the dissolution. It was his inability to lay any of it to rest that broke her heart. She couldn't turn his life around; only he could do that. And he wasn't willing or able to do so.

"Beautiful night."

Fancy whirled around to find Lucien leaning against a gnarled beech tree, dark and still, a cheroot illuminating the solemn planes of his face, his unearthly beauty, the torment in his eyes.

Unable to bear that look, she turned away and closed her eyes, wrapping her arms around her waist. She wanted to cry but couldn't. Perhaps tears would have washed away the indomitable sense of loss. She wanted her life to be simple again. She wanted to turn back the clock and be the carefree girl she had once been, with a brother who adored her and a grandmother whose love had been freely given and all-encompassing.

"Cold?"

Fancy's head jerked up, and she found Lucien standing beside her, his expression unreadable, his eyes as mysterious as the night.

"No." She stepped away from him, the sound of an owl hooting to its mate filling the silence.

"When I was a lad," he said, staring down at a patch of night-blooming jasmine, "I used to sneak over to the West End and spy on the rich people. I'd watch the women dancing in their silks and satins, the men dressed in their knee breeches, not a single scuff on their shoes. I used to wonder how those glorified peacocks could move their necks with their shirt points so stiff and their cravats wound so tightly in all those intricate knots. I once thought I was luckier than they were because I was free. I could come and go as I pleased, while they were tied down to estates and titles.

"It wasn't until I was about seven or eight that I realized being poor was its own trap and that having no money meant you were a lesser person. I had only known people like myself up until then. My mother had never let me venture far, but that year the Thames had frozen and the dockworkers were all let go. So, being the oldest, I went out and found work gathering up pure from the streets."

Compelled, Fancy turned to face him. "What's pure?"

"Petrified horse shit," he answered bluntly, as though daring her to show her disgust. "My father took me to Mayfair and Kensington in the hopes of getting a better price for it. I remember how excited I was. I'd never been that far from home before. I thought it was going to be an adventure.

"The first time I was spat on and called a filthy guttersnipe, I knew I wasn't like those people. It was as though I was a stranger in my own country."

Until that moment, Fancy had fought against feeling anything, too afraid to open her heart as Lucien related his story without a hint of self-pity. But now all she could see was the child who had been deluded by a world that did not care for everyone equally.

"When I told my mother what had happened," he went on, "she took me outside, and we sat together at the end of the wharf. She said that all people were created equal in the eyes of the Lord, but that some of them hadn't been blessed with much sense."

Fancy smiled through a haze of tears. "Your mother was a very wise woman."

He ground out his cheroot beneath his heel. "You remind me a lot of her."

"I do?"

He nodded slowly. "You have that same kind of wisdom in your eyes, an innate understanding of people."

Fancy wanted so desperately to reach out to him, to wrap her arms around his neck and hold him close. He had opened a door, and she suspected he hadn't done so in a long time. But the revelations felt like confessions, and in a place deep down, an unease began to build.

"Would you tell me what happened between your mother and Christian's father?"

He shifted, staring off into space, and Fancy could tell that he struggled with the memory. "It had been snowing that day. I remember how raw it was. My hands were cold." He looked down at them, his thumb digging into the opposite palm, as though trying to warm them. "My mother feared we would all starve that winter because there was no work and my father's drinking had escalated. For more than a month, she had applied for employment everywhere she could.

"One night she fainted in the street, clutching my sister, Jensyn, who was only six months old at the time. My mother had to take her along because Jensyn was still nursing." His profile, limned by shadows, was stark. "I think she had also grown to fear my father more than ever. He had become meaner as the years went by, prone to jealous rages. He seemed to feel it was his duty to keep her pregnant." He looked at Fancy then. "She had three babies that were stillborn and one who died when she was two months old."

He took a deep breath and gazed up at the sky. "When my mother came to, she found herself on a small cot, face-to-face with the Earl of Redding's formidable housekeeper. Whether it was my mother's story about her search for employment or the sight of my baby sister's thin, pale face, the housekeeper took pity on her and went to speak to the earl about giving her work. That night, my mother's determination saved us all. But when my father heard the news, he slapped her so hard he cracked her jaw. He claimed she must have done something to get the job."

Fancy's hands dug into the material of her skirt, understanding what Lucien meant by "something." Never had she hated a man more than she did his father.

"He was a bully."

"He was," Lucien quietly agreed, "but he let her keep the job, though he always found something to berate her about when she came home. That was about the time my brother Dorian began getting into brawls and stealing. I don't think he knew any other way to handle the emotions churning inside him."

"How did your other siblings behave?"

"Jillian withdrew, more so if the neighborhood boys showed her any attention. I think she believed all men were like my father. Hugh and Gavin took to staying away from the house as much as they could."

"You were the strong one, then. The protector."

"That's me," he said in a bitter tone. "The protector. The problem was, I could never protect anyone. If I had, my mother would never—"

Even in the darkness, Fancy could see the tension that coiled through his body, the brittle posture that said he was on the verge of destruction.

"Say it, Lucien," Fancy whispered. "You've held it inside long enough."

He expelled a breath and ran a hand over his face. "The earl raped my mother," he told her in a deadpan voice. "He raped her and had two of his thugs hold me down to watch."

Fancy raised a trembling hand to her lips. "Oh, God."

"He said it was what I deserved for sullying his wife with my fisherman's hands, that I would learn who my betters were and never think of trying to climb out of the gutter again."

Fancy reached toward him, but he angled away, not wanting to be touched. "You couldn't have known he would do something so horrible," she murmured.

His mouth set in a grim line. "The stupid thing was, I really thought Lady Redding felt something for me. I couldn't believe someone so beautiful and socially influential wouldn't think I wasn't beneath contempt. For me, it was never about the physical aspect. Hell, I don't think I even noticed her body. I just wanted . . ." He shrugged. "I don't know."

"You wanted to fit in," Fancy answered for him, understanding, as she had felt the same thing, mostly during the years her parents were alive and her mother would dress her up like a doll and parade her about for her society friends.

The other girls her age seemed to enjoy emulating their mothers. They could sit in a chair for hours with their ankles demurely crossed and their hands neatly folded in their laps. They could curtsey perfectly and smile with an inborn talent. Fancy never could.

She had always been restless, wanting to study things and play with George and his friends. Her mother despaired. Her father wasn't around enough to care.

"My mother never shed a single tear," Lucien said, and when he looked at her, Fancy saw a blackness that eclipsed the night. "Not one. She wouldn't let him defeat her."

"She was a strong woman." Strong for her family, Fancy thought. Strong for her son. "Did you report what happened?" she asked, fearing she already knew the answer.

"To the law, you mean? The justice system that favors the wealthy and pisses on the rest of us? No. The East End breeds its own form of justice."

"What did you do?"

"I followed the bastard all the next night, waiting for my opportunity to strike. My rage was so strong, I was blinded by it, not thinking clearly. He had been ready for me all along. And when I made my move, the men he had watching me made theirs. The blow to my head caught me unaware, and when I awoke hours later, I found myself shackled in the hold of a ship bound for India."

Where he had been kept as a slave. Never had Fancy felt ashamed of the world into which she had been born. She had never had a reason until now. No wonder Lucien held the aristocracy in contempt. She had once thought the vagaries of her life had been cruel, taking her family away one by one, but she had not known how deep cruelty could truly cut.

"What did your father do when he found out about your mother?" she asked.

"He never did."

Fancy stared at him. "I don't understand."

"We didn't tell him. My mother made me promise. She said it had to be our secret, that my father would kill her, and I knew she was right. He would think she had done something to warrant the attack. He had always taken the coward's way out."

Fancy closed her eyes and shuddered, grief rising inside her for a woman she never knew and a young boy who had been forced to keep a horrible secret locked away all these years, eating away at his soul until nothing but a shadow remained.

Taking a step closer to him, she said, "Do you think you're like your father, Lucien?"

A long stretch of silence enshrouded them, filled only by the rustling of leaves, until finally he said, "Yes."

Fancy moved in front of him and took his hand. "You're not."

"How do you know?"

"Because you care. You did what you had to do. You had the weight of the world on your shoulders at a young age." She raised his hand to her mouth and gently kissed his palm. "You're a good man, Lucien Kendall."

He reached out and cupped her cheek, his thumb lightly brushing over her bottom lip, gently touching the small cut. "I'm sorry I hurt you."

"It was an accident." When he wouldn't meet her gaze, she said, "You're not your father, Lucien."

"Sometimes I think I've become him. I see in myself that same detachment, and I can't change it. It's part of me."

"You did the best you could. You lived with violence, and no one expects you to pretend it didn't happen. But you can't let it rule your life."

"I don't know what happened to any of them. The only thing that kept me alive was thinking that some day I'd get back to my family. But when I returned, everything was gone. They never knew what happened to me, never knew if I was alive or dead all those years. And my money couldn't change one damn thing. The only man who might have known the truth told me that he'd take the secret to his grave. And he did."

"I understand why you hate him so much. But if you hold on to that hate forever, he will have won." She stroked her fingers across his cheek and whispered, "I don't want him to win."

"Fancy," he uttered in a wounded voice, curling his fingers over hers. "My sweet, sweet Fancy. What will I do without you?"

She wanted to tell him that he wouldn't be without her, but he leaned down and kissed her, the tender caress sending waves of pure joy through her as she lifted up on tiptoe to return his kiss with everything she felt for him.

One hand slid around the back of her head to hold her close while his other settled at her waist, his arousal a tantalizing heat against her belly.

His tongue mated with hers, swirling and tasting and delving until she was intoxicated. She pressed tighter to him, needing more.

She laid her hand over his at her waist, entwining their fingers, feeling the strength tightly contained in those hands. And with the boldness she had never been able to suppress, she guided his hand over her stomach and then upward to cup her breast, her nipple begging for his touch.

He moaned and gripped her tighter, a feeling so strong bursting within her that she knew it had to be love, for she had never wanted to give a man every-thing, offer all that she possessed. She had never thought she'd be able to walk away from one world and live in another. But she would if it meant having Lucien.

Fancy drifted to the ground with Lucien clasped tightly in her arms, his weight bearing down on her, the smell of crushed grass and the sandalwood he wore an intoxicating blend.

She arched up against him as he tugged her bodice down and laved her nipple, his beautiful mouth suck-ing, creating a throbbing heat in her loins.

"Fancy," he whispered over and over again, his tongue moving from one distended tip to the other, his hands hungry against her, pushing under her skirt, sliding along her calves to her knees, then her thighs, where he gripped her, bringing her up tight against his groin, his erection a hot, hard length, burning her.

She moaned and surged up against him, her fingers digging into his upper arms, hard bands of muscle holding his full weight from her as he stared down at her, his eyes hot with desire.

"Make love to me, Lucien," she whispered in an aching voice, reaching up to undo the buttons of his shirt, her palms sliding across the solid planes of his chest, the satiny disks of his nipples, and then downward, over his stomach, the waistband of his trousers stopping her exploration.

When she flicked open the first button, he took hold of her wrist. "Don't do this to me, Fancy."

"I want you."

He bowed his head and pushed up hard against her, a deep, guttural groan spilling from his lips as she met his thrust, one hand cupping her breast, toying with the tip before he leaned down to draw it deeply into his mouth.

Fancy whimpered and sought for her breath as her hands reached between them, praying he didn't stop her as she undid the next button on his trousers, and the next, until he slid into her hands, silky and hard.

He watched as she gripped him with both hands, touched him as he had touched her, discovering more with each moment what he liked, his teeth gritted as he pumped in her hands.

When he pulled back, she reached for him, thinking he meant to deny her. But instead he separated the material of her pantalets and stroked her wet folds with his erection, guiding the head of his shaft over her swollen nub, the pleasure building with each glide until her release washed over her with surprising force.

When she opened her eyes, she found Lucien staring down at her. He swept her hair away from her face and caressed her jaw with his thumb. "I love watching you when you're being pleasured," he murmured. "You're going to make some lucky man very happy."

Fancy froze, all the warmth draining from her. "What are you saying?"

He rolled to his back and braced himself on his elbows. "You know what I'm saying."

She stared at him. "You still want me to marry."

"I never stopped."

"But what just happened—"

"Is another guilt to add to all the others I've accumulated. My special talent has always been doing the wrong thing. But I won't compound it by taking your virginity. You were never mine, Fancy." He glanced sideways and said in a soft voice, "But God knows I wish you were."

Fancy closed her eyes. "So I was just your responsibility, is that it?"

"Your brother never would have wanted this."

"What about what I want?"

"If you want Slade, I won't stop you."

Battling tears, Fancy remained silent, hating his blind conviction and the way he could so easily hurt her, even when he hadn't intended to. And when he finally pushed to his feet and walked away, she promised herself that it would be the last time.

Seventeen

The rookery was a place no one went if they didn't have to. Where on any given day a mother might lace her baby's sugar water with laudanum to keep the child under so that it didn't disturb her sleep, or cry incessantly because it was slowly starving to death.

It was a place where weak souls crawled into bed as soon as the sun set and lay awake listening to the rats scurry beneath the floorboards. Where only the faintest sound of church bells could reach, and no one believed in God.

To Lucien, it was home.

He stood on the curb and watched the hackney rattle off into the darkness, the nearest streetlamp a dozen houses away, the cracked pavement showing intermittent pools of yellow from the gaslight. All else was black.

Since the night he had first ventured back into the slums where he was born, waking from a delirium to find himself bruised and bleeding, he had tried to stay away. But he was tired of fighting it.

Tonight he needed to forget how close he had come to making love to Fancy. And how, in the end, he had opened the door for Christian Slade to walk through. Redding had as much as said he would marry Fancy, and though the idea was killing Lucien, he couldn't deny her the chance at happiness.

She was right. It was time to let go of the past. He had lost. Tomorrow or next week, or perhaps next year, he would start over again. But for the present, he would find heaven in the arms of the only mistress he couldn't hurt.

Fancy stood in the front parlor, looking out the window. Christian would be arriving soon to take her to the theatre and a late supper.

She had spent the last three days with him, meeting him each morning for a ride in Hyde Park. While they trotted among the daily crush of people, he amused her with anecdotes from his youth, impressed her with the depth of his knowledge, and charmed her with his ready smile. He possessed all the qualities a woman could hope to find in a man, yet Fancy could not summon up any feelings for him.

She wanted to blame Lucien for how she felt, but it was not his fault that she didn't love Christian. She had discovered she didn't want a man who was so perfect, so predictable. But what she wanted, she could not have.

The doorbell chimed, and Fancy moved to answer the summons, never having had a butler to get the door for her at Moor's End. Pierce had gently chided her for doing his job, yet it seemed silly to simply stand there, especially when it was most likely Christian.

Though a headache earlier in the day had nearly been her excuse for canceling the evening, Fancy knew she could no longer put off the inevitable. She had to let Christian know how she felt about him. She should have done so before now, but she had wanted to strike out at Lucien by doing exactly what he had given her his blessing to do. She soon realized it would not make Lucien love her, though, and only made her like herself less.

But when she opened the door, it was not Christian she found standing there, but Heath. For a moment, Fancy could do no more than blink.

He swept her into his arms. "Dear God, how glad I am to see you. You don't know how worried I've been about you."

"Heath, put me down. You're squeezing the breath out of me."

"I'm sorry," he said, looking chagrined as he lowered her to her feet. "I just didn't think I would find you before Kendall did something horrible to you."

Before she could remark, Pierce appeared, his brow drawn together in disapproval, though whether it was due to Fancy opening the door or to their newest arrival, she couldn't be sure.

"May I help you, sir?" he queried, an intimidating figure in black.

"I'm here to see Fancy," Heath replied, clearly not appreciating the interruption.

"Lady Francine, you mean?" Pierce corrected in a reproving tone.

"Yes, Lady Francine. Now, will you please give us a moment?"

Pierce looked to her. "Is everything all right here, miss?"

"Yes, Pierce. Thank you."

Giving Heath a cursory glance that could have been construed as a warning to behave, Pierce disappeared down the corridor.

"Insufferable servant," Heath said. "Are they all so lofty here?"

Fancy didn't intend to discuss the servants. "I don't understand why you're here."

"Is there somewhere we can talk alone?"

Fancy was growing to dread such conversations. But she said, "Follow me," and led Heath into the library, where he closed the door, taking a moment to scan the ceiling-high shelves packed with books.

When his gaze returned to her, it drifted over her in a way that made Fancy uneasy. It was the way a man looked at a woman he found attractive, and while Heath had often told her she was beautiful, she had never seen the blatant desire that she saw now.

"You have blossomed into a stunning woman," he said, moving forward to take her hands in his.

"Thank you."

"Is this outfit one that *he* picked out for you?"

"If you mean my guardian, the answer is no. This dress was my choice, as were all my others. Lucien would never dictate what I should wear."

"Lucien . . . how very familiar that sounds. Have the two of you become better acquainted since he brought you to London?"

Fancy stiffened, hearing his subtle undertone. "I don't see what business that is of yours."

"There was a time you used to confide everything to me."

"I was a child."

"So you've outgrown me, then?"

Fancy tugged her hands from his and took a step away. "I don't know what this is all about."

"It's about your guardian," he said, tossing his gloves onto a side table and moving toward the liquor cabinet to take down a bottle of port.

Though it was not her house, Fancy bristled at the way he acted as though he had the right to do as he pleased.

Once he had poured himself a healthy glass of the strong wine, he shifted to face her, leaning a hip against the edge of the table and regarding her over the rim of his glass.

"How much do you know about your guardian?"

"Why do you ask?"

The tensing of his jaw told her he didn't appreciate having his motives questioned. "Perhaps I'm wondering what he's told you about his time in India . . . and about George's death."

The mention of her brother brought Fancy to attention. Heath knew she had always wondered about the circumstances surrounding George's death, as they had never been quite clear.

"What about George's death?" she asked, forcing herself to meet Heath's gaze squarely.

"That night you were to meet me at the cove, do you remember it?"

"Yes."

"You didn't come."

"Because of the weather." And Lucien. When she had come upon him in the library and seen him gently holding the kitten in his arms, she had felt the earth move beneath her.

Perhaps that was the moment she had first fallen in love with him. And there had been many other moments since. She realized that she wasn't ready to give up on him and walk away.

"Yes, the weather," Heath said. "Then you went off to London, and I was left in the dark about where you were. I had to squeeze it out of Jimmy. The brat wouldn't tell me for the longest time."

"You didn't threaten him, did you?"

"Of course not," he replied tersely, scowling at her. "I simply thought he would take my money and be done with it. But it seems your guardian gave him a considerable amount *not* to tell me your whereabouts. The lad was disgustingly noble to the cause."

It bothered Fancy that Lucien had used his money to buy Jimmy's silence. But perhaps Lucien's motives hadn't been entirely self-serving. In many ways, Jimmy's life seemed to mirror his. Maybe what he saw in Jimmy, he saw in himself.

"So how did you get him to tell you where I was?" Fancy asked.

"I told him it was a matter of life and death, and that if I didn't find you, something terrible might befall you."

Fancy's temper flared to life, and she swept across the room to face him. "That was a loathsome trick, and I can't believe you could even face me after spouting such a lie to that young boy."

"It wasn't a lie," he said, suddenly gripping her upper arms and giving her a shake. "Your life *is* in danger."

"You're talking nonsense."

"Am I? Have you ever queried your guardian as to what exactly happened to George? Or have you stopped caring, now that Cornwall is a dust speck behind you? Perhaps you've forgotten the horrible way your brother died."

Fury gave Fancy a strength she hadn't realized she possessed. She wrenched an arm free and slapped him across the face. "How dare you question my devotion to George! You know how much I loved him, how I could barely go on. I cried on your shoulder too many times to count, yet you stand here telling me I've forgotten about him? I'll never forget! Now get out," she demanded. "And don't come back."

"I'm not leaving until you've heard me out."

"Then say what you have to say and leave."

"Fine," he said through clenched teeth, his gaze raking over her as though she had become something to be loathed and pitied. "You've changed, you know. You were once a sweet girl; now I barely recognize you. I would have married you, taken care of you and that run-down house, but you wouldn't have me. You wanted nothing more than to hold on to Moor's End. I thought that when you almost got caught by the gaugers, you'd cease in your behavior, but it only made you more determined. I truly thought you'd have to be arrested before you'd learn you wouldn't win."

"You never believed in me, did you?"

"I indulged your whim. That's all it was—you would never have been able to save Moor's End without financial help."

"But you never offered, did you?"

"That would have defeated the purpose, wouldn't it? I wanted you as my wife."

"And you were willing to watch me be run to ground in order to get me?"

"If that's what it took."

Fancy recognized the depth of her gullibility. "It was you who alerted the gaugers when the shipments would be arriving, wasn't it? You set out to keep me from making that money." When he didn't refute her claim, she felt the final piece of the life she had known fall away. "No wonder George didn't name you as my guardian. He knew what a fraud you were."

"And you think he made a better decision with

Kendall?" he scoffed. "At least my only crime was try-ing to get you to see how foolish your quest was. I never murdered anyone."

Fancy went completely still. "What are you saying?"

"What I wanted to say two months ago. Your guardian is the reason your brother is dead. The bullet that killed George was from Lucien Kendall's gun."

Fancy felt as though the earth had just opened beneath her feet and sent her tumbling into a dark abyss. "No," she said in a barely audible voice. "He would have told me."

"And why would he do that? You didn't know the truth, and there wasn't any reason for him to enlighten you. Perhaps he hoped you'd marry him. He knew about the trust you would be inheriting, and his chances would be considerably lessened if you knew he had caused your brother's death. If that wasn't enough incentive, then there was your stature as an earl's daughter, which would have given him social status."

"And you," Fancy found the strength to say, strug-gling to absorb it all.

George had taken a bullet to his side. The wound had slowly and irrevocably bled into his stomach. They said he had been killed in the line of duty, but never anything more. Not how or why or where.

"I wasn't the one who kept this from you," Heath retorted angrily.

"No? Then how do you know all this now?"

He shifted under her scrutiny. "George wrote to me the day before he died. He didn't want you to know."

"You're lying."

"Would I have come all this way if I didn't have proof?" He extracted a folded piece of parchment paper and handed it to her. "Go ahead. Read it."

With shaking hands, Fancy unfolded the letter that had begun to yellow with age, its edges frayed. Tears sprang to her eyes when she saw her brother's familiar scrawl. She had never thought to see it again. And as she read the last words he had ever written, it was as though he stood before her, his voice a haunting whisper in her ear:

Courtenay,

By the time you read this missive, I suspect I will be dead. I have been wounded and am not sure if I shall survive the night.

But I write to you not about myself, but about Fancy. My only regret in this world is leaving her. While other siblings quarreled and resented one another, Fancy and I had a special bond. Perhaps it was due to feeling we had no one to depend upon beside each other. Perhaps it was simply that Fancy just didn't care that the world had dictated that siblings be rivals.

She never was like anyone I had known, and my heart aches at never seeing the man she chooses to love or the babies she will have, beautiful, smiling children with eyes as green as ferns and an innate sense of curiosity about the world. Sons and daughters who would have called me uncle.

• • •

Tears blurred Fancy's vision, and silent sobs racked her body. Oh, God, how she wanted George back. How desperately she missed him. She couldn't read any more. She could not bear another word. And yet her eyes went back to the page.

I hope she knows that I will always watch over her, no matter where I am. For now, however, I must leave her in the care of another and pray that he will cherish her as much as I do.

I know you will wonder about my decision not to choose you. Perhaps it was simply your feelings for Fancy that kept me from doing so. I hope you will trust that I have done what I felt best, and that the man who is now Fancy's guardian will take care of her. He is my commanding officer, Colonel Lucien Kendall.

When I first met the colonel, I was in awe of him. Nothing made him back down. I doubted he had ever known a fear in his life. Time proved me wrong. We are all fallible. Even heroes.

A man came to visit him one day. No one knew who he was. But shortly thereafter the colonel left, telling no one where he was going. Patrols were sent out, seeking to arrest him. A week later he returned, and he was not the same man. Something had happened to him.

We found out that had had gone to Anandpur Sahib, home to the Sikhs, and a place no foreigner, most especially an officer in Her Majesty's Infantry, would travel if sane.

No matter what disciplinary action was threatened, he would not speak of what took him to Anandpur. He was thrown in the hole for three weeks. Most men could not have survived one. But the colonel did not break.

The first night of his return to duty, two days ago, he went into his tent and didn't come out. Concerned, I checked on him and found him unconscious on his bunk. When I turned to call for the medic, I found a Sikh standing inside the tent, a sword pointed at my throat. He spat words at me that I didn't understand and lunged toward the colonel. The next thing I felt was the bullet.

I remember waking and seeing the colonel kneeling over me, his eyes glazed and his face pale, a gun in his hand. The Sikh lay beside me, dead, the bullet having gone through him and into me. I don't think the colonel knew what had happened. It was as though . . .

"*He wasn't there with me,*" Fancy read out loud, a wave of despair rolling through her, vividly recalling the look her brother spoke of, that vacant stare. That utter lack of recognition. Lucien had known all along how George had died, and he had never said a word.

She remembered wondering if guilt was the weight on his shoulders, if he felt as though the death of his men were somehow his fault.

This time it had been his fault. He was to blame for her brother's death, and whatever she had felt for him withered and died as she read on.

I don't know if I've made the right decision, but the colonel needs someone to believe in him, someone to turn him around, and Fancy has always been a healer. I think she can heal him.

Watch over her, my friend. Never tell her what I have revealed to you this day. She might never forgive Kendall. I already know he will never forgive himself.

Farewell,
Fitz Hugh

Fancy closed her eyes, and the papers fluttered to the ground.

"Do you believe me now?" Heath asked, a hint of triumph in his voice. "I told you Kendall was a murderer. He should have been hanged instead of honorably discharged."

Fancy turned away from him. She couldn't think. It was as if she had lost George all over again, and she feared the anguish would defeat her.

"Come back to Cornwall with me, Fancy," Heath beseeched, coming to stand in front of her. "Now. Tonight. You need never see Kendall again."

Fancy dropped her head into her hands, and she hadn't the strength to fight when Heath drew her into his arms. Every image of her time with Lucien flashed behind her eyes like a timeline.

She didn't hear the knock on the door or Pierce clearing his throat until Heath demanded, "What is it, man?"

"Lord Redding is here for Lady Francine."

"Send him away, Pierce," she begged. "I don't care what you tell him."

"Perhaps you'd like to relay the message yourself," came the earl's voice, bringing Fancy's head up and her gaze to the doorway where Christian stood, stoic in the face of her rude dismissal.

"Dear God, what's happened?" he said when he caught sight of her tearstained face.

Fancy could only shake her head. She couldn't bear it. Picking up her skirt, she ran from the room, to the sounds of Heath calling after her and the scent of scattered rose petals from the bouquet she had knocked from Christian's hand as she raced by him.

Before colliding into someone.

She looked up to find Tahj holding her at arm's length, wind blowing in through the open front door, the smell of incense clinging to his orange robes.

"You are needed," he said in an urgent tone. "You must come with me."

"No." Fancy shook her head. "Leave me alone."

He looked over her shoulder, and Fancy knew the men were standing there. She backed away from Tahj and whirled toward the stairs.

"He's killing himself."

Fancy gripped the banister. Everyone and everything she had known was crumbling before her very eyes. She didn't want to care about what Lucien did, yet George's words reached out to her.

Fancy has always been a healer. I think she can heal him.

She couldn't heal him. She didn't want to even try. She wanted to believe the inner voice that said she hoped he suffered for what he had done to George, even as she turned back to face Tahj.

"Come with me," he asked again, holding out his hand to her.

And Fancy took it.

Eighteen

Fancy said nothing to Tahj as the coach rattled down the nearly deserted streets of Mayfair and into a part of town that she had never entered.

The farther they went, the more inhospitable the area became, with fewer and fewer lamps dotting the street to give even the illusion of safety, small groups of rough-looking men congregating in alleyways and dark corners, bursts of bawdy laughter filtering out tavern doors.

Fancy could still feel the impact of each word in her brother's letter, hear each labored breath as he fought to write the last entry of his life and forgive the man who had been the cause of that life ending too soon. Nothing could hurt George now. The same could not be said for her.

The coach came to a jarring halt on a narrow side street. Fancy could see no signs of a bordello or run-down tavern or gaming hell, only a single, nondescript door.

"Where are we?" she asked, peering down at Tahj, who stood on the curb holding his hand out to her, once more expecting blind faith.

He led her toward a door and opened it to reveal a long hallway like a tunnel with an odd blue phosphorescent light glowing at the end.

A strange odor coiled around Fancy as she moved down the corridor with Tahj, the scent sweet and pungent, making her lightheaded. She fought a need to turn back, not sure she wanted to know what she would uncover in that strange blue mist.

Then it was too late for retreat. As she stood at the entranceway to a vast room, she gasped at what she saw. At least fifteen people lay on the floor, some completely motionless and sickly pale, others glassy-eyed with long tubes in their mouths, white puffs of smoke a cloud above their heads.

"What are they doing?"

"Smoking opium."

Fancy's gaze jerked to his. "Opium?" She knew what opium was and how, if administered correctly and in small doses, the drug could ease pain. Abused, it could cause death. "Why did you bring me here?"

The moment Tahj's ebony eyes met hers, Fancy knew. It all seemed so dreadfully obvious now, and so horribly surreal.

"Where is he?"

Tahj pointed a finger toward the farthest corner, where barely a slice of light illuminated a huddled figure, set away from the rest. And not moving.

Fancy lifted the skirt of her evening gown and stepped around the mass of bodies, both male and female. She muffled a shriek as a hand clamped around her ankle.

"Give us a kiss, lovie," came a creaky voice, bringing Fancy's gaze downward to the hollow-eyed female grinning up at her, two bottom teeth missing, her lips cracked, her face looking as though all the youth had been drained from it. "Come on, Princess. Y'll like it."

"Release her," Tahj ordered.

The grin faded from the woman's face as she slithered back, allowing them to continue.

Fancy's first glimpse of Lucien made her stomach wrench. "Oh, God. He looks . . ."

"He is not. But he shall be if we do not get him out of here."

Fury rose in Fancy as she turned on Tahj. "Why didn't you take him out of here before this?"

"Because he ordered me away."

"And you listened?"

"The decision must be his. It is Buddha's will."

"I don't care about Buddha's will! He's your friend, first."

"Which is why I came for you." He peered at her long and hard. "Are you his friend?"

Fancy met his gaze for a moment and then looked

away. She could walk away, turn around now, and no one would stop her. Lucien's just due, for George's death.

Instead she knelt down next to him and touched her palm to his brow. He was burning up. "How long has he been like this?"

"Since the night of the Fordhams' event."

For a moment, Fancy could not breathe. "That was three days ago."

"He has been gone longer."

Fancy closed her eyes and finally understood it all. Lucien was addicted, and had been for a long time. Then she noted the black box, the same one she had seen that night in the library. It was open now, the contents of a secret life revealed.

"Lucien," Fancy murmured, leaning close to his face, struck to the marrow by the unhealthy pallor of his skin, the sunken hollows beneath his cheekbones. She glanced up at Tahj. "Help me lift him."

"I cannot take him unless he says he will go."

Fancy stared at him. "What?"

"He must go willingly."

Fancy surged to her feet and faced him. "You will help me get him to the coach, or I promise I will make every day of what remains of your life a misery."

She prayed the threat worked, for she could not move Lucien without assistance, and none of the people around them would help. Desperation pounded away inside of her. She *had* to get him out of there. He needed a doctor. He would die, otherwise.

"He must go willingly," Tahj repeated firmly.

Fancy whirled away from him and dropped down beside Lucien again, lifting his head and lightly slapping his cheeks.

"Wake up," she demanded. "Please, Lucien, *wake up!*"

He groaned and tossed his head. "Fancy . . ."

"Yes," she breathed. "Yes, it's me. Open your eyes, Lucien. I want to see your eyes." Those beautiful aquamarine eyes that had entranced her the first time she had looked into them.

Slowly his eyes opened, but they were dull and unfocused. Still, he looked at her. "Sweet Fancy," he murmured as his head began to roll to the side.

"No, Lucien. Stay with me." She shook him. "You need to come home. Tell me you'll come home."

"Home," he mumbled, though it was clear he didn't understand.

Her gaze lifted to Tahj. "He said it. Now help me!"

Tahj hesitated, then nodded, reaching down and hauling Lucien from the floor with a strength that seemed impossible in a man of his size.

Together they got Lucien into the coach, which hastened them out of the dark alleys of the rookery and raced through the night toward Charring House.

Only one light glimmered through the windows of the mansion on Charring Lane. The butler was awaiting them, helping to transport his employer to his bedroom, where he and Tahj deposited him on a massive four-poster of dark burl wood.

Tahj and the butler both looked at her, as though expecting her to make the decisions. Glancing at the butler, she said, "Call for the physician immediately."

"Will Mr. Kendall be all right?"

"Of course." Fancy wouldn't allow herself to think otherwise.

The butler inclined his head, but Tahj stopped him before he took two steps. "No doctor," he said.

"But he must have a doctor!" Fancy protested vehemently.

"By morning everyone would know of his shame. I cannot allow that to happen. I have given a solemn oath to protect him."

"This is not the same! He needs someone to take care of him."

"You will take care of him."

"No." Fancy shook her head and stepped away from him. "I can't." The very thought scared her senseless. If he died . . . She blocked out the image. And what of George? How could she nurse the very man who had taken her brother from her? She whirled around to face the monk. "It's impossible."

"You waste precious time." Tahj turned and propelled the butler toward the door.

"Where are you going?" Fancy demanded.

"Whatever you need will be sent up on the lift." He pointed to a panel in the corner of the room. At the threshold, he faced her. "Take care of him well, *saba priya.*" Then he closed the door. The next sound Fancy heard was the key turning.

He had locked her in!

Fancy took a deep breath and forced her riotous thoughts to calm. She had to think clearly. Tahj had left her no choice but to tend to Lucien herself.

She turned to look at her patient, sprawled out on the bed, thinner but still intimidating. The first time she had taken care of him had been against her will; it seemed nothing had changed. This time, however, his wounds were not so simple to treat.

Moving to the bed, she sat down beside him, seeing him clearly now. Perhaps more clearly than she had seen anyone. He had been an idol to a young man. A hero to a country. A son to a broken legacy.

To her, he had been the man she loved.

Fancy heard the well-oiled hinges of the lift and hastened to the wall to open the panel. On a tray was a large pitcher of water, a glass, a bowl, and a cloth. She removed the items and set them down on the bedside table.

She poured some water into the glass, then leaned over Lucien. Lifting his head, she tipped the glass to his mouth. "Drink, Lucien," she whispered, and felt him stir, parting his lips to allow a little of the water to drizzle in.

Next she poured water into the bowl and dipped in the cloth. She gently smoothed it over his forehead; he was still far too warm. She needed to cool him down, and would have to undress him to do so.

Her fingers hesitated at the buttons of his shirt. They trembled slightly as the soft cotton slowly opened, revealing the chest she had felt beneath her palms, still smooth, still hard; his shoulders incredibly wide as her hands glided over them to remove the material and slide it down his arms, lightly trailing her fingertip over his bicep and down his forearm before realizing what she was doing.

There was a tattoo on his other arm, up near his shoulder—a fierce depiction of a tiger and dragon, done in black ink. A Shaolin symbol, she realized. The mark of a warrior.

Fancy noticed other signs of battle: a small scar above his right nipple, a jagged one along the left side of his stomach. Several others on his arms.

When she lifted him to pull the shirt out from underneath him, her hands found the raised lash marks that crisscrossed his back.

Fancy closed her eyes to keep from crying, but the tears slid down her cheeks and onto Lucien's shoulder. They continued to fall as she rolled him to his side and gently swept the cool cloth across his back, wishing she could make each scar disappear.

She ran the cloth down his arms, his hands, across his palms, where hardened calluses gave testimony to years of labor.

For long minutes, she kneaded the tiny knots with her thumbs, applying the same light pressure at his wrists, massaging his forearms, feeling the supple pliancy of his skin.

The cloth fell to the side as she worked her way over his chest, dipping her hand directly in the cool water and wetting him down, hesitating when she came to the waistband of his trousers.

Scooting to the edge of the bed, she removed his boots and socks, then undid the buttons on his trousers and peeled them down, remembering how Olinda had told Lucien that Fancy had never seen a naked man, that she was a good girl. Yet Fancy felt distinctly bad whenever Lucien was near.

Abruptly, she rose from the bed and pulled the sheet over him, recalling his teasing words to protect his virtue when he had been lying on her bed in Cornwall. If only he knew how indecent her thoughts had become since that day, how often she had pictured him like this, but awake and holding her in his arms.

The vision dissipated as he began to toss, his body shivering uncontrollably. She had seen this the night she had stayed with him and *hillas* had plagued his sleep.

Sitting down next to him, she took hold of his hand. "Ssh," she murmured. "I'm here." She stroked his cheek, her fingers drifting into his hair, the feel of it like silk against her palm as she whispered softly to him, trying to calm him.

He stopped thrashing but the shivering continued, and without thought, Fancy lifted the embroidered bedding and slipped beneath the sheets with him, pressing her body close to his side, murmuring softly in his ear until the shaking began to subside.

She lay with her head nestled on his chest, listening to each beat of his heart, lulled by the strong and steady rhythm, and feeling, for the first time since she had seen his unconscious form, that he would make it.

She turned her head into the crook of his neck, the heavy elixir of sleep pulling her under.

Fancy awoke to the feel of Lucien's body on top of hers.

His hands tugging at her bodice.

Her skirt pushed up to her waist.

His hips between her spread legs.

His erection hard against her.

She panicked, her hands fisting against his chest to push him off, but his strength outmatched hers and she could not budge him.

She could feel the tension rippling through his skin, the wildness about him, and she whimpered as his mouth came down on hers, his hands gripping her wrists and pulling her arms above her head, leaving her helpless and burning with fear and anger and a burgeoning desire.

"Don't leave me, Fancy," he groaned as he pressed down against her. "Don't leave me."

Fancy knew then that the drug still held him in its grip, and yet he thought of her. She was now the *hilla* that stalked his dreams, and she wanted to banish the nightmare. She couldn't bear to be another pain he held deep inside.

He kissed her fiercely, hungrily, a moan rumbling up from deep in his chest each time she gave in another bit to his demand.

He rocked against her, his hard length sliding back

and forth along her sleek valley, his chest abrading her nipples with each movement he made until Fancy clung to him, never wanting the pleasure to end.

She closed her eyes and arched up against him as he drew her nipple into his mouth, his tongue flicking the sensitive peak. One touch at a time, he was siphoning away her ability to reason. She knew everything he had done now, yet her heart could not deny him.

He rolled her to her side and moved behind her, taking her hands and lifting them over her shoulders and onto his, his arms coming around her, strong and muscular, those beautiful, masculine hands cupping her breasts, leaving her nothing to do but feel him in front and in back. Yet she needed him to know she was not a dream; that she was there with him and she would not leave.

"Lucien, please . . ." She bit her lip as he gently rolled her nipples. "I need you."

"I'm here."

And in that moment, at least, Fancy knew he was.

"Put your leg over mine," he urged in a husky whisper, gripping her thigh, spreading her, making her vulnerable as one hand slid over her stomach and down into the nest of curls to dip inside her wet heat, coating his finger before stroking the ripe tip of her sex. One finger lightly circled her nipple while another circled her nub.

"You shouldn't have come for me. I didn't want you to see me like that." He pushed a finger partway inside her, and she moved against him.

"You're destroying yourself."

"Walk away."

"I can't." She didn't know why. She should never have gone to him, never have made his healing her responsibility. But she couldn't leave him. She was tied to him, whether she wanted to be or not, and when he touched her, she could barely think.

He pushed his shaft between her spread thighs, letting her feel him there, moving back and forth. She reached down and took hold of him, feeling his silky texture, his hardness, wanting all that heat and power deep inside her.

She pumped him until he removed her hands, wrapping one of her arms around his shoulders so that he could lean over and suckle her while he increased the friction against her taut peak.

Fancy writhed, nearly incoherent with need, but a small bit of reason remained. She couldn't let him do this, wouldn't let him leave her with one more memory of his hands and mouth, never knowing all of him.

"No." She pulled away and rolled to the other side of the bed to face him, and heaven help her, it was a mistake. For the way he looked at that moment would be forever emblazoned on her mind—his hair mussed and skimming his shoulders like dark silk, his body a monument to perfection, with its sculpted planes and taut surfaces, his manhood stiff and thick.

But it was his eyes that would be her downfall, the lost and vulnerable expression, the endless depths of hurt, the fear of being hurt again. And she understood then that as long as he was in her life, she would never be immune to him. Never be able to shut him out.

She crawled over to him and pushed him to his back. "Fancy . . . ," was all he uttered before she kissed him, giving him what he had given her, taking his wrists in her hands and lifting them above his head as she straddled him, stroking her wetness along his hard length until they were both on the edge of madness.

Then she sat up, her gaze intent on him as she took his erection and positioned it beneath her, knowing with one downward stroke she would no longer be a virgin.

He grabbed hold of her hand, stopping her. "Don't, Fancy. Not for me."

"I know what I want, Lucien. I won't cry foul tomorrow. I won't say you forced me. No one is going to hurt you because of me."

And with those words, she took control of the only area of her life where she had ever felt any power, praying he wouldn't stop her as she slowly lowered herself onto his erection, feeling the stretching, the nearly unbearable fullness, and the barrier of her maidenhead.

"Break it," she urged. "Please."

He hesitated, then took hold of her waist, and before she could prepare, he thrust up into her and she cried out. He stopped.

Fancy shook her head, waiting for the throbbing to subside before she glanced down at Lucien, seeing the regret in his eyes. "You didn't hurt me."

She lifted up slowly and slid back down, the ache ebbing with each silken glide, her movements growing more frenzied as a renewed pleasure built.

He guided her, slowing her, letting her feel his full and total possession of her body. He sat up against the headboard and kept her straddled across his lap, the new position heightening the intimacy, allowing her to look at him with each movement, allowing him to see every expression on her face.

She tossed her head back as he leaned forward and mouthed her nipple, looking up at her as he gently tugged and licked, everything tightening inside her until the first deep pulse spiraled down through her body and tightened around him, over and over again.

In a fluid motion, he rolled her to her back and entered her in one swift thrust as the molten spasms rippled through her. She clung to his arms as he pumped inside her until he found his release, his body stiffening, shuddering, and then pulling out to spill his seed on the counterpane.

Nineteen

❧

Fancy stood at the frost-etched window as the sun began to rise, the ground dusted with the winter's first snow.

She had heard the winch raising the lift earlier and found breakfast and a note asking if she needed anything. Her request had been met with a one-word reply: no. Tahj would not release her from her prison, a place that had become both heaven and hell for Fancy.

During the night Lucien had slept fitfully, awakening two more times, and both times they had made love. Behind these doors, in the dark, with Lucien's body moving in hers, his past was relegated to a place where it could not reach them.

Fancy sat down at the writing desk with ink and paper, staring at a water-filled globe of a village, the tiny inhabitants enclosed in their safe world, unaware of any turmoil that existed outside their glass home. Much as she felt now.

She quickly penned a note to Lady Dane, explaining where she had gone, and saying that Lucien was ill. Then she sent the letter down the lift.

An hour later, she received a missive back from Clarisse, who was clearly relieved to find her well. She had been dreadfully worried. She went on to impart news that struck at Fancy's heart.

> *Someone tried to harm Lady Rosalyn last night. The intruder must have scaled the side of the house and entered through an unlatched window. The prowler bound and gagged the poor girl. How terrified she must have been! He very nearly succeeded in kidnapping her. Only Pierce's tendency to sleep light saved her from whatever fate awaited her. What would I do without the man?*
>
> *Upon hearing the news, Lord Manchester appeared on my doorstep and quite literally barged into the house! He demanded Rosalyn immediately pack her belongings, to her protests and mine, which were both ignored. Then he spirited her away, not even telling me where he was taking her. Rosalyn made me promise I would tell you she was fine and not to worry; she would be in touch with you soon. My dear, I must say that I'm very concerned about you both.*

Fancy folded the paper and tucked it into her skirt pocket. Never had she felt so helpless. Rosalyn needed her, and she had not been there for her friend.

"Bad news?"

Fancy turned to find Lucien propped up against the pillows, the sheet pulled to his waist, the thin material hiding none of his virility. To look at him now, she would never have known how sick he was, except for the shadows under his eyes. And in them.

"How are you feeling?" she asked, coming to the end of the bed, noting the way his gaze narrowed on her, telling her he did not miss the purposeful distance she kept.

"Good as new."

"Do you feel feverish?"

"No, but I feel hungry."

"There's a tray." Fancy pointed to the food she had placed on a small round table in the corner, but he made no move to get up. Instead he continued to regard her, until she could no longer meet his gaze. "About last night," she began.

"You regret what happened."

Fancy frowned at him, then realized he had misinterpreted her words. "That's not what I was referring to. Lucien, I thought you were going to die."

"I'm too stubborn to die," he said lightly.

"This problem is serious."

"*This problem*," he said with a sharp look, "is not your concern, so leave off." He swept the covers aside and swung his legs over the edge of the bed. He closed his eyes, and put a hand to his forehead.

"Are you all right?"

He gave a brief nod. "It's about the same as a hang-over."

"But it's not, and you can't delude yourself that it is."

Lowering his hand, he squinted at her, as though the light hurt his eyes. "Your persistence is one of your more annoying habits."

Fancy wouldn't allow him to shift the focus onto her. "Why do you do it?"

"Do what?" he said, stepping into his trousers, leaving the top button undone as he moved around the bed to get a cup of the rich-smelling brew that had been sent up.

"Please do not play games."

Steam rose from the cup as he stood holding it in his hand. "Why do people do anything? Compulsion? Self-destruction? Boredom? It's all the same thing."

"It's *not* the same thing. You were in there for three days, Lucien. Three days! It's a sickness, not bore-dom."

"I can handle it. I have for more than ten years."

Fancy's mouth dropped open. "My God."

He ran his hand across his face, where several days' worth of whiskers had accumulated. "Jesus, I feel griz-zly." He moved to the bell pull.

"They won't come."

He swiveled around. "Excuse me?"

"No one will come. We're locked in."

"Like hell we are." He strode to the door and yanked

on the knob. When it didn't open, he drove a fist against the wood. "Open this damn door!" he bellowed. His demand received no response, so he grabbed the handle and rattled the door until Fancy was sure it would come off the hinges. "I swear I'll end your life this time, you bloody pious monk!"

As silence reigned on the other side, he growled loudly and spun around, leaning heavily back against the portal and banging his head once against the wood.

The sounds of the cables creaking brought his gaze jerking to the lift.

"Supplies," Fancy told him. Moving to the wall, she opened the panel and retrieved the tray. "Shaving supplies. Seems the bloody pious monk knows you well." She placed the tray on the bureau.

"I haven't shaved myself in years. I'll cut my damn throat."

"Maybe that's what he's hoping."

Lucien shoved away from the door, scowling. He stared down at the items in disgust and then glanced at her. "You could help, you know."

"I could—but you may not want the sister of the man you killed at your neck with a razor."

A heartbeat passed, and then he said, "So you know."

"Yes, I know. But I never would have heard the truth from you, would I?"

He ran a hand through his hair and closed his eyes. "So many times, I wanted to tell you. I never could find the words."

Fancy fought to hold on to her anger and pain, but she couldn't forget the times he talked about George, the true regret he had expressed over his death, the way he had agonized. But she also couldn't forget the senseless way her brother had died. It would have been easier for her to accept had his life been taken in battle.

"You were smoking then, too, weren't you?"

He nodded slowly. "I thought I had beaten it, started over."

"What changed?"

He moved to a chair next to the bookshelf and dropped down into it, his elbows on his knees, his head in his hands. "A man came to see me. Elhamed Jahmar. I had hired him to find Sanji's body. I owed it to her. My life had been saved, while hers had been forfeited. I knew her family would not bury her in holied ground. She deserved that much.

"It took nearly three years, but Jahmar finally found her in a graveyard for Untouchables on the outskirts of Anandpur Sahib. I thought I would find peace once she had been laid to rest, but something took hold of me." He shook his head. "I guess I couldn't deal with it."

He sat back in the chair, his gaze fixed on the ceiling. "I was beyond comprehending anything the night the assassin entered my tent in camp. I had defiled a grave, dishonored a family. I had escaped retribution once, and they would not let it happen again.

"I don't even remember grabbing my pistol. I only remember how loud it sounded when it went off. All I saw was one man. But after he fell . . ." His fingers dug into the ends of the chair.

"But your guilty conscience didn't stop you from taking the opium, did it? That's why you didn't realize what you had done."

He came out of the chair and reached for her, but Fancy moved away. "I tried to stop," he said. "I swear I did. But it got a hold on me. Smoking became the only way I could open my eyes every day. If I could have changed places with your brother, I would have."

Fancy could see by the look in his eyes that he meant it, but her heart still ached. In time she would forgive him. But not now. It was too soon; the hurt too fresh.

"Sit down," she told him.

He frowned. "What?"

"In the chair. You need a shave."

When he still stared at her, she took him by the hand and pushed him back into the chair. Then she stirred the mixture in the bowl and put the lather on the brush.

He watched her warily as she leaned down and lathered his cheeks and jaw, his gaze following her when she picked up the razor, which glinted wickedly in the light.

He took hold of her wrist as she put the blade against his neck, but he didn't say what she expected. "Why did you let me make love to you last night?"

Fancy stared down at his hand. "You needed to."

"You could have said no."

She hadn't wanted to say no. "It's done. Now, would you hold still so I can shave you?"

He looked like he wanted to say more, but she tilted his head away from her and began scraping his whiskers. The task felt intimate, and she didn't want to acknowledge that she enjoyed doing this for him.

Once she was done, she took his chin in her hand and patted his face with the towel, the look in his eyes as he stared up at her almost too much to bear.

"I'm sorry," he murmured, his hands settling at her waist, slowly pulling her down into his lap.

"I know," she whispered, gently brushing his hair back.

"I'm sorry," he repented in a raw voice that threatened to tear down her defenses.

"Lucien . . . ," she softly beseeched, an ache squeezing her chest.

"I'm sorry."

A tear slipped from her eye. "Don't . . ."

"I'm sorry." He wiped the tear away with his thumb, his gaze searching hers, asking for absolution—for more than just the death of her brother; for all those he believed he had failed.

Fancy combed her hands through his hair and lightly kissed his closed eyes. "You're forgiven, Lucien," she breathed against his warm flesh, feeling the tension flow out of him, as though a weight had been lifted.

His gaze never left hers as he undid the bodice of her dress, or when he raised her skirts and gripped her thighs, or when she reached between them and freed him from his trousers.

Or when he entered her, holding her tight as he thrust deep, an emotion far stronger than any she had felt for him before binding them in that moment.

Each time he touched her was better than the last, and Fancy had grown to need this from him, her head dropping back as he slid in and out of her with deliberation and precision, his hands massaging her breasts.

He cupped the back of her head, her hair fisted in his hand as he brought her mouth down to his, his hips grinding up into hers, his arm around her as her hands clutched his shoulders.

She whimpered and he groaned, their mouths barely meeting as the pleasure expanded and intensified, the feel of him inside her erotic and torturous. With one last deep thrust, she convulsed.

Fancy closed her eyes as he tenderly brushed the hair from her face, which she buried in the crook of his neck. She wanted him to stay inside her, for only when they were like this did nothing else matter.

She was drowsy when he lifted her into his arms and carried her to the bed, climbed in beside her, and took her in his arms.

"Did you make love to me just now because I needed it?" he quietly asked. She pressed a finger to his lips to silence him, for he must already know the answer.

When she next opened her eyes the afternoon had settled into dusk, snow whirling in a gust of wind, creating a fairy-tale landscape. This time it was Lucien who stood at the window. He turned when he heard her stir.

"Hungry?"

Fancy nodded, watching as he moved to the table. New dishes had arrived, and the food smelled delicious.

Rising from the bed, she found that all she had on was her shift. "I thought you'd be more comfortable without the gown," Lucien explained. "I left one of my robes on the bed."

"Thank you," she murmured, slipping her arms into the long silk dressing gown, which trailed behind her as she walked to the table.

Lucien put a plate in front of her, piled high with thick slabs of ham in a rich honey glaze, braised leeks and artichokes, thick wedges of Stilton cheese, and a flagon of wine. Fancy sighed in rapture as she took a bite of the ham.

Lucien chuckled as he poured her a glass of wine. "Good?"

"Delicious," she replied, devouring a piece of cheese. "I can't believe how ravenous I am."

"Lovemaking will do that to you."

Heat prickled Fancy's skin as evocative images rose to her mind—of him moving above her, whispering sweet words in her ear and against her lips, the rush of breath she felt with his first penetration, how he saw to her needs before his own, and how he held her afterward as though he would never let her go.

"Do you think Tahj will ever let us out of here?" she asked.

He speared a leek on his fork and held it out to her. "I don't know if I care anymore." He paused, then asked, "Do you?"

Fancy wasn't sure how she felt. Bit by bit, he was making her want to stay. But how could she ever be with the man who had caused her brother's death? She had forgiven him, but could she forget?

"Rosalyn needs me," she said instead of answering. "It seems Calder has found her again."

Lucien's hand tightened around his wineglass. "Damn that maggot. I only wish I had been able to get my hands on him back in Cornwall. I would have tied him into a knot and tossed him off the cliff."

"Calder has always been slippery." Over a bite of artichoke, she added, "It seems Lord Manchester has come to Rosalyn's rescue." From beneath her lashes, Fancy waited to see Lucien's reaction, considering he had played the role of savior up to that point.

The corner of his lips quirked up into a grin. "Derek is going to have his hands full."

"What does that mean?"

"That Lady Rosalyn is about as much trouble as you are."

Fancy glared at him. "*I'm* trouble?"

"Let's put it this way: you're the only woman who's ever shot me."

Fancy slapped her napkin down on the table. "How long am I going to have to hear about that? It was an accident."

Lucien leaned back in his chair, amusement in his eyes. "You don't think you're just a little bit of a handful?"

Fancy folded her arms across her chest and shrugged. "Perhaps a little."

He raised a brow. "I've come to think of the scar on my ankle as a battle wound." When her face clouded over, he hastened to add, "One I'm honored to have. The fire poker aimed at my manhood—now, that might take me longer to forget."

Fancy snorted. "Of course. Then you couldn't be a ladies' man."

"I'm not a ladies' man now."

She harrumphed, and the lout had the nerve to grin at her.

"You're jealous," he said, clearly pleased.

"I am not! Fancy shoved her chair back, but he grabbed her around the waist and pulled her onto his lap. "Let go of me!"

"Ssh," he murmured. "I only want to hold you." He gently stroked her arm. "I haven't told anyone this, but I lost interest in women entirely for a long while. There were times I thought my desire was gone for good. And then you came along."

Fancy relaxed a little against him. "What did I do?"

"You were just you. Vibrant and strong and brave. You were sunshine. And you made me want to be a better man."

Fancy couldn't help herself. She glanced at him. "I did?"

He nodded. "There haven't been many times in my life when I was able to put aside where I came from, where I had been. But for a while, you made me forget."

Fancy faced him fully. "You can change, Lucien. Everyone can change."

"I can't do it alone, Fancy."

"You won't be alone. I'll help you."

"Why?"

Fancy was afraid she knew why, but she couldn't say it, even to herself. "Because you owe it to George," she answered solemnly. "And you owe it to me."

"I know," he murmured, making her feel a spark of hope as he brought her head down for a kiss—praying they had turned a corner.

A noise awoke Fancy in the middle of the night. She rolled over and realized that Lucien was not in bed. She sat up and reached to turn up the wick on the lamp.

"Don't," came his gruff reprimand out of the darkness.

Blinking to clear the sleep from her eyes, Fancy found him pacing in front of the window, a wedge of moonlight giving him a ghostly appearance and showing the extent of his agitation.

"Lucien . . ."

"You have to get Tahj to let me out. I have to get out." When she made no remark, he snapped, "Do you hear me? Get him to open the goddamn door!"

"Lucien, please, come back to bed." She held out her hand, but he didn't seem to notice. He stalked about the room like a caged tiger.

"I need to get out. Just for a few minutes." He turned to her suddenly. "Please."

"No, Lucien," she murmured. "You promised you'd try."

"I will. I am." He ran a hand through his hair, which looked wild, as if he had been doing the same thing for hours. "I can taper off. You can't expect me to just stop."

"I know it'll be hard."

"Hard?" he bit out, swinging around and striding toward the bed. "What do you know about it?"

"Nothing. But I do know that if you don't walk away from it now, you might never be able to. Please," she whispered, "lie down with me."

"God," he growled, gripping his hair in his hands. "You are so bloody self-righteous."

Fancy left the bed and stood before him. "You asked for my help."

"This is not the kind of help I need."

"Then what kind is it? Do you want me to just say, Go ahead, kill yourself?"

"That's not going to happen."

"Do you want a wife, Lucien? Children? Is there anything that means something to you?"

"Damn you. I know what I'm doing. Now call for Tahj."

"No."

He took a step toward her, and it was all Fancy could do to stand her ground. "Call him," he ordered.

"No."

He picked up the lamp on the bedside table and hurled it across the room. *"Call him!"*

An urgent pounding sounded at the door. "My lady," came Tahj's voice, "are you all right?"

"I'm fine."

"Shall I open the door?" the butler asked in an anxious tone.

"Yes!" Lucien bellowed.

"No," Fancy countered just as loudly.

Lucien backed her up until he had her pressed against the wall. "Tell him to open it."

"No."

"Do it now, Fancy, or I'll—"

"What?" she demanded as she glared up at him. "What will you do, Lucien? Hit me?"

A horrified look came over his face, but she needed to open his eyes, to see what the drug was doing to him.

He reeled away from her to the opposite side of the room, unable to remain still as his hands moved over the books, the table, the top of the chair, his fingers flexing and unflexing.

Then he leaned back against the wall and slowly sank to the floor, where he crossed his arms over the tops of his knees and pressed his forehead to them. "I can't do this."

Gathering up her courage, Fancy padded over to him, staring down at his bent head before kneeling before him.

She lightly touched his hair, smoothing the wild strands, wondering bleakly if they would both have the strength to see this through. He had been addicted for so long; what made her think she could help him? What did she know about what he was going through? All she knew for certain was the terrible withdrawal he would have to suffer.

She had seen it once before when her grandmother had nursed a friend for nearly a week while the man overcame his craving for morphine, which had taken hold of him after he lost the lower half of his leg to gangrene. For months afterward she had nightmares, remembering the ghostly sound of his moaning issuing from the attic room.

But as she looked at Lucien, she knew she would do whatever it took to get him through. "Come to bed," she murmured, tilting his face up to hers, seeing the barely suppressed hunger in his eyes, but not for her. He needed something else far more desperately, and the realization broke her heart.

She rose to stand before him, slowly slipping the straps of her shift from her shoulders, the material sliding down her arms and pooling at her feet on the floor, leaving her naked and vulnerable.

"Come to bed, Lucien." She held out her hand to him.

He looked up at her for a long moment, then lifted a shaking hand and put it in hers, rising unsteadily to his feet, his gaze drifting over her, his body tautening.

With a growl, he swung her into his arms and moved with urgency to the bed, laying her across it as he ripped at the buttons on his trousers. Then he spread her legs, coming down on top of her with a frantic need as he entered her in one swift thrust, taking the breath from her lungs as he pumped inside of her until he was spent.

Then he slept.

And she stared up at the moonlit-driven shadows on the ceiling, cradling Lucien in her arms, knowing the worst was yet to come.

The delirium began the third night, shaking Fancy from a fitful sleep to find Lucien crouched in the corner of the room holding the razor she had used to shave him against his wrist.

Alarm welled inside of her, but she was afraid that if she moved too fast it would startle him, and the sharp blade would slice across his flesh.

"Lucien," she whispered, inching toward the end of the bed.

His head bobbed and slowly rose, as though it was too heavy to lift. His eyes were bloodshot, his face dangerously pale. With each passing hour, he became more and more like a person who was passing to the next life.

He had not eaten since the day before, and the hollows in his face had become more pronounced. Whiskers once more darkened his jaw, but he had refused to allow her to shave him that morning. Delusions surfaced whenever she came near him with the razor. Why hadn't she thought to get rid of it?

"Please, Lucien, put that down."

He tapped the blade against his wrist, and she could

see he had been doing it for a while. Tiny slashes marked his forearm. "He made us bury 'em beneath the tree," he said, rocking back and forth, his voice tinged with a cockney accent. "I told 'im we couldn't. It weren't right. They needed a proper burial."

"Who, Lucien?" Fancy quietly asked as her feet slid to the floor. "Who did you bury beneath the tree?"

He jammed a hand over his eyes, an anguished moan rumbling up inside him. "The babies," he responded in a choked voice. "He said he couldn't afford no burial, and dirt was dirt."

Despair closed Fancy's throat. "Your mother's still-born babies, you mean? Your father made you bury them beneath a tree?"

He nodded. "Me and sometimes Dorian, but I didn't want Dorian to see, so I'd make him turn his back." His laugh came out a sob. "I stole holy water from the church in Bluegate to put over their graves." He glanced at her, his eyes tortured. "Do you think it was a sin, stealing water like that?"

"No, love," she murmured, shaking her head. "You did what was best for them."

"I waited for the vicar to go into the confessional," he said, his words their own confession. "Then I scooped the water into a glass and ran." He held the blade up and turned it into the light. "I didn't know any prayers, so I made one up."

"You were a good brother," she crooned, cautiously inching closer to him, her gaze focused on the hand holding the razor.

"A good brother," he repeated in a raw voice. "That tree was gone when I returned from India. Everything had been leveled to the ground—like my life." His gaze suddenly cut to hers, the blade slicing the air as he thrust it out toward her, just a foot away, the tip directly between her breasts. "Where are they?"

Her body trembling, Fancy reached out and gently curled her fingers over his wrist, lowering his hand. "We'll find them," she said, turning his hand over and carefully easing his fingers from the handle.

He watched her, the air vibrating with potential anarchy, until he loosened his hold and she slipped the razor from his grasp.

Relief rushed over her, and she closed her eyes, her heart beating like a hummingbird's. She had not realized until that moment how long she had been holding her breath.

"Don't leave me," Lucien begged her in a haunting whisper, his fingers trailing across her cheek.

"I won't," Fancy softly vowed, a promise from her heart.

Twenty

It took nearly eight days for the drug to work its way through Lucien's system.

There had been times when they almost hadn't made it, when the shaking and delirium got so bad that Fancy thought Lucien would disintegrate, seeming on the verge of madness, and other times when he would break down and cry, sinking so deep inside himself that she feared he might never resurface.

Now, as he slept for the first time without the nightmares, Fancy watched the sunrise on her ninth day of captivity, knowing that at last the worst was over. What would become of them now, she did not know. And perhaps that, more than anything, was what frightened her the most.

Lucien had left her no way to harden her heart

against him, with his midnight confessions, poured out to her in heart-wrenching detail, painting vivid images of his youth, of the brothers and sisters he had loved and lost. Of the days he had thought to end it all.

There had been moments when she wanted to clap her hands over her ears and not hear another painful word, to think only of the brother she had lost at the hands of the man she had come to love.

Yes, she loved him. Loved him with all her heart and soul, though she admitted it only to herself in quiet moments like this. He had slipped into her heart and torn down every barrier she had erected to save herself from despair.

A knock at the door roused her. She turned her head and quietly called, "Come."

Tahj stood in the threshold, bearing the morning tray. He looked different somehow, at peace, much like Lucien. A silent message passed between them, no words necessary as he padded to the table on slippered feet and removed the items from the tray.

When he turned to face her, hands folded calmly in front of him, dark eyes solemn, Fancy knew she would never see him again.

"You," came a groggy voice from the bed, bringing both of them around to find Lucien sitting up, his hair mussed, his eyes heavy-lidded from sleep, but his gaze clear and direct for the first time.

"I see you have not lost your way with words, *vajra*," Tahj murmured in a dry tone. "And may I say that you look like a heaping pile of camel dung."

A smile teased the corners of Lucien's mouth, and deep, rich laughter rumbled up from his chest. It was a wonderful sound.

"I do, don't I? But I feel damn good." He looked at Fancy, his gaze tender. "You think you might be willing to shave me again?"

She folded her arms in front of her and said sternly, "You have two hands."

He shook his head, amusement glinting in his eyes. "You're not going to allow me to play the invalid at all, are you?"

"No."

He sighed. "Well, I guess I better get up then and start looking like a human being again."

Throwing the covers back, he swung his legs over the side, the impact of his presence just as dazzling to Fancy's senses as the first time she had seen him, her gaze drinking in every inch of him as he reached for his trousers and then walked to the table.

He was thinner now but still remarkably virile, his muscles standing out in stark relief on his leaner frame. The hungry way he had loved her during their confinement made an ache of yearning well up inside her.

What would happen now that he had recovered? The life she had wanted only a few short months ago was no longer enough to fill what was missing inside her.

"I must say my good-byes."

Cradling a steaming cup of coffee in his palms, Lucien frowned at Tahj. "What did you say?"

"I am leaving. It is time for me to go."

"Leaving?" Lucien faced his longtime friend and companion, his expression disbelieving. "But I've just gotten used to your annoying presence. You can't go now."

"You do not need me any longer."

Fancy's heart ached. The two men had a special bond, one she feared would leave Lucien adrift now that it was being severed.

"So that's it? You're just going?" He slammed his cup down on the table, coffee sloshing over the top. "Well, go then. Get the hell out."

"You will be fine without me."

In a way, Tahj had been Lucien's crutch, carrying him through the bad times. Now that Lucien had turned a corner, Tahj was not going to give him an excuse to fall.

He laid his hand on Lucien's shoulder, crossing the barrier between mentor and student. "You have found your true path, my friend. Now you must walk it alone. I will never be far if you need me, but I do not think you will," he added with a glance in Fancy's direction. "Good-bye, sweet angel of the night." He bowed his head to her, then looked back at Lucien. "Good-bye, *vajra*. May your life be one of many blessings." Turning silently on his heel, Tahj disappeared through the door.

Lucien walked to the threshold and placed his palms on the jamb, his head bowed. Fancy moved behind him, laying her hands on his arms and pressing her cheek against his back, the faint sound of the front door opening and closing drifting up through the hall-way.

"He's gone," Lucien said in an empty voice. "I finally succeeded in pushing him out of my life."

Fancy gently turned him to face her. "You didn't push him out of your life. You've found your life. Don't you see? That's why he left."

He curled his fingers around her wrist, his thumb lightly tracing a vein. "What have I found, Fancy? What's waiting for me? Do you know? Because I sure as hell don't. All these years, I believed that I had lost everything. I raged against what had been denied me. And now I've awoken to discover that all the things I tried to put behind me, tried to forget, are still out there. I'm still alone."

Fancy slid her fingers through his and held his hand. "You're not alone."

"I won't ever be fully cured, you know—I suspect the need will always be there. I'm afraid of what might happen if I can't control it."

"We'll cross that bridge when we come to it."

He gazed down at her with eyes like a wild Cornish sea. "Why, Fancy? You could have any man you want. Why would you want to be with me?"

At that moment, the answer seemed so clear. "I always thought I would instantly recognize the man I was suppose to love, and that I'd be able to catalog every reason why I loved him. I envisioned a sort of fairy tale. But it hasn't turned out that way."

Lucien closed his eyes at her admission, his hands sliding away. "I'm sorry."

Fancy captured his hand and held it against her cheek. "I'm not. I thought that I would never be able to forgive you for George. Perhaps I believed I shouldn't. But when Tahj came to me and told me you were hurt, I knew that I had to go to you. Nothing else mattered.

"And during these last few days, I realized what I was truly feeling—that the need to be with you was love, strong and steady." She shifted his hand and kissed his palm. "What I want is something real, Lucien. My heart skips a beat whenever I see you." She placed his hand over her heart, letting him feel the rush of emotions that flooded her whenever they were together. "My brother had far more foresight than I had ever imagined. He sent you to me."

"Fancy . . . ," Lucien whispered in an aching voice as he leaned down and pressed his lips to hers, holding nothing back as he gathered her tight against her body, his arms encircling her.

Love, the tie that would carry them through good times and bad.

Epilogue

~∞~

Christmas Eve

The Cornish lights twinkled above a frothy night sea, scattering golden stars across the glassy surface and reflecting off the newly cleaned windows of Moor's End.

Fancy hugged herself, feeling sublimely happy as she stood where generations of Fitz Hughs had proudly surveyed their slice of heaven.

Once she had given herself over to loving Lucien, he had wasted no time; he married her by special license the same day they gained their liberation from his bed-room.

Since then, he had shown his love for her in so many ways. He had brought her home to Cornwall. He had found out about the taxes due on Moor's End and had secretly paid them, handing over full ownership of the house to her the day he carried her over the threshold. He had brought her life full circle, renewing the hope she had once believed gone forever.

A rush of anticipation sluiced through her as she spotted him balancing an armful of chopped wood for the fire, an image of him making love to her in front of it, as he had nearly every night that week, causing butterflies to dance in her stomach. Snow clung to his hair and shoulders. It had been coming down all day, ushering in the first of what Fancy hoped to be many beautiful Christmases to come.

Swinging away from the window, she hastened to check her appearance. Who would have thought a breeches-clad hellion would actually enjoy looking like a lady?

Fancy gave her cheeks a pinch and pivoted to face the door as her husband strode in with his burden, bringing a brisk snap of winter air and snowflakes.

"Need any help?" she asked with a coy look and a blatant shifting of her hips.

He smiled devilishly at her as he hunkered down in front of the fireplace to stack the wood. "I could use a kiss. Know anyone who might be willing to give me one?"

Fancy canted her head and tapped a finger on her chin. "I think I might be able to find one willing female."

"Do you think she could hurry up? My lips need a little warming."

Fancy needed no more incentive than that. She hastened to Lucien's side and sank to her knees before him, taking his cold, handsome face into her warm hands and pressing her mouth to his. It took only a second for him to fan the flames of a simple kiss into something much hotter, dragging her tight against his body, holding her as though it had been an eternity since he had seen her, rather than an hour. He had a way of making her feel loved, and she would cherish the blessing, for she knew George, in his way, had sent this man to her.

The sound of someone clearing his throat seeped into Fancy's consciousness, her eyes slowly blinking open to find Lucien's butler, Henry, framed in the doorway, his normally ashen cheeks ruddy with color, his gaze averted to the ceiling.

"What is it, man?" Lucien grumbled, his tone rough with desire.

"A package has arrived for you, sir." He produced a large envelope from behind his back and deposited it in Lucien's hands.

Lucien stared down at it; the imprint on the wax seal was unmistakable. The emblem of the Earl of Redding.

"If you require nothing further, sir?"

Lucien shook his head and ran a hand through his hair. "No. That will be all."

The butler bobbed his head and departed.

For a long moment, Lucien stared down at the envelope. Fancy watched him, fearing what the missive contained, her gaze following him as he walked across the room.

Moonlight streamed in through the window, revealing the vulnerability in his eyes as he held the envelope out to her.

Her hand trembled as she took it from him, then slipped the letter opener along the seam to pull out the papers inside. The top sheet was written in a delicate female script.

"*My dearest Lucien . . .*" Fancy read aloud the words written by Lady Diana Slade.

> *I hope this letter finds you well and happy, and if you have not thrown it in the fire by now, then I feel a measure of hope for the future.*
>
> *I suspect it would be too much to ask that you do not forever despise the name of Redding. I do not despise you, nor does Christian, though I doubt you will believe me. I understand far more than my dear sibling thinks, and I believe I understand you, as well.*
>
> *My wish for all of us is that we can move beyond the sins of the past and look toward the future. To that end, I have enclosed several items I recently received from my father's old solicitor. Apparently these files were lost for a number of years, and forwarded after my father's death. Please do not think Christian had knowledge of this information and kept it from you. The box was not found and opened until yesterday.*

*I hope that you will find within these pages what
you are looking for, and that it will bring you some
measure of comfort. I truly wish to see you happy.*
                                        Merry Christmas,
                                                Diana

Fancy looked into Lucien's eyes as she handed the
documents over to him. He swallowed hard, hesitating
before he lowered his head to read what Diana had
sent.

Then he closed his eyes tight, the sheets curling in
his fist. Fancy pried them loose, and as she skimmed
the words, a tear slipped from the corner of her eye.

His mother's grave had been found.

The sun was budding in the sky when the coach rumbled to a stop the next day. Lucien had not spoken a
word during the ride. He held out his hand to help her
down from the coach, his bearing somber, and her
heart ached for him.

Golden rays dappled the barely tended grass that
marked Paupers' Field, where Lucien's mother had
been buried for nearly twelve years, after she had contracted pneumonia in a debtor's prison. She and her
husband had been sent there when they were unable to
repay a loan.

Albert Kendall had been killed there, shivved in the
back by a fellow prisoner when he tried to steal a dead
man's shoes, and was now buried elsewhere.

There was one glimmer of hope, though. Included

among the papers was a ship's passenger log dated only a few years earlier. On it were the names of Lucien's brothers and sisters. The vessel had been bound for America. So the Kendall clan was out there somewhere, and she and Lucien would not give up until they found them.

Lucien drew her to a halt in front of a nondescript marker that served as the only means of identification among the crowded rows.

Fancy knelt down and wiped away the dirt covering the small plaque, arranging the flowers she had brought with her.

"They buried her here like she was trash," Lucien said, a lifetime of bitterness in his voice.

Fancy gave his hand a gentle squeeze as she rose to her feet. "She can be moved. And I know a wonderful place."

"Where?"

"Alongside my grandmother. It's a beautiful spot, high on a hill overlooking Meadow's Cove. I think she'd like it there."

Lucien reached out and stroked his hand along her hair. "I love you, you know."

"I know." Fancy walked into his embrace and held him tight. "I'm sorry about your mother."

"I always expected that my father's end would be ignoble. But my mother . . ." He turned his head away.

Fancy cupped his cheek and made him look at her. "Your mother loved you. She would have been proud of the man you've become. And I know she would want you to be happy."

"Do I make you happy?" he asked, a tentative question in his eyes.

"Very happy," she vowed, kissing him. "And this is not the end, Lucien. Your brothers and sisters are still out there. We have a place to start. We'll find them."

"Do you really think so?"

"Yes," she said. "You are my family now, and you may have noticed that I'm very protective of those I love. I've been known to clout a few heads."

"I know," he said with a chuckle, his hand going to the back of his skull.

"Keep that in mind, husband, for you have an obligation to fulfill."

"And what is that, my love?"

Fancy leaned into him and wrapped her arms around his neck. "To bless me with many babies to love and cherish."

A roguish grin tipped up the corner of his lips. "That, you may depend on, dear wife."

Pocket Books Proudly Presents

Melanie George's
Next Book

Turn the page for a preview. . . .

*R*osalyn dreamed of him.

Velvet blue eyes, piercing and intense, hair as glossy as a raven's wing, and a tall body of rugged elegance, brawny beneath his tailored exterior, his beauty mocking all those around him as he smiled wickedly at her from across the ballroom.

She shivered as she watched him approach, noting how he moved with careless grace.

When the darkly beautiful stranger stopped before her, his voice a low, deep hum that tripped along her nerves in the most disconcerting fashion, she knew. Oh yes, she knew.

She was doomed.

She could read her downfall in the glance he leveled on her, as though he knew a secret he had no intention of telling.

"Derek," she murmured in her sleep, reliving the kiss he had given her in Lady Senhaven's garden, the scent of honeysuckle surrounding them. It was a scandal in the making, the other guests no more than forty yards away, yet Rosalyn could think of nothing beyond Derek's lips on hers.

The dream suddenly evaporated and her eyes snapped open as a hand clamped down over her mouth, her gasp muffled into a man's callused palm.

"Utter a single word," a foul-smelling voice hissed, "and y'll be one very sorry miss. Now, get up. An' be quiet. There's a man waitin' most impatiently for y'."

Her stepbrother had found her.

He must have trailed her from Cornwall to London after his unsuccessful attempt at kidnapping her from Moor's End, Fancy's home, where Rosalyn had been staying since learning of Calder's twisted plot to marry her and do away with her, so that he could obtain her inheritance.

Rosalyn was jerked to her bare feet. A rough-looking man stood before her dressed in dark, filthy clothes, the left side of his face obscured by shadows. As his gaze crudely raked over her she felt exposed and frightened, garbed in only a nightgown.

She straightened her spine as the man pushed her toward the window. She swallowed back her fear as she looked down from her room on the second story to the ground below, where a hemp rope swayed unsteadily in the night breeze.

"I'm takin' my hand away now," her kidnapper said in a muted voice. "Make a peep an' I swear I'll gut y' like a fish."

Rosalyn nodded and sucked in a deep breath of cool air as the man's rough palm dropped from her mouth. "Thank you," she murmured as she met his gaze.

"Quite the polite little thing, ain't y'? So sweet and nice, but I've been warned about y'. I knows y'll put a sticker between a man's ribs an' not blink an eye."

"That's absurd," Rosalyn scoffed.

"Y'll not lure me with y'r siren's body an' angel's face, missy." His gaze slid over her, his perusal missing nothing.

"Are you quite finished, sir?" she asked in the haughtiest tone she could muster.

"Sir?" He gave a low bark of laughter. "Aye, I'm finished. Now through the window with y'." He gave her a shove.

Rosalyn stumbled forward, her mind working feverishly.

"Out the window," the beast urged, his tone brooking no argument.

Rosalyn glanced down at her bare feet. "May I at least get some shoes?"

"No," he snapped. "Now get movin'—or do y' want me to toss y' over my shoulder an' carry y' down?"

Rosalyn blanched at the thought of being carted down the swaying rope ladder on the brute's shoulder. She'd rather fling herself bodily from the roof.

Hoisting up the hem of her nightgown, she straddled the windowsill, fervently wishing a white knight would suddenly appear to save her.

"This ladder looks most unsturdy," she stalled. "Are you sure it will hold? Perhaps we should go by way of the front door?"

"Missy," he said, pressing his face close to hers, his eyes devoid of any compassion. "Y're wearing mightily on my patience and that ain't a good thing."

Rosalyn shivered. "I'm sure it isn't," she murmured.

Reluctantly, she placed her right foot on the first rung. Once steady, she swung her left leg over, her mind whirling with the possibility of making a run for it the moment her feet hit the ground.

Her left foot had just settled into the rung when

her bedroom door suddenly flew open. A huge, menacing figure loomed on the threshold, backlit by the flickering sconce in the hallway, casting him in black shadows.

A glint of steel told her that a gun was trained in their direction. "Step away from the lady," the man's voice said, "or I'll blow your bloody head off."

Derek?

Rosalyn's breath expelled in a rush, knowing the brawny highland lord was more than a match for her midnight intruder.

The thug lunged toward her, causing Rosalyn to swing back, one hand slipping from the sill, her feet losing purchase on the rung. She cried out as she began to fall, dangling by a single hand and scrambling for a foothold on the rope.

Her abductor jammed both legs out the window in an attempt to escape, his booted foot smashing against her fingers, nearly causing her to fall.

Derek's arm thrust through the open window to grab the man by his grimy shirtfront, attempting to yank him back inside.

"Hold on, my lady," he called out to Rosalyn as he fought to maintain his grip on her struggling assailant. The man cried out a moment later, falling past her and hitting the ground with a hard thud.

Rosalyn stared down at his unmoving form, her

fingers twisted painfully in the rope, sheer dint of will all that kept her from the same fate. Then a hand clamped around her wrist.

"It's all right, Lady Rosalyn," Derek said. "I've got you."